Russell Celyn Jones is the author of *Soldiers and Innocents*, which won the David Higham Prize, *Small Times* and *An Interference of Light*. He was the recipient of a Society of Authors award in 1996. He has taught at the universities of Iowa, USA; East Anglia; and the Western Cape, South Africa. He lives in London and is a regular book reviewer for *The Times*.

Also by Russell Celyn Jones

Soldiers and Innocents
Small Times
An Interference of Light

THE EROS
HUNTER

Russell Celyn Jones

An *Abacus* Book

First published in Great Britain by Abacus 1998

A CIP catalogue record for this book
is available from the British Library.

ISBN 0 349 11045 X

Typeset in Cheltenham Book by
Palimpsest Book Production Limited,
Polmont, Stirlingshire
Printed and bound in Great Britain by
Clays Ltd, St Ives plc.

Abacus
A Division of
Little, Brown and Company (UK)
Brettenham House
Lancaster Place
London WC2E 7EN

For Rachel and Ben

THE EROS HUNTER

My name is Alice Harper and I murdered my father, they say.

I say: they've got my name bang to rights, but Alice Harper's no patricide.

So let's try again. Who I am depends on the play of light.

And landscape, literature, language.

But you can't expect the police to be acquainted with these determinants. And it's the police who bestow upon me my identity, one of two they have in stock. I'm a killer or I'm not. And if I'm not, I soon slide out of their mind's eye. It wouldn't occur to them I may have an altogether different identity – the one I invent, the *made* character.

I know what that is even if they don't.

Murder police can't see beyond their job description. They trade in victims and victimizers. There is no third dimension, middle ground, no island normal for someone like DI Robert Clyne investigating my father's murder, who holds on to me dearly so long as I remain a suspect.

He's a good cop, good father, someone the world needs around. Too good to be true, perhaps. But so caught up with the hunters and the hunted, he never gets to taste the fresh air of the green fields that stands between, nor relate to anyone who can.

If I can make my character I can surely make his. For his is relatively simple. There are only two places he can be.

From the moment he wakes at the start of a new day . . .

. . . he tries to make the world disappear by concentrating on sounds inside his room. As kids we can do this, but he can't even hear himself breathing over the car alarms and sirens. All the trouble out there . . . it's now inside the bedroom. In this asthenic state even the rustle of the river ebbing a mile away he can hear. Smell it too, like the dank odour of crows. Off the landing, water clatters into the bath. A medicine cabinet door slides open and shut. His two children collude outside, their bare feet sticking on the polished floorboards. He can identify each by their different weights descending the stairs. Two dishes are taken down from the rack in the kitchen. Two mugs unhook from the dresser. A kettle boils. Cereal packets rustle. The fridge door opens with a gasp. And then nothing. It's preternaturally still.

The children are sitting at the kitchen table, watching their father approach. Their faces are blank, their hands rest on their knees. He has never seen them so inanimate. Clyne sees the third person the moment he enters through the kitchen door. With his back to the fridge stands a tall, built man. There is a balaclava over his face and an over-and-under twelve-gauge Browning pump in his hands, the stock seated into his hip. He says to Clyne very casually, reasonably almost: You've destroyed my life. Now I'm going to destroy yours. I'm going to take the children out and let you live to contemplate the ruins.

Clyne's body ejects from the bed. He is moving for real now, but that's all he can be sure of. He pads across the bedroom carpet, the bare landing boards, down the stairs. Cold tiles under his feet stretch to the kitchen. The door is open and the children sit at the table where they are having an altercation over the

2

radio. They draw their father into the argument, about which station they each want to hear. And that's how he knows it's all right.

What follows is Clyne's story, and mine also.

ONE

Bob Clyne is a friend of Sam Ridley and Sam Ridley is a friend of Kelly Stokes. Clyne, Ridley and Stokes are all police and ride around in unmarked cars. Clyne is higher-ranking than the other two but never pulls it in the car, where those friendships are nurtured, en route from one cooked corpse to another.

They are on their way to one again.

They collected Clyne from his house and it was Ridley who went to the door. He has been into Clyne's house on occasions and Clyne into his, although Clyne has never seen sight of Stokes'.

Ridley gets in behind the wheel and Clyne sits in the back behind Stokes.

'St Katharine's . . .' Ridley is saying.

'Yeah.' Clyne leans his arms on Stokes' headrest. 'St Katharine's Dock.'

'It's your bottom office down there, right, Bob?' Ridley asks.

'I took you there a year ago, remember?'

'That's right,' Ridley says. 'Two quid for a bottle of Budweiser.'

'Two pound *fifty*,' Clyne says, glancing at him in the rear-view mirror. 'It's two pound fifty for a bottle of Bud.'

'Yes, you're right, now I remember. Two pound fifty. Can you believe that, Kelly? Fiver a pint. And he drinks there from choice.'

'What can I say? It's my sailing club,' Clyne says. 'And I tell you something else. It's why Manny jacked me out on my day off. Because he knows it too.'

Stokes opens her account. 'When you sailed around, you know, did you ever get off your boat?'

'Of course,' Clyne says. 'Tuamotus atoll I liked very much. Bora Bora, Moorea. I saw an active volcano in Vanuatu.'

'I've never heard of those places,' Ridley says.

'People there have never heard of England.' Clyne thinks for a moment. 'In Aitutaki . . .'

'I've heard of that,' Stokes interrupts. 'There's Cook Islanders there who speak the Queen's English.'

'That's right.' Clyne is impressed. 'The Queen's English.'

'I'd like to see those places. Some of those places,' Stokes amends.

'Trouble with land, I always got sick.'

'What you mean, sick?' Ridley asks.

'Viruses. Wounds festering in polluted air. And a few other things I picked up I didn't want. Weevils in the Panamanian pasta, for instance. A rat . . .'

'A rat? Jesus Christ.'

'That rat was with me all the way 'cross the Pacific.'

'*All* the way across?' Stokes asks.

'Most of the way . . . sharpening its teeth on my bulkheads. When it ate through the PVC coating on the cabling and shorted out my electrics I knew I'd have to kill it.'

'You killed a rat on board?' Ridley asks. Clyne can tell he doesn't believe him.

'I shot it with my .38 that I had for protection.'

Ridley laughs and briefly loses course, crossing a double white line.

'No, really,' Clyne says. 'Lying down in the galley. Such was the angle the bullet passed through the rat and out the doghouse window.'

'The doghouse window,' Stokes grins. 'That sounds good.'

'I had water pouring in there for weeks.' He lights a Camel and opens the window a crack. 'But you know something, when you come to these islands by sea you understand what a place means, how one fits in with another. For thousands of years that's how people arrived.'

'Before the Boeing 747,' Ridley adds.

'Exactly. Flying is like supermarkets.'

'What did you discover?' Stokes asks. 'About yourself.'

Ridley and Clyne catch each other's eyes in the rear-view mirror.

'Nothing,' Ridley answers smartly.

'Come on, you must have discovered something?'

'I discovered Eden is the sea. The Fall is man's entrapment by women, standing on the shore, ruling the tides with our progeny.'

Stokes turns round in her seat. She looks indignant. 'You missed your kids, you mean?'

'I missed my kids. Otherwise I might have gybed at Plymouth and gone round the world a second time.'

'Okay. Just don't blame the women,' Stokes says.

'I don't. Honest.'

'We're here, folks.' Ridley points through the windscreen.

'Yacht heaven,' Clyne replies.

Quite a crowd has gathered on the jetty to stare up at the masthead of a forty-foot Westerly Corsair. The yacht itself has been cordoned off. Halogen spots erected on the jetty favour the white overalls of forensics crawling on their knees across the teak deck. *Eclipse*, the name on the yacht's transom reflects in the oily water. At the top of the mast in the bosun's chair is a slumped body.

They step out of the car to the sound of rigging lines clipping aluminium masts. The wind is a force three to four with a little Arctic bite from the north. Clyne leads the way to the jetty with his hands buried in his overcoat. Whispers from the crowd encapsulate the uniformed police meditating on the body. A WPC tells them where the HQ has been set up: in Clyne's yacht club on the riverfront.

They climb the stone steps to the hinged black doors, guarded by two brass cannons. Clyne can feel Stokes flinching the moment they walk through the inner frosted-glass doors. The size and grandeur of the place is impressive to a first-timer. The coffered ceiling in the hall is double-height and a mahogany staircase with ornately carved newel posts sweeps up to the en-suite bedrooms and snooker room upstairs. An iron art nouveau fireplace with elaborate oak mantel supports silver trophies. In the cat's corner by the river-facing window are two chesterfields.

The three detectives advance across the pitch-pine floor to the bar nook teeming with forensics, fingerprint teams, scene-of-crime officers, bag carriers, training inspectors, their cigarette smoke excavated through vents in the ceiling. A stained-glass window on the half-landing casts a yellow light on to their massed black shoulders. Behind them on the wood panelling hang pictures of yachts listing, seaspray veiling brightly coloured spinnakers, with the volcanic ocean bearing down, frozen at the moment of its greatest passion.

Manny the DCI is there, conducting. With his long arms hooked around beer pumps he looks to be thwarting a stampede to the bar. And he is complaining as usual: 'I can't believe this went off and no one saw it.' He clocks Clyne walking in with Ridley and Stokes and disconnects his arms from the pumps. To the teams he says, 'Usual routine, gentlemen. Start with the twinkies on their yachts.' He strolls over with that lope of his until Clyne is face to face with his tangled eyebrows. 'A George Harper owns the tub. You know him, Bob?'

'I know him, vaguely. He's in and out of the club, like me. That him up the mast?'

'The pathologist hasn't been up yet.'

A stray shard of light striking the wedding band on Ridley's finger distracts Clyne for a moment. 'Harper's a doctor, as I recall.'

'A philosopher?' asks the DCI. 'Or the kind who saves lives?'

'Some kind of consultant. Goes by Mister Harper.'

From the yacht club they walk to the jetty. Above a police helicopter hovers, its snout pointing upstream. Manny's arm is around Clyne's shoulders, his stentorian voice breaking up under the noise of the chopper. 'We have to get the pathologist up the mast,' Manny says. 'Have you seen how big that fucker is?'

'Fifty-eight foot.'

'I mean the pathologist.'

The minutes fall away. Ever more voyeurs leave their tables in the restaurants to come see the show. Clyne turns his back to them, rolling his shoulders around, trying to stay concentrated.

A training inspector coaxes the pathologist out of a nearby watering hole and down to the pontoon. One of the private Frankensteins on a four-year tender with the Met, he'd been having a sly jar in the Charles Dickens.

His lips are wet and his eyes glazed. On his face are small black moles that look like dead flies. Clyne smiles when he belches. In a minute he is going to break the bad news to him.

The forensic crew consider routes in, routes out to the scene of the crime – the masthead. There is not a man amongst them who can work it out. They haven't the vaguest idea. The one obvious way up has already been booked by the body, winched up on the main halyard, with another loose rope tied to the bosun's chair.

It would have been hard, but not impossible, for one person to do all that. Second thing that occurs to Clyne: this is advertising.

Manny's face is a blank sheet.

'He could have been installing instruments up there, Manny, I suppose. Like navigation lights. Anemometer. Repairing a broken shackle. Any of those things. Fixing a St Christopher to the cap, maybe. But someone had to winch him up.'

'You're the expert, Bob.'

'I heard about this man once killed top of a mast. Electrocuted himself. He had a drill on an extension lead and the socket box dropped in the water. That was an accident. This doesn't look to be.'

'This wasn't an accident. Whoever sent him up would know something about boats, you think?'

'Definitely. Crew for instance, yeah.'

'So how do we get the pathologist a ride?' Manny's hands are cupped around his mouth.

'I'm working on that.'

Manny wanders off, his toes tapping against the pontoon slats. He comes to a standstill beside the topsides of the yacht, his face taut with uncertainties.

Clyne gains a purchase on the pathologist's Burberry. Like many pathologists he is pale as a lily – inlaid with those moles. Bad luck for him in the UVs. 'Put out the cigar, Doc. You a sailor by any chance?'

'No I'm not. No way.'

'You're going to have to go up on the jib halyard. It's the only clean forensic route I can see.'

He doesn't know what Clyne is talking about.

'That okay with you?'

'The spirit's willing.'

'It's the flesh I'm concerned about.' Clyne looks at the top of the jib halyard – six foot short of the body. 'How much you weigh?'

'Fifteen stone.'

'We can winch you up most of the way, but the last few feet you're going to have to climb.'

'I'm not an old man, Inspector.'

'You will be by the time you come down.'

'What about my equipment? I can't carry that as well.'

'I'll send it up in a bucket.'

Clyne tells Ridley what he needs. Then the forensics lead Ridley over the clean routes to the cockpit locker. He forces the padlock on the locker and throws a canvas bucket and twelve feet of rope on to the jetty, then travels below in search of a safety harness.

With the rope Clyne makes a bowline on the bite – an improvised bosun's chair – and secures it to the jib halyard. As the pathologist climbs into it Clyne draws hard on a cigarette. From inside the yacht he can hear Ridley cursing.

Ridley reappears with a blue harness and throws it to Clyne. 'There's a fuck load of blood down there,' he says, diminished by what he's seen.

Diminishing he can't afford. Ridley is the shortest man in their investigation pool, a whole seven inches under Clyne, who's never quite got used to lowering his face to talk to him. Ridley may be small but he's perfectly formed. That's what his wife once said to Clyne.

Clyne fits the harness over the pathologist's shoulders. 'When you get there, clip this harness shackle on to the shroud.'

'The what?'

'Shroud . . . the shroud. There's no other word.' Clyne indicates the wire at the top of the mast. 'Look where I'm pointing. You see what I mean? Climb it the best you can.'

He rolls three turns of the jib halyard around the port-side winch. Sam helps him on the handle while two scene-of-crime officers tail the rope.

The wind is in his hair, the chanting of the crowd in his ears, the halogen light in his eyes. They make millimetre-by-millimetre progress. The pathologist rocks back and forth, the boat listing with him.

He manages to clip on to the shroud, then starts climbing it like a monkey, pinching with his feet, hand over hand, until he loses his footing, falls and hangs from his harness. The wind snatches greedily at his coat.

He climbs again, conquering the bare pole. At the top, nose to nose with the body, he twists his head over one shoulder and vomits on to the deck. The forensics all moan.

The wind belts into him. Clyne can just see him falling.

The canvas bucket with the pathologist's equipment is sent up the forestay. Even before it gets to him he is shouting down: 'He's dead all right.'

A few minutes later he asks to come down. Ridley and Clyne hold his dead weight, over two hundred pounds on the scales, on an eighteen-inch handle. They ease out in short jerks, bouncing him down. Then the rope gets a riding turn around the winch and jams.

Clyne vents off at the officers tailing even though it isn't their fault. 'Not at an angle! Tail straight back from the winch!' They just look at him, like deaf mutes. '*Stroll on!*'

The pathologist swings alarmingly in the wind. 'Can you take your own weight for a sec, Doc?'

He uses the last of his strength to lift himself as Clyne pumps the halyard. He feels the wire biting into his flesh and a trickle of blood runs between his fingers.

They keep paying out the halyard even after the pathologist's feet touch the deck, until he is down on his hands and knees.

Manny joins them on deck. He places a hand on the pathologist's shoulder. 'Give up the smokes, son,' he advises.

The pathologist's face is hot and angry. 'That body was either winched up dead, or winched up alive.'

11

'Sorry if I'm missing something here,' Manny smiles, 'but what other ways are there?'

'There's a gag around his airways.'

The pathologist has had a busy half-hour. He is helped off the yacht by two WPCs and looks to be enjoying their company more than he liked Clyne's. The first thing he does on stepping on to the pontoon is light up a fresh Havana.

The police photographer is next to go up. He is half the weight of the pathologist and half as strong. He tries shinnying up the shroud four times before quitting, swinging back and forth in the improvised bosun's chair. His camera and flash gun lie unused in the canvas bucket.

The police are fucking up under the eyes of the City boys gathered on the jetty. Heads lean out of apartment windows à la Stanley Spencer. No messiah passing by, but plenty of crucifying anxiety. They watch from hotel rooms. The pub empties and drinkers hunch against gusts of wind with pints in hand. Great show for them, but no policeman likes to work this way, under surveillance. They make Clyne nervous until he can't think clearly. Their endeavours look like amateur dramatics. More DIY than CID.

Then the press corps arrive, cameras firing. They see the police photographer failing and mock him. What a quitter!

'Send us up, we covered the Gulf War.'

For a moment Clyne considers their offer.

'May I suggest something?'

He turns to see Kelly Stokes behind him.

'What 'ya know about yachts, Kelly?' he snaps.

'Nothing, not really.'

In a year or two, DS Stokes will make DI. Then Clyne won't be able to give her orders. He makes the most of the time left.

'Leave this to me, would you?'

'I was only going to suggest . . .'

'I said leave it!'

'. . . that you bring another yacht alongside, send the photographer up that mast. Perhaps we could lean that boat towards this one?'

Clyne dredges out a Camel and rips off the filter. Sometimes he does this when needing a stronger smoke. He torches the cigarette with a flaring lighter.

'Might be the best forensic route,' Manny says softly, going gentle on Clyne's open wound.

'Sure. Okay. Go see if you can find a yachtie to volunteer his tub.'

They stand around as statuesquely as possible waiting for Stokes' return. Clyne tries a look of enigmatic efficiency for the benefit of the nation's press. They have begun arriving by the truckload now, from nearby Wapping.

The DCs Manny sent out earlier start to trickle back in, having made their local enquiries. No one saw anything.

Manny is having none of that. 'There's two watering holes in this dock. Hotel, shops, apartments, yacht club, a hundred boats moored up. And no one saw a fucking thing? Wouldn't it have been noisy winching him up there, Bob?'

'Not with all this rigging tapping away,' Clyne says. 'But I can't believe no one *saw* it go off.'

Stokes reappears aft a forty-eight-foot customized Moody racer, with a sunshine-handsome at the helm. A half-a-million piece of work transporting her across the marina has done a job on her sex appeal. Her colleagues all stall to watch her glide in. With one hand she steadies herself on the pushpit and with the other she holds back her blonde hair against the wind. Her coat is open and her breasts push hard against a white sweater. Her eyes are expansive and her mouth spills silent laughter, and winds Clyne a little.

The skipper throws a line across to *Eclipse* and rafts up alongside. They attach bow and stern lines to his port-side cleats and bring them over both decks, tying off around the

13

dolphins on the pontoon. Pulling the lines as tight as possible they tilt the Moody racer until the two mastheads touch.

The photographer goes up in the racer's bosun's chair, smoothly, like in an elevator. From the jetty the pathologist watches in contempt.

The photographer shoots off some film and returns without trauma.

Lowering a dead man from a masthead is a lot harder than lowering a live one. The corpse is limp and can't help in the operation. It hangs out in all directions and tangles in the rigging. Clyne can't even shift it with the line. The forensics dust four mast steps before he climbs to a height from where he can break the body free using a boat hook, swinging it out beyond the shrouds.

The pathologist makes a more detailed examination of the corpse where it lies on a white polythene sheet spread across the deck. There is duck tape around the mouth of the corpse and the arms are tied back. Clyne confirms the victim as George Harper, owner of the yacht, a slight figure around fifty years old, groomed black hair dusted with a little grey, and well turned out to meet his maker, in Armani trousers – torn and bloodstained around the crotch – blue Kenzo shirt, Timberland docksiders – one missing. Not gear you'd wear for yacht repairs.

The pathologist prods around the crotch area with his Parker pen, but there is not a lot to see. The genitals have been excised. He removes the tape around the mouth and discovers where the genitals have got to. The photographer shoots off another half-roll.

The pathologist qualifies his earlier diagnosis. Burst blood vessels on the retina, congested engorged pallor to face and neck, an absence of skin trauma where the hands have been tied suggests death by suffocation.

The design is intriguing, the advertising graphic.

The coroner bags the corpse and seals it both ends. The DCI

hands over to the exhibits officer who starts removing for the lab everything that will come away. Walking to the car Manny calls the East Ham mortuary on a mobile and tells them to jack up a post-mortem in an hour. He and Clyne then leave together.

The PM revealed multiple micro-haemorrhages in the eyelids and conjunctivae, indicating asphyxia; an impression of a ligature around the front of the neck suggested he was strangled from behind. Blood loss from the genital area was minimal, indicating the penis and testicles were removed after death, timed at around 0400.

He was sent up the mast post-mortem rather than antemortem.

The pathologist stitched up the St Bartholomew's – a long Y cut traced around the neck down to the navel. A mortuary attendant packed the fingernails into a dead-hand box and the entrails in other plastic bags ready to go to Guy's for DNA and toxicology tests. Bags against the wall contained the victim's clothes: shoes, trousers, shirt – each packed separately.

There was a powerful odour in the examination room. Not from Harper's corpse but one brought in an hour before, fished out of a skip. Nothing else smells like decomposed flesh and it made Clyne's eyes bloodshot. He ripped off his green plastic apron and plastic overshoes, gagging to get out.

The pathologist disappeared into the clean room to wash up. The mortuary superintendent slid Harper's chrome tray off the supports and on to the trolley. Clyne and Manny followed him to the fridge, where three other Specials lay, waiting second post-mortems by legal defence teams.

Harper was eased on to a rack between the other bodies and the door slammed shut. No more rent to pay. He now belonged to the coroner.

Outside the mortuary it had started to rain. Standing on High Road South with Manny, Clyne still had that taste in his mouth.

15

Like almonds sautéed in body odour. Behind them was the low-rise mortuary building. In the mirrored windows of the examination room, that separated the living from the dead, Clyne observed his own reflection staring back at him.

Manny stayed silent for a long time after leaving the mortuary, his knees crushed against the glove compartment. He meditated on the headlights spilling on to the road, the markings vanishing under the car.

He broke the mood with a loud declaration.

'That bloke's been up there all fucking day and no one reports it till late afternoon. Doesn't anyone care no more?'

'Those days are over Manny.'

'It's taken twenty-five years in the Met for me to come round to the Christian way of thinking.'

'You're Jewish, Manny.'

'My father was Jewish. So not quite.'

'So what is the Christian way of thinking?'

'Don't act on instinct. Basic instincts are not nice.'

'We need proper sanctions, is what we need.'

'Like Hell is a proper sanction.'

'We've got Wandsworth, look on the bright side.'

'Why do we rarely have any bother with the Christians, Bob?'

'Catholics we have a bit of bother with. Protestants as well.'

'Only when they're fighting each other.'

Manny opened up his Gauloises to discover an empty packet. Clyne sent his Camels across the seat. Manny opened the pack and lit up, casually sampling the easier brand on his throat. Thoughtfully he brushed cigarette ash from the trouser leg of his £800 Italian suit. Half of Manny's income went on clothes. Only his overcoat was tat, a sentimental inheritance handed down from an uncle who died in '55. Forty years on and the style was back in fashion. A deep blue-black herringbone with a

16

high collar that he always turned up, his ear lobes flapping over the edge. A long time ago, low ear lobes were considered by an Italian criminologist as a characteristic of a criminal personality. But then he'd never met Manny. Manny was proof that villains have no monopoly on low ear lobes. Low self-esteem, maybe.

'I tell you what it is,' Manny continued. 'People who fuck with the law, they're like spoilt children. Don't like others having more than them.'

'That's right, villians are immature.'

'You got to teach children fear, or they go out into the world and destroy it.'

'Bullshit, Manny. They're precisely the ones who do go out into the world and destroy it.'

Clyne looked solemnly across the seat. Manny didn't have children. That was his blind spot. And the reason he could afford Armani suits.

Manny stared back, frustrated by his colleague's sentimentality.

They arrived at the station from the mortuary at 1930. They got a sandwich from the canteen. Roast pork for Clyne, beef for Manny. The incident room was up and running as they walked in. Receiver and action allocator sat at the table nearest the door. Behind them was house-to-house/family liaison controller. Sam Ridley was on the same table as the statement document reader. Kelly Stokes stood over two civilian women entering the information as it came in on to the HO computer.

Manny's presence quickly established dominance in the room, this hard-visaged son of a northern shipbuilding family. At fifty-one, he was younger-looking than some of the DCs. All that ballroom dancing. Each Christmas party he showed off his footwork and the women in the AMIP lined up to waltz with him. He'd still be going at 4 a.m. The forty French cigarettes he smoked a day hadn't left a mark.

The office manager at the back of the room was numbering

actions on a white board. He waved as Manny was bartering his sandwich onions for Clyne's tomatoes. The manager had it confirmed that George Harper was a psychiatrist.

'A shrink. My word. Where'd he work?' Manny asked.

'Marwood Hospital, sir, in the adolescent unit. He was a TV consultant, radio commentary as well. Bit of a star.'

The receiver told Manny that the press had already put in eighteen calls, which immediately depressed him. They had picked up on the MO but not yet the identity of the victim.

'The family need to be notified before a press statement's released. Job for you, Stokes, but please don't take flowers like you did the last time you went out on this kind of action. Department can't afford it.'

'I paid for those flowers myself, sir,' she says.

'I'm talking about the sentiment we can't afford.'

Manny walked off to compose the one and only press briefing he'd give before routeing all enquiries through the press bureau at New Scotland Yard. But before he disappeared from the incident room he turned to Clyne and said, 'Bob, my office in five.'

Manny told Clyne to close the door behind him.

'You knew this guy. What was he like?'

'I don't think I said more than two words to him,' Clyne said. 'Nice enough.'

'This isn't a slag on slag, obviously. Media's already booting in. I don't want us to look like we're sitting on it.'

'The two other incident rooms running . . .'

'You're in this suite until it's over. You belong to the same sailing club as this shrink. You got inside track. If that isn't providence I don't know what is.'

'The pathologist says his nuts came off after he died. So we can count out the possibility Harper did it to himself?'

'Shrinks may be crazy, Bob, but samurai they're not.'

'Perhaps, at this early stage, we might like to consider whether it was a contract execution?'

'There was a lot of style there, sure. My feeling is the killer was known to the victim.'

'Another thing . . . he was topped in St Katharine's. That's where Conrad's ship sailed from. Evil begins and ends in St Katharine's Dock.'

Manny laughed. 'That's good, Bob. That's what I call quality evidence. Killer's a literary type.'

'I'll do house-to-house. Anybody with a copy of *Heart of Darkness* on their shelves, I bring in under Section Two.'

'Champion. I'll make sure it's recorded in my policy file. Why don't you go with Stokes to see Harper's wife. But give her a half with the woman before you poke your bugle in. Go in with the forensics after the grief-letting with your big boots.'

Driving over to Islington, Stokes' face was moonish and glazed with tears. Tears were Sam's department, but since he wasn't riding with them Clyne had to cover. 'Are you okay?' he asked.

She started sobbing so Clyne wound his window down.

'What's wrong then, Kelly?'

'Oh, my boyfriend dumped me two weeks ago.'

'This your main squeeze?'

She looked affronted. 'I don't have any other boyfriend.'

'Forget him.' Clyne changed down too quickly and crashed the gears. 'Plenty of others out there.'

She turned in the seat to face him, her expression one of exasperation. 'Why do men always do that?'

'Because they're stupid.'

'I'm talking about you.'

'Sorry?'

'Women talk these things over. Men don't give you time to grieve. They say, Forget it, let's go have a game of snooker.'

'I never said anything about snooker.'

The car radio played quietly on Capital. As Clyne thought of a way to surreptitiously turn up the volume, Kelly leaned over and switched the radio off. 'He's gone off with a tart he met in the amateur dramatic society.'

'I bet an actress won't look after him like you used to. He's going to have to do all the running.'

'An *amateur* actress . . .'

'Excellent.'

Her eyes were translucent, her face pale and thin; delicate features that disguised a strong willpower. Some stray hairs that had got loose from her clip were stridently individual, like horse hair. Clyne always found her presence very sexual. More so now, now the boyfriend had upped and left. He recalled what Sam had once said, about how her bed was the first thing you saw as you walked into her flat. He thought that was probably the reason he'd never gone into her place. Sam had also betrayed one of her confidences, how she had trouble buying a new bikini each summer: small in the bottom, large in the top.

She said, 'When I'm in work it's okay. Soon as I get home I fall to pieces. All he left behind are some plastic coat-hangers. I feel such a fool. Manny's been understanding.'

'Manny! What's Manny know about women?'

'Quite a lot actually. It's down to him none of the girls get called treacle, turtle or pik. Or get a hairy arm up the skirt. Manny'd beat the crap out of them.'

She stared out of the window into the dark Islington streets. 'I told Manny I'm seeing a psychotherapist. I think that's why he sent me out to see Harper's widow.'

'Because you know the score.'

'Yeah, I know the score.'

'Does it hurt . . . the therapy?'

'Not as much as the acupuncture.'

'You do that as well?'

'You should try it sometime.'

20

'If I want acupuncture I go into the garden and throw myself on to a thorn bush.'

'What about therapy?'

'Never tried it.'

'That time you had a sort of breakdown . . .'

This was Clyne's own private business. He tried to head her off at the pass. 'I got out of Dodge City for a while.'

'You sailed round the world. Well, therapy's a journey too. I see this biodynamic therapist. He gets me to lie in a bath of water and I speak to him through a snorkel.'

Clyne laughed. 'I got a yacht, not a submarine.'

'You don't talk to anyone, Bob?'

'What you mean?'

'You can talk to me if you like.'

'Sure. So who do you think's gonna win the Coca-Cola Cup this year?'

'I mean about yourself. I've had four years of therapy. Something's rubbed off, the theories. Talk to me.'

'Four years! It only took me a year to circumnavigate the globe.'

'But you learnt nothing, you said.'

'Of course I learnt something. Like I found out how we're made. In vitro.'

'Let me be your counsellor.'

'I don't think so, Kelly.'

'We can do it in the car.'

He said: 'The best sex I've ever had was in a car.'

'Is that a proposition, Bob?'

Clyne considered this. He risked a glance at her chest, and imagined her naked thighs that were hidden in blue cotton trousers. But it was just too incestuous.

'Tell me, Kelly, what do you miss most about the boyfriend?'

'Let me think . . . No, can't think of anything. Yes I can. He was hung like a bear.'

21

'Then try going out with blokes with small dicks next time.'
'Why?'
'They try harder.'

While Kelly was doing the consolation work with Mrs Harper Clyne took a stroll around her neighbourhood. Nothing under half a mil. He saw so much artwork looking through the windows it was like visiting the Tate. Although he did have doubts about people who shun lace curtains, blinds, some kind of screen between the interior and exterior worlds. They seem more self-conscious about *not* having them than people are who do. There's an inverse logic to it.

Three forensics arrived in an estate. They composed themselves, straightening ties, buttoning jackets before approaching the house with Clyne. On the pavement outside the house a young couple sat in their sleeping bags. The girl tried a beg on them, while her significant other, holding a vanity mirror in one hand, plucked out rogue hairs from his eyebrows with tweezers.

They stepped over them to get to Harper's front door.

Kelly answered the bell. 'What's she like then?' Clyne whispered.

Mrs Harper appeared behind her, looking intimidated by the sheer force of numbers trying to enter her house. Clyne followed Kelly into the lounge, noting the Impressionist watercolours, the fleshed-out bookcases swollen with psychiatry journals and texts. On a mantel was a single photograph of two children, a boy and a girl in school uniform.

Clyne took a measure of her, a lacquered blonde monument in white silk blouse, red tartan skirt. Like a Tory wife, he thought. Something about her narrow hips and waistline suggested they weren't her kids on the mantel.

She didn't sit down nor invite them to. Clyne started in with the routine. 'I'm sorry to trouble you at this moment. But we have to act swiftly on this.'

'Of course. Ask your questions.' Her eyes were distant, clear and empty as water.

'Did he arrange to see anyone the day he died?'

'He was due to go sailing today. He went down to get everything ready.' She was focused on remembering. 'Yes, and he slept on the boat last night.' Mrs Harper was high church, the schooling all there in the voice.

'Do you know if he was sailing with someone?'

'Alastair.'

'Alastair what?'

'O'Kane. He's a BSkyB television producer.'

'I know him from the sailing club,' Clyne said. 'Quite well. Do you sail too, Mrs Harper?'

'I get seasick.'

She had yet to show any emotion. Clyne tried a more personal touch. 'How long were you married?'

'Nearly eleven years. He was married before, but his first wife died.'

'Before or after you met him?' Clyne went in heavily.

'That is not any of your business.'

Stokes buttoned Clyne with a hostile look and took over the interviewing. 'You and Mr Harper,' she began, 'do you have children?'

'He has two children by his previous marriage, but he was estranged from them.'

'Why?'

'They didn't like me.'

'Where are they?'

'One lives abroad – the son, Max – and his daughter Alice here in London.'

'Do you have her address?'

'It's not an address exactly. She's with those New Age travellers.'

'That's interesting,' Clyne said. 'Where's her camp at?'

'George thought she was on Wanstead Flats. But they move around quite a lot.'

'His funeral . . . his children will turn up?'

'We'll have to wait and see, won't we?'

'Do you mind if we look around the house, Mrs Harper?'

'You may see his study, if you wish, but that is all I'm prepared to show you.'

The study was conservatively furnished. There was a salmon chaise-longue with a box of Kleenex beneath, cherry sofa, rose Chippendale armchairs with footstools, a seascape-at-dusk painting on the wall. Above the oak desk a framed monochrome photograph depicted a racing yacht on a starboard tack, the crew harnessed to the deck, winching in sheets.

Two clocks ticked noisily, keeping the exact same time, both five minutes fast.

'Did your husband see patients here?'

'Yes, when there was a need for confidentiality. When the clients were public figures.'

'Like?'

'Anorexic daughters of cabinet ministers. Cocaine-addicted sons of Anglican bishops.'

'Is that his computer on the desk?'

'Yes.'

'We'd like to take that away with us, Mrs Harper, and any disks, software that go with it. Diaries, notebooks, the contents of his filing cabinet.'

'I'd like it all back in the same condition,' she requested.

The forensic team went to work, unplugging the computer, emptying the desk, the filing cabinet drawers, covering everything in polythene sheets. Mrs Harper stood sentinel with her back to the wall and her arms crossed.

As the forensics were near finishing Clyne asked, 'May I use your toilet, Mrs Harper?'

Her cheeks hollowed as though she were sucking a mint.

Then she uncrossed her arms and for a moment Clyne thought she was about to point him in the right direction. Her hand, laden with engagement and wedding rings, indicated through the window. 'There's a public house over the road.'

You remember when we were kids, how we dressed up like fairy-tale princes and princesses? From the age of two I wore only flowing dresses that I could lift by the hem and dance to the music in my head. While my brother tooled up with a stick, broom, shovel for slaying dragons, witches. We used vocabulary from the texts that we couldn't even understand. At three I'd go up to my two-year-old brother and say, 'Marry me, Max, or you won't get your inheritance.' We've been constructing our characters from fictional models since the first fairy story was read to us. Not reality, not the news, but from heroes and heroines who do not exist. You with me?

Well, the process doesn't quit just because we get older. What *has* changed is this new generation make themselves over from what they see on TV and in the movies. From actors, in other words, not the text. They construct their characters from actors. Look at the magazines next time you go into a newsagent for your fags and your semi-skimmed milk. Actors on every cover. But actors are nothing, they're messengers. It's not the message that's important any more, but the messenger.

This is all by way of a preamble to explain why I interview actors, musicians, pop stars for a living. It's not as frivolous as it sounds. Politics and politicians don't have so much clout as they used to in editorial meetings of the features department. Actors, sportsmen are the new ambassadors of the national psyche. If a Premier League football star gets caught with his pants down in a nightclub, papers next morning vilify him as though he were an archbishop.

My latest subject is a young actor who's recently quit the stage and screen at the height of his fame to work as a news presenter at BSkyB. He's a face you'd recognize. But I won't say who, I'll let you read the interview instead in *Esquire* (May issue), who commissioned the piece.

At BSkyB, I ask him why he's abandoned acting. That is the peg. Had he lost faith in the job after someone had threatened to murder him while playing Macbeth at the RSC last year?

'That was the last straw, yes,' he admits. 'Until that moment I admired men who risked their lives to further ambition. I liked playing those kind of characters. But acting is not meant to be life-threatening. A hundred times as Macbeth I died on stage. But I always got to go home at the end of the night.'

I'd interviewed him once before, for a listing magazine, while that threat to his life was live. He was in the Scottish lochs making a film and I'd gone up to meet him. At one point in the filming a policeman noticed a small motorboat on the loch was coming too close for comfort. The set was evacuated in seconds. But the helmsman was only a vapid film buff who'd come for a closer look.

The actor shrugged it off, wanted no more delays. 'If it's on the cards you've got to go, what's the point in trying to avoid it?' At the same time he admitted he was 'bloody frightened'. About his would-be assassin, a fan or jealous actor, he said, 'The man is sick. I feel sorry for him.'

The Scottish lochs had been petrified by a severe winter. Birds were mute in the naked trees, the mountains white with snow. The loch was black, and as smooth as glass. The press corps, who outnumbered the film technicians, were all hoping to witness the real thing, a murder. 'Journalists are cowards,' the actor said to me, refusing to talk to any of the other hacks. For some reason I was exempt. As a girl, I suppose. Under normal circumstances I might have been offended. But why look a gift horse in the mouth?

It was a ringing downpour that sent everyone packing for a second time. Except the actor, who remained staring up into the heavens, an easy target, the rain ruining his make-up. He was locked into that landscape, transferring his emotions on to it, minute by minute transforming himself into . . . well, I won't say who or you'll guess the actor.

He went back to Stratford from Scotland to finish his run as Macbeth, where his antagonist threatened to kill him, actually on stage. On the last night there were police all over the theatre, on the stage door, in the wings as he went out to give a final dangling performance. He expected to die that night, and not only as Macbeth. He looked out into the capacity audience and put them all through the wringer. They knew the rumour too. They were there for the Show. He played the last act with mad energy, on fire with insane power. This was the ultimate Macbeth, a Captain Maximus. When Macduff kills him and he knew he'd made it through the night, Macbeth's dying breath was his life-enhanced sigh.

He says to me at the BSkyB studio: 'If that was going to be my last show I was going to make it *the* performance, you know. I went out and thought, you bastard, come and get me.' Death threats coupled with that other consequence of fame – drinking – was the turning point for him. He was 'speeding up inside, heating up'. The other thing that pissed him off was, as an under-educated Welshman, his colleagues in the theatre. They were almost exclusively educated English people. The English and the Welsh have never liked each other, he said. The English have a proclivity for cruel irony, the Welsh for cathartic rage.

28

When the English get bitchy the Welsh get punchy. 'People goaded me in the theatre, my accent they mimicked. And I'd take it deep inside myself.

'I always used to say that when I'd got to the top I'd stop drinking. But it just got worse. I couldn't get out of the bar. I'd frighten my wife and children. I can't say I blame them now for ditching me. I didn't have then what Peter Hall said was necessary to survive. It's not enough to have a great talent, he said. You have to have a talent for handling the great talent. Oh, the vanity of that business, the ego of it all . . . I hate and detest it.'

His new wife is a silent, plain woman who helps him keep on track. He returns to her metronomically from the BSkyB studios each night. In real life he has forgone Cleopatra for Octavia.

I visited his childhood village in Wales in preparation for this piece. Terraces with outside toilets, rugby ground, chapel, pubs – you get the pitch. It is forlorn now, scarred for life, down. Steelworks nearby, now defunct, have left it looking unwashable, despite its proximity to the sea. The village is traversed by an inter-city railway line and a motorway. Fast cars and faster trains pass overhead, leaving it behind. Front doors open to the street are for entrances not exits.

I met the actor in a café there. He was down visiting his sister, who lived nearby. As I waited for him to show I thought about the reason why he'd been a better film actor than a thespian. Maybe his ordinary celluloid roles had more in common with his ordinary background. And then his face appeared round the door. Despite it being a freezing day he was wearing just an open-necked shirt.

We took his car and drove around the village, making a pilgrimage to the past, as he put it. 'There are pieces of my puzzle missing and it's always here I come looking for them.'

'Do you ever find them?'

He didn't answer me. As we drove past a library, now closed, he said, 'I used to dream about that place. In my dreams I'd walk inside and find books filled with truth.' He said his favourite book was *The Great Gatsby* and quoted the final lines: 'So we beat on, boats against the current, borne back ceaselessly into the past.'

Of the steelworks he said, 'My primary school teacher used to tell us about the Fall of Eden and I thought she was referring to the steelworks. It was one of my earliest religious visions.

'My life is all riddles and paradoxes,' he continued, telling me everything and nothing at the same time. 'Most people have something to hide and that's okay. As an actor I found it useful to bury these secrets in the roles I played. Secrets from the audience, but also from myself. It's what put the terror into the performance. Something that exists outside analysis.'

I wanted to see the house where he grew up, but the actor refused to take me. Instead he dropped me at the café before speeding off back to his sister. I asked several locals where his childhood house was situated but nobody knew. Rain was pitching horizontally on a cold icy wind and night was falling. I didn't want to still be there in the dark.

I walked into a pie shop. This was going to be my last call. An old woman sat knitting behind the counter. A one-bar electric fire heated the entire shop. I asked if she'd known the actor in his childhood. 'You a reporter then?'

I said I was.

'Local paper . . . or English?'

'American,' I said.

'Well, then I did know him. He was very lonely. They say his father was violent to him, or something worse. You never know what goes on behind closed doors, do you? I remember him as someone who always played by himself. Wild as nettles, he was.'

'I'm trying to locate his house.'

'It's next door, love.'

The actor's family house next door to the pie shop had been gutted by fire. I climbed over the back wall and entered via a broken window. Up the burnt stairs I found his bedroom that he'd described to me, facing the sea. It was a charcoaled pit, strewn with glass. A gale-force wind blew off the sea and shrieked through the young actor's room. From his window I watched the London express train shoot past, glowing in the dark like a fairground train.

TWO

A few years ago Clyne had a conversation with Alastair O'Kane in the sailing club about how he'd grown up in the same Glaswegian neighbourhood as Hugh Collins and Jimmy Boyle. He survived his childhood while the other two went down. Alastair covered his tracks to London and became a journalist. Clyne had seen his TV documentary on the Special Unit at Barlinnie Prison, where both Boyle and Collins ended up.

Now he worked at BSkyB, a television redoubt behind chain-link fencing in Isleworth. Clyne and Ridley got to him fifteen minutes before his current affairs programme was due to go out live, at 2200.

His PA asked the police if they didn't mind waiting until it was over.

Did they mind?

Is TV more important than murder investigations?

Is news of the events principal to the events themselves?

Researchers beavered away at screens bolted on to long lines of desks, like pews in a Baptist chapel. No prayer books, just the paraphernalia of news-gathering. Earphones and tape recorders tossed into heaps, telephones with twelve lines, direct numbers into Westminster on a paper drum.

Clyne took a peek in an election constituency guide, which told him where the Conservative defence battlegrounds were, if he cared to know. Banked up beside him were televisions, VDUs that wouldn't yield without the password, white boards like they had in the nick.

Stories\Rep\Prod\Guests\Costs!\Recording
Israel\Clive\Feed 22.15 ex: J'salem

Programme logs, actor and contributor files, viewers' letters . . . and so on. Sam and he exchanged bored expressions.

O'Kane sat with his interviewer in an office, rehearsing their moves. A junior minister was currently en route to the studio. They could hear the two men giving each other a lot of static, acting out a political discussion.

'How long can you hold on to power with a majority of THREE!' There was a thespian's lilt and emphasis in the interviewer's voice.

'We need to go on another year because then people will understand how strong the economy is.'

'If there's any demur on his behalf . . .'

'Kick tha' cunt in the ass.'

A lot of laughter escaped the room. It was as if they knew, once in the live studio, it was no joke.

The daily newspapers were spread around. There was Pamela Anderson, the *Baywatch* minx, on a front page. 'You think she's a babe, Sam?'

'I'd rather fuck a hole in the fence.'

'My son's a fan, he's only seven. Should I worry?'

'I'd worry more if he was catching *Baywatch* for the plot.'

O'Kane's voice swept across their bows. To his PA: 'The script's printable. Let's see it.'

Clyne stood up. 'Mr O'Kane . . .' Formal address.

'Not now . . .' He raised his hand. 'I have a minister in reception.'

Clyne watched his back recede through the busy office. O'Kane hadn't even recognized him. He caught a young male researcher smiling at him. 'What the fuck you looking at?' Clyne said. The researcher turned his head away quickly.

O'Kane's PA came back. 'Alastair's going to be tied up for at least half an hour. Would you like to go to the viewing gallery to watch?'

From the gallery Clyne and Ridley watched designers prepare the set, lower the table, raise the seats, position the mikes. Then the interviewer came in with the minister and sat down at the table. The bright studio lights burnt shadows to cinders, turning the politician into a phantom.

The interviewer's voice mumbled over the PA system. 'I seem to be on open talkback. I want to be on switched, fellas.'

'Preview credits for me,' O'Kane told someone in the gallery. 'Richard, you have switched now.'

'Isn't that guy down there Richard Moss, the actor?' Ridley whispered to Clyne.

'Fuck, yes.'

'I'd heard he was doing this, but never believed it.'

The atmosphere in the gallery became hysterical. People went into a gallop as the interview began. Angles from five cameras showed up on screens, the autocue script on another.

O'Kane sat nearest the gallery window, his hand resting on a telephone, looking down at the set and scanning an enlarged script in front of him. Clyne stared at the back of his head, where he was balding. Each time the politician talked O'Kane picked up the phone and told Moss his next line through his earpiece, like Cyrano de Bergerac.

'*The Scott report, it's gonna be very damaging.*'

Moss repeated back verbatim: 'The Scott report, everyone, ah, thinks it's gonna be very damaging.'

As the minister squirmed his way out, O'Kane went off again, talking down his hotline to Moss.

'*Innocent men could'a gone to jail.*'

'Innocent men could have gone to jail . . .'

'*Move off Scott. Move off it now, Richard.*'

The PA barked, 'Ten minutes left. Ten minutes.'

O'Kane lifted his phone and put it down, listened, picked it up ten seconds later.

Through Richard Moss, O'Kane questioned the minister on the White Paper on Europe *(Gonna be divisive, innit?)* Tony Blair *(Can't land any punches, can ya?)*, privatization *(So many excesses!)*.

When the interview finished the boys and girls in the gallery threw paper in the air. They whooped and cheered. The interview had gone out on air and no longer existed.

The people's hero may have been the former actor Richard Moss but Clyne knew otherwise. Now he knew how the power worked. Moss was O'Kane's little puppet.

The film to end the programme had been in a bicycle courier's shoulder bag until a few minutes ago. They slotted in this report, and that was a wrap. The minister limped off the stage.

Now at last they had O'Kane to themselves.

But first he had to visit the green room. He had to eat something.

In the green room were sandwiches, sausage rolls, chicken drumsticks, cheeses, wine, beer, tea and coffee. The minister was five feet away. Moss was there too, flirting with a female researcher. He didn't sound so sharp without O'Kane to write his poetry.

Clyne strolled over. 'I enjoyed your show, Mr Moss,' he said.

Moss smiled, but even that seemed rigged.

'When Alastair says jump, you jump, right?'

'Would you sign your autograph for me?' Ridley asked Moss.

'I don't do that any more,' he said sharply.

They all looked across the room then at O'Kane, his yellow kipper tie leaking from his throat. They watched him pluck the wooden cocktail sticks from a dozen drumsticks and arrange them into a miniature bonfire. He stuffed the drumsticks into the pockets of his red jacket, then took a wedge of Stilton and put that in with the chicken. You can take the man out of the slum but you can't take the slum out of the man.

Clyne and Ridley watched his pilfering in amazement. So too did the minister, who complained loudly that he'd bagged that Stilton for himself.

No wonder Alastair wanted out of there. He wasn't going to lose his Stilton. He walked over to Clyne. 'Let's go to my office, gentlemen.'

As they walked through to his office Clyne said, 'That was an education. I never knew TV worked like that.'

'My interviewer likes the guidance.'

'He likes the guidance . . . You controlled the whole show.'

O'Kane smiled at the flattery. 'All I'm trying to be is a good civic journalist.'

'The actor . . . does he help the ratings?'

'That was the idea behind hiring him, yes.'

O'Kane sat down on a black leather sofa in his office and began eating the cheese with a fixed smile. His neck and jaw were thickening, his stomach bulging. It was his eyes that had the muscle. He stared hard and piercingly at the world and kept the detectives the wrong side of the door frame.

His stare held good while his jaws worked on the contraband Stilton. He couldn't talk, was waiting for Clyne. Clyne edged further into the room. And said nothing. O'Kane had kept them hanging around; now it was their turn to stall him. O'Kane's hands twitched behind his head. Slowly his composure broke up.

'What do you want to see me for, Bob . . . Inspector? What do I call you?' His lips were frothing with cheese.

'Bob's fine. Your friend George Harper . . .'

'What about him?'

'He was found dead earlier this evening.'

O'Kane broadened that fixed smile. 'George and I are going sailing in a couple of hours.' Then he laughed. A big, fruity laugh.

'His body was found on his yacht.'

'I don't understand. What are you telling me?'

'He was murdered at four a.m.,' Ridley said.

O'Kane came to his feet. 'I've somewhere I've got to go.'

The police quickly looked at one another.

'I don't have time for this. I'm sailing on tha flood tonight.' His Scottish accent thickened the more anxious he got.

'Mr O'Kane . . .' Ridley sounded as sympathetic as he was able. 'I think that trip's off.'

O'Kane sunk his hands into his trouser pockets and his eyes into the floor and disappeared for a moment. What he said he said to the floor. 'You're telling me George was muthered?'

'Yes. I'm sorry. When was the last time you saw him?'

'About three days ago.'

'At the club?'

'No, here at the studio. To discuss the business with the teenagers who stabbed their teacher.'

'Did you have to tell George what to say, like Richard Moss?'

'Of course no'. George was th'expert. He was very good.'

'He was very good. What did he say?'

'I can get you a transcript . . . Why am I being asked this now?'

'Just a summary will do.'

O'Kane considered his answer. His delivery was ice cold, over-rational. 'George said . . . the initiation of boys into manhood is necessary for a healthy society. Anthropologically speaking. That initiation once took the form of apprenticeships. Now boys who have never known work are initiating themselves through crime.'

'I broadly agree with that,' Clyne said. 'Don't you?'

'Yes, I do.'

'What else can you tell us about him?'

'He's an anti-authority figure. R.D. Laing's heir apparent. And he was my best friend.' O'Kane looked as if he might fall apart any moment.

'You want to sit down again, Alastair?'

'No, no, a' don't.'

'He worked with delinquents. Did any of them threaten him, do you know? Their parents, perhaps?'

'This is a shock, like.'

'Do you know of anyone who might have done this?'

'Who'd want t'kill George? He was a gentle, loving man.'

'His widow said he'd gone to St Katharine's to prepare for your sailing trip.'

'Yes.'

'Whoever killed him was probably known to him. And a sailor.'

O'Kane suddenly looked wide-eyed.

'We're still trying to construct a motive,' Ridley explained.

O'Kane walked over to the door and removed his calf-leather coat from a hanger. The hanger was padded with red velvet. The coat reached his knees, its leather smooth and soft. He ran the palm of his hand across his hair and pulled a snarl across his top lip.

He started for the door. 'Alastair, where are you going?'

'I've got to get some air. Please.'

Clyne stepped back to let him pass. 'If you think of anything else, call me at the station.'

As he brushed by, Clyne held him by the arm, offering another space should he have any other half-forgotten thoughts to fill it with.

O'Kane obliged. 'There was a time when we were sailing. We got caught out in a force-ten storm. I didn't think we would make it, you know, I thought we'd had our chips. And he says, in the middle of it, the storm, "For many people what gives their life design is the certainty a' dying. For me what will give my death design is the certainty a' living."'

Clyne let go of his arm and he bolted.

In the elevator on the way out Ridley said, 'What the fuck was all that about?'

'Don't know, Sam, I'm sure. I was more interested in the way he runs the show. That politician never knew where the punches came from.'

They had one more call to make. On their way Clyne checked in at home. Looking up at his house he thought it looked different somehow. The door and window frames had a gloss shine like they'd just been painted, although he knew this wasn't possible.

Ridley was less than helpful. 'They say this happens when you've been away for long periods.'

'No, it has to be the moonlight.'

'Such a big moon tonight for such a small place,' Ridley sighed.

The house was a two-storey late Victorian in Wilton Square, with Regent's Canal right there, where it passes under New North Road. Borough's Islington, on the border with Hackney.

As they walked to the door Ridley said, 'A lot of blokes in the force think you're on the take to afford such a gaff, Bob. You realize that?'

'Let them think that.' The truth was more embarrassing. His ex-wife paid the mortgage in exchange for child maintenance.

He opened the door and skidded on unsolicited mail selling satellite TV. 'A special package for family choice.' Clyne showed it to Ridley before hiding it in his pocket, should his kids get bright ideas. 'Family choice my ass. It's a bloodbath out there on the airwaves.'

They progressed through the hallway, stepping over green charity bin liners. Something small and plastic crunched under

Ridley's feet. An unidentifiable missile whistled past Clyne's ear. From the kitchen his seven-year-old son, dressed in football shirt, followed the missile down the hall.

'Why aren't you in bed?' Clyne said.

David came to a sudden stop six inches in front of his father and started ranting into his stomach. 'My teacher made me play in fucking goal again today.'

'Watch your language, son.'

'It's all right for you, you're six foot three. I'm only four foot and he puts me in goal.'

'So what you want me to do, write a note to him?'

'Tell him I'm a striker.'

'Where's your sister?' Clyne asked.

'In her room.'

'Did you talk to her about this?'

'Lucy doesn't listen to me. All she thinks about is getting kissed by Richey Edwards.'

'Where's Mick?'

'I'm out here, in the kitchen,' came a voice.

David veered off into the living room, dumped himself on the couch and channel-hopped with the TV remote.

In the kitchen Mick had his arms deep inside the sink. Mick was Clyne's houseboy, aged fifty-three. He stayed home with the kids until Clyne got there. Sometimes that stretched twenty-four hours. Mick cost more than the mortgage. To look at him you wouldn't think he was cut out for this work. Second-hand cars, maybe. His hair, what was left of it, was ash-grey and greased back, with sideburns to the jawline. His eyes were so black you could get lost in there very quickly.

'What's David doing up still?'

'He wants to sleep in the living room.'

'Okay, but no TV, tell him.'

'You home now?' He took his arms out of the sink. His hands were like buckets of soap suds.

'I've just been to BSkyB. I've got to go out again.'

'Isn't that what you get from beef?'

'BSE you're thinking of,' Ridley informed him with a grin.

Mick gave him the eyeball. He was the man who never smiled.

Ridley was always amused by how his colleague had procured Mick from the parole board. But Clyne had his reasons. Mick had done time for GBH and thus would be handy if a couple of bur-glars broke in while he was there. Clyne also believed in support-ing ex-cons who made an earnest attempt at going straight.

Mick took off his apron. Two of the buttons on his shirt were missing. At the interview for this job he had arrived in a blazing orange sweater *tucked into his belt,* a red plaid sports coat over the top, cream flared trousers and white PVC loafers. Clyne's daughter Lucy took one look at him and told her father that if he dared employ him she'd go live with her mother, even though her mother didn't want her. That's how bad he looked.

His gastronomical skills were what turned Lucy round. He made such choice meatball sauce they should have cast him in *Goodfellas.* Now she went shopping with him for his clothes.

After he'd been with the family a while Clyne asked why he was doing what he was doing. Didn't he think it a strange job for an ex-villain of fifty-three? Mick said he never had any ambition to be anything other than a stay-at-home. There was an old-fashioned mother trapped inside him.

When Clyne's ex-wife first met him, all she could say was, I guess you won't be fucking this au pair like you did all the others.

Clyne had never fucked any au pair. Moreover, no au pair they'd ever had could cook like Mick.

'And another thing,' Clyne said. 'Did you teach my son to swear like I just heard?'

Mick started to protest, then said, 'Oh sure, Bob. I even teach him how to spell them.' His lips were as thin and straight as a hairpin.

41

'You can't read, Mick.'

'Some things I can.'

'Some things you can. Well, I never used to swear like that until I was in my twenties. Lucy upstairs?'

'Tooting on my bag of cocaine.' Mick wiped his hands by running them over his head.

Clyne left Mick talking over old times with his DS and went to find Lucy. From the hall he could see the screws in her door handle vibrating from the viscera-thumping bass of her stereo. He forced open the door, pushing back a gale of violent sound.

His daughter was sitting on the edge of her bed, painting her toenails a sinister black. Snuggled under her chin was the portable phone. How could anyone have a conversation over that noise? She couldn't hear her father shout. He leant a finger on the volume control.

Lucy kept painting her toenails in the ensuing doldrums. Without looking up, she said, 'Hi, Dad. Make the streets safer to walk today?'

'When was the last time you walked anywhere? Who you talking to?'

'Mum.'

He stalled. 'Give her my love,' he managed.

'Dad sends you his love.'

Lucy shrugged. Clyne knew what that meant.

'I'm going to have to go out again.'

'Sure, Dad. Go get the scumbags.'

'Actually I was wondering whether you'd hold the fort here for an hour or two.'

'What about Mick?'

'I can't afford him as it is.'

'I'm not a registered charity either.'

'I'll pay you three pounds an hour.'

'Some deal!'

'Please, help me out this once.'

'All right,' she sighed. 'Just tell David that I won't take any shit.'

'Good girl. See you later.'

Ridley caught up with sleep on the way to Wanstead Flats. No problem with that normally, except he was driving the car. Every time his chin dropped Clyne slapped him round the head.

The scoot over to Wanstead cuts through Leyton, where the spirit takes a fall; sex drive, self-esteem are pitched downwards. Like Walthamstow and Chingford further to the north, Leyton is a pointless epic of autistic architecture. Mini-cab depots, doner kebabs, Spar grocers, Chinese takeaway, caff and pet shop with a flat above each. Away from the strip, a woman walks out of her bungalow straight on to the hard shoulder of the dual carriageway.

'How can anyone emerge from this swamp and still say they're ready to rock and roll?' Clyne said.

He and Sam Ridley had motored through a lot of urban desert like this one, often with a foot to the boards. They didn't make a mark on this city but the city made a mark on them. Ridley's face was a mirror of Clyne's and looked shunted by city-blast, by the heavy loads.

To help Ridley stay awake Clyne turned the car radio up loud. Frank Sinatra ('What is this Thing Called Love?') clung to the sparse foliage of the trees on that bruised February evening.

As Wanstead Flats developed ahead Clyne became sentimental. 'I was born here, Sam. I ever tell you that?'

'Yes, but I suspect you're going to again.'

'After the Blitz the government put up prefabs here. For soldiers' families.'

'That's how come your dad got one?'

'That's right. He and my mum lived in it until 1958, the year I was sprogged.'

'It was very harmonious in those days.'

'How'd you know that, Sam?'

'You told me, Bob.'

'Yeah, well, it was. Economists, dockers, civil servants . . . all gypsies for a while.'

On the Flats a convoy of coaches, trucks and horse boxes were drawn into a circle like a wagon train. The vehicles were fitted with wood-burning stoves that puffed smoke into the grey London night. Coachwork was painted in psychedelic colours and designs. The New Age travellers.

Clyne remembered having a run-in with them ten years ago. In uniform then, he was drafted into Stonehenge where they'd descended for the summer solstice. Their argument was that they had spiritual rights of dominion over Stonehenge; that they – natural, free, their faces painted – were the heirs apparent of this profound pagan site. The National Trust and English Heritage who administered the site didn't quite see it their way and got the festival banned. Enter the police. As a tactic to prevent the travellers getting into the site the police 'decommissioned' their vans and buses. But their vehicles were more than just wheels – their one possession that set them free – and they all ended up having an almighty scrap in the mud and rain. It became known as the Battle of Beanfield and attained the status of folklore. It was their Agincourt.

As Clyne and Ridley waited at traffic lights on Dawes Road, several of the travellers' kids of about nine or ten rushed over to the car and started to wash the windscreen. Squeegee artists.

Clyne rolled down his side window. 'Fuck off the lot of you before I run you in.' He flashed his police ID and they beat it back into the camp.

Harsh justice, but Clyne also had scars from the Battle of Beanfield.

Ridley was laughing, looking at his watch. 'Half past fucking twelve. Kids stay out this late when you lived here, Bob?'

'No. They never washed windscreens either.'

Making their approach on foot Clyne looked back at the bay-windowed terraces and gave a passing thought to the residents watching through grey net that tribe of openly hostile punks hunkered down around camp fires, their dogs fighting in packs. Such displays of existentialism were unwelcome in an age when existentialism had gone out of fashion. The travellers were dedicated to doing nothing when we were all meant to be doing something.

They ambushed a group sitting round a fire. In the flame Clyne could see their clothes and skin encrusted with dirt. They wore rings through their noses and tattoos on their faces. Self-mutilators. Mohicans and dreadlocks dyed green and blue. And KO'd on a homemade hooch the colour of diesel fuel.

The air was cloying with smells of rotting fruit, rancid fish. Voices locked together; mocking cries and whispers. Clyne's gently probing questions about whether the council had tried to kick them off the Flats were received politely. Two minutes later that politeness wore off and he and Ridley were asked the nature of their business. They couldn't hide their society by virtue of their dress.

Clyne said he was looking for Alice Harper.

'She's a friend of ours,' Ridley added.

One of them said, 'Then it's a lapsed friendship . . .'

'What you mean?'

The travellers laughed among themselves, laughter like a corral fence. 'She's in the yellow bus, man.'

They turned to where the fingers pointed. A single-decker coach painted canary yellow backed into an impenetrable copse of prickly hawthorn bushes. A windmill on the coach roof turned in the breeze and a diesel generator rumbled.

They made their approach through a colosseum of fighting dogs.

We are not a politically organized tribe, but by the nature of our lives, are politicized. In our defence against an artificial urban life we are perceived as anarchists but really, few would know what the word means. And ask a crustie who the current PM is and he'll struggle to get the guy's name out. Until the Criminal Justice Bill we had nothing to do all day but fuck, sleep and drink. That single piece of legislation made us. It gave us reason to get up in the morning. Up, out, climb a tree, dig a tunnel.

These people need such focus, even if it is only playing hide and seek in tunnels below new motorways. Any activity that can keep solipsism at bay. For we are not a happy band of brothers. It's hardly a choice to become a traveller. You don't wake up one day and decide it would be hip to join a tribe. We're fucked up in the head, more than most. Ending up here is an evolutionary thing. If it wasn't a travellers' camp it would be jail or the nuthouse for many of us, the black sheep of our families. For one reason or another few can fend for themselves in conventional society. We leave that behind and change our names. In this life I'm called Wave. Max is Fawn.

It's been Wanstead for the past six months. Then who knows where. The only consistency is our bus. Let me give you the tour. The front section of the coach is the lounge, with sofas and rugs and coffee table, heated by a wood-burning stove. A few half-empty silver dishes of takeaway chicken tikka masala litter the table but otherwise it looks dinky, with fresh flowers in vases. A photo of me and Max as kids in school uniform is propped up in the window. A tie-dyed cotton hangs from the walls. A mural painted on the ceiling depicts a Last Supper attended by dreadlocked crusties. The driver's cab draped in a Union Jack looks like a piece of situationist art. Max's bicycle lies against a hip-high stack of magazines containing my copy. There's a small step up to a galley area. A bulkhead beyond the galley isolates the two bedrooms from the rest of the bus, curtains between each. An old carpet runs the whole length of the bus and tears the heels off my shoes.

Max, in boxer shorts and vest, and our heavily pregnant friend Rainbow, stretched out on the sofa and working her way through a tray of chocolate eclairs, are watching *Four Weddings and a Funeral* on the TV. As the only chick with a job I can afford such luxuries as a TV/VCR. Twelve-volt batteries, split charger, step-down transformer, AC/DC converter fires it up. The wind turbine keeps the batteries topped up, producing half a kilowatt a day in a force five or over. When the wind won't blow we turn on the diesel genny.

I don't care much for TV and take myself off to bed. I'm halfway into the house of sleep when I hear a knock at the door. It's Max who pads over to open up.

'I'm looking for Alice Harper.' Hearing my old name used rings alarm bells.

'Don't know if she's awake,' Max replies.

'Who are you?'

'I'm Alice's brother, Max.'

'I thought you lived abroad?'

'Who told you that?'

'Your stepmother.'

47

'You met my stepmother?'

'May we come in?'

'Who are you?'

'Detective Inspector Clyne. This is Detective Sergeant Ridley.'

The bus moves on its suspension as two heavy bodies enter the bus. 'What's this?'

'We're watching *Four Weddings and a Funeral*,' Max says.

'Good film?' the one called Clyne asks.

'Bit overrated actually.'

'You Alice?' Clyne asks.

'That's Rainbow,' Max answers for her. 'She hasn't a kip of her own at the moment.'

Rainbow doesn't answer the next question either: 'You flying solo, love?'

''Fraid so,' Max says.

I hear the sofa sigh as Max flops down into it. I wait. But it's obvious he isn't getting up again. He's gone back to watching the film.

'I'd like to talk to you and your sister if that's not too much trouble?' the detective sings.

'Sorry. Yes . . . Alice.' Max approaches at speed. He pushes open the curtain to my room.

'I heard, I heard,' I say.

I wrap a sheet around me and go out. On seeing the two suits in my lounge I become self-conscious of my nakedness under the sheet, my hair in knots. The one called Clyne is in his mid-thirties and very attractive, with full lips, big eyes, strong nose. The other cop's short and stocky.

'What's going on?' I ask.

'Alice Harper?'

'Possibly. I'll have a better idea in the morning.'

'I'm Detective Inspector Clyne. This is Detective Sergeant Ridley.'

'What do you want? It's almost midnight.'

Clyne sought out Max, wanting to include him too. 'It's to do with your father. I'm afraid he was found dead earlier today.'

'My God . . .' I say. 'No kidding . . .'

'We'd like to ask you some questions.'

I glance at Max; his eyes have not roamed from the TV.

'Give me a moment to get dressed.'

'You want to hang around in that sheet, s'all right by me,' Clyne flirts.

'Max will make you some coffee.'

'That will be nice, thank you.'

'Max!' I shout. 'Make these coppers some coffee.'

Max suddenly looks crestfallen. 'What . . . now?'

'Tomorrow's likely to be too late.'

'I'm watching a film on TV, Alice!'

'It's a video, you berk. Make some coffee. Do as you're told.'

'Okay, sure. Right.'

Rainbow freezes the video, the most strenuous exercise she's done all day. I leave the cops looking perplexed by our strange sibling relationship. As I dress I leave the curtain pulled aside and watch Max and the two police in the galley. The small table hinged to the wall is heaving with empty wine bottles, overflowing ash trays. Nobody has done the washing-up for a week. Max handles the kettle on the calor-gas stove well enough. But when he starts pouring ground Columbian coffee straight into mugs Clyne steps forward to give him a hand.

'You got a pot somewhere?'

Max presents him with a cracked brown teapot, which Clyne first has to empty. He puts in a few dessertspoons of coffee and Max fills it up with water; before the water has actually come to the boil.

'Got any cigarettes, Inspector?'

'Sure,' Clyne says, handing Max his Camels. 'You working, Max?' he asks, knowing it's a racing certainty that he isn't.

'I don't have a job.'

49

'Oh really, that's too bad.'

'I've never had a job, actually.'

'Who pays your way, DSS?'

'Alice does,' Max says, wrong-footing the cop, examining the cigarette between his fingers as he exhales the smoke through his nose.

'She's got a job?'

'Sort of.'

'Role reversal, is it?' the one called Ridley says.

'Maybe I'm frightened of getting a job,' Max confesses. 'Of being somebody. I don't want to be somebody. I want to be me. Does that sound odd?'

'Not at all,' I intervene. 'Work's not the only means of defining who you are.'

My reappearance makes Clyne stagger backwards, seeing me dressed in a black mini-skirt and white shirt, with a little red lipstick applied and my hair brushed. I've confounded his prejudices about travellers. I don't have my tongue or eyebrows pierced and I don't wear tattoos. His eyes go up and down my bare legs. He recognizes good legs when he sees them.

'How's the coffee, gentlemen?'

'It's pretty good,' Ridley grins.

'The last time I asked Max to make coffee he heated up a cup of Bailey's Irish Cream.'

'Thought you wouldn't notice the difference?'

'Exactly.'

'Can we talk here, or somewhere else?' Clyne asks.

'Here's fine.'

Rainbow will hear us but I don't particularly care. I look at Max. He's still not really with it yet.

'I understand you haven't seen your father for some time?' Clyne says.

'Who told you that?'

'Your stepmother. She told us where to find you.'

'Really? That surprises me. That they knew where I was. I haven't seen either of them for years.'

'Why did you fall out with your father?'

'Children often do . . . drift apart from their parents.'

'Your stepmother thinks it's because you didn't like her.'

'Does she?'

'Is she right?'

'Not really. But you know . . .'

'Would you have any idea who could have killed him?'

'Killed him! He was murdered then?'

'Yes.'

'I don't know who my father mixes with.'

'I knew your father as a passing acquaintance. From the sailing club.'

'You sail, do you, Inspector?'

'I do, yes.'

'That's interesting.'

'I own a boat too. A Rival 38.'

'On a policeman's salary?'

'Me and two partners. My father passed some information on, from his colleagues in the Customs. They seized this drug smuggler's yacht up in Newcastle. I went up and bought it in the auction for eight grand. It was worth thirty.'

'Worth more with the drugs.'

'Drugs'd been taken off.'

'What a good dad you have.'

'Had. He died a couple of years ago.'

'Sorry.'

'I sailed it round the world.'

'Round your father . . .'

'What?'

'Did it make you wiser?'

'Why do women always ask that question? Did it make me wiser? I don't know. I read a lot of books.'

51

'You could have done that at home.'

'Not me. Too restless, aren't I, Sam?'

This Sam guy nods, too overwhelmed to speak.

'Alice . . . ?' Max interrupts. He has my black leather handbag on his arm. I lift the handbag, and find my purse inside. I hand Max a crisp ten-pound note.

'Max's pocket money,' I say smartly as Max starts ripping off his vest.

'You going out?' Clyne asks.

'Yeah,' says Max.

'No mourning period?' Ridley sounds offended.

'Can you both account for your whereabouts at four a.m. today?'

'I was here.'

'What about you, Max?'

'Me too.'

'Listen . . .' I say angrily. 'There is more than one way of killing someone. My father, we cut him out a long time ago.'

'Are you going to his funeral?'

'I'd like to see some of my relatives.'

'But you won't be sending flowers?' Clyne asks, draining his coffee, grouts and all.

'Deadly nightshade, maybe.'

In his jeans now, Max drapes three different-coloured shirts over his arm. 'What one should I wear, Alice?'

'The black denim one.'

'Right,' he says and stuffs his arms in the sleeves.

'Do you have to dress him as well?' Clyne asks.

Despite the sarcasm I sense that Clyne likes my brother, his benign insouciance, his impudence. Max's face is a perennial child-like phenomenon, the kind of bloke who makes police work simple. His lies would be easy to scope. 'How would you like to foster a grown man, Inspector?'

'Thanks for your time,' he says.

'Good luck,' I say as they are leaving, and detect a falling in Clyne's eyes, as if he didn't really want to go. He glances again at my naked legs, at the full catwalk display.

'You going out as well?' he asks.

'Me? No. I'm going back to bed.'

THREE

There were three women sitting on the edge of the sandpit. Three generations, but unrelated. A north London Jewish grandmother, a middle-aged Turkish Cypriot and a Hungarian girl of nineteen or twenty. The grandmother talked most, the Hungarian hanging her head sadly. Their clothes looked like they'd come off the same Brick Lane stall: Indian cotton wrap-arounds, raw silk blouses, white tights, Moroccan slippers. Each woman's hair was thick and unmanaged. They were not beautiful, but attractive in other ways, sparking off each other debating children, grandchildren, gardens, cooking, books, politics – breaking it up every five minutes to check where their own respective wards were in the playground.

Clyne feigned to read his newspaper and tuned in to the women while his son David was polishing up the slide. He was taken by the way three women of different ages and ethnic backgrounds could find common ground. Put three men in a sandpit and you'd have a competition.

This Hungarian girl, looking about to break into tears, was being counselled by the other two. 'Don't worry, don't worry, it gets better,' the grandmother was saying. 'When my husband left me I cried for three years. The next thirty years I haven't stopped laughing.'

'Is true,' said the Cypriot, 'you will be happy again.' Then she complimented the grandmother on her lemon silk dress.

'You know, I never wear dresses,' the grandmother explained. 'All my old dresses I've cut off the bodices. It was my grand-daughter who found this one. I think the reason I cut them up, because my ex-husband always wanted me in one. And not just dresses either. Little skirts and knee socks, a nun's habit once. Depending on his sexual fantasy at the time.'

'Your husband, he is not Jewish?'

'Oh yes, but he converted to Buddhism. Said it was easier to understand.' The grandmother turned back to the young Hungarian. Stroking her hair she said, 'So your husband's left. But you'll find other things to love. Your children, friends, gardens, a job well done, pets.'

Whereupon she produced a rat from inside her dress. A large black and white rat which they passed around, woman to woman, generation to generation. For five minutes each they allowed the rat free range inside their blouses, their bras, next to their breasts, feeling its warmth on their bare skin.

The roads around Hampstead are as winding and neurotic as country lanes. Cars peeled round bends, clipping wing mirrors, forcing Clyne on to the kerb. Every one was a Merc or a Beema; none of them with manners.

'Fucking hell!' Ridley covered his eyes as an Audi convertible skimmed them. 'If I'd a car like that I'd treat it with respect.'

'Sam, folks round here skin up dope in twenty-pound notes.'

You never get to see Hampstead residents moving about their manors. They are always away in the Caribbean, Provence. Or sitting tight inside, comforted by the whine of their electronic security systems. At best, you see a gate to some driveway opened by the hired help, a Filipino on two pounds an hour, and one of those cars mentioned slides out with a well-groomed shadow at the wheel.

55

They found Marwood Hospital shielded from the road by a line of wind-breaking poplar trees, discreetly signposted with a bronzed number on the gatepost. At 0915 Clyne drove through the frigid gardens. The lawns were cropped shorter than a golf tee. Flowerbeds had been patted down for the long winter nights. Plants were bound with string and gagged with polythene sheeting. The driveway wound through a couple of switchbacks and concluded outside a large red-brick Victorian building. They parked the car and headed on in.

The hospital was mute and deserted. Seeing no reception area they started to walk down a long white corridor. All the doors had peepholes and heavy locks.

'This is a place where the dogs don't bite,' Ridley said.

They jumped when a door swung open and a woman in a white smock floated out, her benign smile undone by her bleeding fingernails that stretched for Ridley, pressing up against a sealed window. A rotund psychiatric nurse stepped from the cell and prevented her patient from coming closer.

Clyne asked where he might find the adolescent unit and she told him to keep going. The unit was an annexe at the back of the hospital.

They carried on their way and didn't spare the horses.

Still that corridor wouldn't quit. The end was a vanishing point that never got bigger than the eye of a needle. There was a slap and a whistle, a howl and a laugh from behind closed doors.

By the time they reached the exit they were both in bad humour. Clyne threw his body against the door and fell among branches of a rose bush climbing the outside wall. Thorns tugged cotton threads out of his jacket and scratched at his face. Acupuncture on the NHS.

They saw what they'd been looking for. Also chained in these barbed tendrils was a prefabricated single-storey nexus of huts, recently built and colour-coded with the main red-brick building.

The annexe seemed empty at that time in the morning. Inside were more closed doors, but no peepholes. Clyne heard what he thought was his name whispered, but it was his shoes squeaking on the rubber floor.

A young man sat behind a sliding window reading a magazine. On his T-shirt was a logo, DAZED AND CONFUSED in blurred white lettering. Clyne's emotion, identified. When he asked where he could find the senior consultant the man pointed them into a waiting room. Clyne saw him ring a bell on the wall. There was no sound from it, but by and by a secretary came to the waiting room. She was about thirty-five and well practised in aloof warmth. Did they have an appointment? Clyne showed his badge. She told them to wait.

At 0930 two teenage boys entered. One, in reversed baseball cap and built-up Nikes, sprawled in the seat as far away as he could get. He didn't seem to know the other kid, in a parka zipped up to the chin. Clyne tried figuring out their problems, to pass the time. When he was their age he'd have been in pretty bad shape before consenting to therapy.

This was what he decided: the kid nearest, he saw his father murder his mother. The other had a coke habit. He'd got a tooter's nose.

Clyne flicked through the magazines on the table. *Maxim* and *Loaded* and stuff like that.

She didn't introduce herself when she came to collect the police, but stood at the door and pointed down the hall. Clyne and Ridley were only too pleased to get out and followed her blindly. A few strides later, she turned round and said, 'I'm Mary Oppenheimer. I never introduce myself in the waiting room.'

It was then Clyne noticed her ankle-length Dorothy Perkins, her vegetarian's canvas shoes.

'Those two boys waiting to see you?' he asked.

'I don't see patients, I'm the senior consultant.'

Her office was tiny and narrow, partitioned, with a couple of

Vermeer prints on the walls. Their perspectives recalled the main hospital corridor, the geometrical shapes converging into vanishing points.

They sat facing one another, Clyne and Oppenheimer's knees separated by a couple of inches. Hair was sprouting through her shins. He ran straight into her eyes behind orange-rimmed glasses the wrong shape for her face.

'You've come to ask me about George?' Oppenheimer was straight in, in no mood for small talk. 'I found out earlier this morning. I'm stunned, I have to say. Absolutely devastated.'

'How long has he worked here?'

'Five years.'

Clyne wrote that down in his notebook.

'This is an NHS hospital?'

'Yes, but our unit's private.'

'I didn't know that. Your clients have money?'

'Most of our patients are extra-contractual referrals. There's a shortage of NHS places. They get immediate admission here.'

'Those two boys in the waiting room, they're NHS referrals?'

'Private, actually.'

'That surprises me. You can't tell anything from appearances these days.'

'Perhaps you shouldn't even try.'

Clyne looked up from his notebook and felt her admonishing him like a school teacher. 'Truth hides behind appearance, not the other way round,' he said. 'Mr Harper, why did he work in the private sector, to earn more money?'

'What's the basis of this prejudice of yours, Inspector?'

'I don't like it conceptually. I go to see a private shrink, how do I know he's not going to overdiagnose my problem just to get his hands on my wallet?'

'It would be easy to pathologize an adolescent. Of course that's true. Some child with violently abusive parents, say, when clearly what he needs is to be separated from those parents. He'd need a social worker, not therapy.'

'But you run a tight ship here?'

'In an ideal world we would still be in the NHS. It's not us who demolished it.'

'Mr Harper have that view also?'

'Yes. Absolutely. I believe so.'

'Absolutely. You believe so. Which is the right answer?'

'He went on television to say why more adolescents are being recommended for therapy now than at any other time. He said it was a direct result of the government's social policies.'

'Or lack of them.'

'Absolutely.'

'Was that on BSkyB?'

'Yes, I think it was.'

'The adolescents he saw, what kinds of problems did they have?'

'Could you be more specific?'

'Did he have violent patients?'

'I don't know how well you know our work here, Inspector, but adolescent trauma's rarely dramatic. Very often they have nothing more than depression from loneliness. Or they can't make friends in school. But it feels to them like the world's caved in. Adolescents are on a springboard, trying to leave infantile longings behind and leap into the next stage of life. They want independence. They still depend on parents. Disturbed adolescence is almost a tautology.'

'So I should send my daughter for counselling?'

'Ask her.'

'I will. George . . . did he have any patient who might have wanted to kill him?'

'That's not something I wish to comment on. It would be an infringement of patients' confidentiality.'

'Okay. What about his colleagues. Anyone on the staff . . .'

'Want to murder him? That's almost risible, Inspector.'

'Well, someone killed him. I'm trying to build a profile of Mr Harper, Mrs Oppenheimer. Learn something about him.'

'I'm sorry. That's the consequence of psychotherapy existing outside of culture. We don't always know how to behave in public.'

'People don't like therapists . . .'

'We're regarded as disreputable.'

'Did he give out drugs?'

'Never. George offered explanations of experience. That's it. He helped kids clarify the codes. You see, the way adolescents behave is linked to how their parents want them to behave. They erect false selves to please their parents. George helped them eliminate their humiliation and find independence. That's why he had a running battle with parents who wanted his help in making their children . . . *obedient*.'

'Any of those parents psychopathic?'

'He didn't believe in seeking self-knowledge.'

'Why not?'

'Because there's no original character. If you try and look for one, some mythical self, you'll end up damaging yourself. He used to say, don't go on that journey, it's a waste of psychic energy. Life is greater than self-knowledge.'

'Like an onion, you mean?'

'Sort of.'

'May I see his case reports?'

'Absolutely not. They're confidential.'

'I'm trying to solve his murder, not pry.'

'You'll need a court order to force us to make a disclosure. Even then it'll be partial. The GMC's policy is to disclose only that part of what we feel is relevant to your inquiries.'

'How would you know what was relevant?'

'Are you an expert in adolescent psychology?'

'No more than you're an expert in police procedure. It might be nice to work together on this.'

'I don't think that's possible.'

'Then I'm going to have to come back with a court order.'

'I'm afraid so.'

Clyne and Ridley were both feeling bruised from their encounter with Ms Oppenheimer. A woman had taken them out. It was by common consent that they dropped the subject as they drove back to the Commercial Road station.

'Manny thinks it's a two-hander. Alice and Max Harper? A double patricide. What d'you think about that idea, Sam?'

'What's their motive?'

'Oh, we'll get to that.'

'Alice wears the trousers over there. But Max is a bit cleverer than he looks.'

Last September one of the glossies asked me to track down Claude Vignisson and interview him. Claude is a fallen star. A one-time gangster for several of the now defunct East End firms, a hurt-addict in his time, a knife merchant, he'd even gone up and down the road with Ronnie Kray – the Colonel.

I had an in with Claude. He was a member of the same sailing club as my father. And it was there I tracked him down, by telephone.

When I introduced myself, Claude said, 'I've only spoke to your father once or twice but he was very nice.'

I then asked if I could interview him.

'Any daughter of George's can ask me what she likes.'

We met face to face in the Ruskin Arms, Manor Park – a short walk from Wanstead Flats and from where he lived in East Ham with his fourth wife. I arrived early and sat at a table by the emergency exit. I felt nervous, whether on account of Claude's violent reputation or as an acquaintance of my father, I did not know. Drinkers sat around tables against the walls, looking into the empty space as if waiting for dancers, cock fights, wrestlers to appear. Originally an establishment with four separate lounges, the Ruskin Arms had been converted into one universe. A super-bar sold a dozen different real ales. In the far corner was a pool table.

Claude arrived punctually; a whiskered octogenarian with bleached blond hair, dressed in navy-blue blazer with a white hankie in the breast pocket. His sailing club tie was tightly knotted around his thin neck. He wore a Rolex watch, probably fake. What all this gear couldn't hide was his slight hunchback (from creeping about) and his nose broken in so many places a fly'd have trouble landing on both feet.

Claude would not hear of it when I offered to buy him a drink. It was something a 'girl like you' simply shouldn't do. He bought all the drinks we were to consume that night, making the pilgrimage to the bar alone.

Claude drank rum and blackcurrant from a wine glass. I stayed on lager.

'When was your last brush with the Old Bill, Claude?'

He said, 'Couple of years ago,' then began the kind of monologue I was to hear much of. 'Someone put eighteen stitches in Jackie Prior's face, snout from Whitechapel. I was innocent of that one as it transpired but they booked me anyway. Eighteen stitches might seem excessive for what had been a minor misdemeanour on the snout's account, but the commissioning rate went by the stitch. Economics is economics. Next morning you go by your client's place with the morning's newspaper and work out, from the crime report, how much wages was owing.'

'Who do you work for now?'

'I don't do nothing fancy any more. I'm retired.' He smiled, but his eyes remained in the shade.

'Come off it. There's no pension in your business. You can't afford to retire.'

'No, listen, I was a legend. I'm taken care of by my old friends. They put clothes on me back, give me eats and drinks and do everywhere I go.'

'Well, you're looking gentle on the sauce, Claude, whoever's putting it on your plate.'

'I've always been gentle, Alice.'

The friends of Claude Vignisson were in no position to give him anything. They had all been shot dead in the streets, or gone insane in Broadmoor. His friends had been succeeded by less visible, less flamboyant individuals that the police still had to put a face on. Ethnics who used Semtex rather than the sawn-off, traded in pharmaceuticals rather than bonded goods. They'd have no use for an old-time dandy like Claude.

We were the only white patrons in the pub full of Indian males, doing the English thing and stealing a crafty pint away from the women. It seemed a strange venue for Claude and I called him on it.

'Pakis are nice,' he said. 'They won't rob yer house. Never had any trouble with any of them in my life. It's the niggers I detest, for leaving their wives and kids in the lurch. A man must spend time with his family.'

'You sound like the Mafia, Claude.'

'I was the Mafia.'

'None of your old friends are here though, are they?'

'Well, no, that's true. No self-respecting villain would be seen drinking in a Paki pub. But I have sentimental reasons. When I was a kid my old man used to play boogie piano here Saturday nights, his pint of mild and bitter trembling on top the piano while his hands roamed the keys. My old mum used to send me out to get him at closing time because he was always too drunk to find his own way home.'

I asked him to fill me in about his early life.

He skipped his childhood completely, said it was not relevant. The rest was straight off the CV. At seventeen he enlisted in the Royal Navy as an ordinary seaman. Three years later he was dishonourably discharged for theft and began his career as a professional criminal. He outlined a sentimental history of long firm frauds, blue corner games, point to points, spielers, orange box hookers, and other erstwhile diabolical liberties.

'Your parents have passed away?'

'When I was eleven, lovely girl.'

'My mother died when I was eleven.'

'Then you know, don't ya.'

'What happened to you after your parents died?'

But again, he would not be drawn on this. Childhood was off limits. Instead he kept me entertained for another half-hour, telling how he helped the community more than the Old Bill ever done. All the Bill could do was file a complaint, he said, while he and his associates would know who did what within two hours and give them a smack. Putting them all away was the worst thing they ever did. He said, Sorry Alice, but it was us what reduced local crime, we was the first community watch. It's all fucked up now since Freddie Foreman, Eddie and Arif went down. The drug gangs have taken over the manor. All this crack and shit, brought over by outsiders. Bunch of non-English snouts, never see their faces in the clubs. In the old days no self-respecting villain would touch drugs, wouldn't even put up the scratch.

Claude Vignisson might have maimed and killed a few people in his time, but he do have his morals.

At closing time Claude insisted on walking me home. I'd have preferred he didn't. I didn't want him to see where I lived. But Claude had the mentality of a pit-bull and hooked my arm inside his. We strolled through the Flats like father and daughter, him talking less and less as we entered the travellers' camp. Crusties were roaming around in the dark like apparitions, putting the frighteners on him with their orange mohicans and face paint and adornments clinking.

I tried to sever our ties outside the bus but he followed me in through the door. Max was there to greet us, in his underwear.

The way Claude looked him up and down I feared for Max's health. 'This is my brother,' I said rapidly.

Behind Max a couple of chicks were sitting on the floor, fucked up on something chemical. Their faces and necks were ingrained with dirt.

Claude had seen enough to know he'd wandered into uncharted territory. 'Lord above. Even Rachman's slums looked better than this. In the worst of all my days I've never seen anyone living like this. What's the matter with you, girl? Where's your dad? He should be taking you home. Those girls are covered in shit, look . . .'

One of the girls fired back at him: 'The dirt's all on the outside. Our souls are pure.'

'Honey,' Claude said, 'no man I know likes their crumpet to have fallen in the mud.'

I pushed Claude back through the door. Outside he held my hand in the dark, his eyes full of pity. 'What are you, Hansel and Gretel?'

'Not a bad guess, Claude.'

'Can't you find a little kip with taps and a cooker?'

'It's a long story, Claude.'

'Ain't they all. What's your father think, is what I'd like to know. Next time I see him down the club I'm going to have to give him a slap.'

'He's out of the picture, Claude.'

'Well, for fuck's sake. I got kids. If I found any of them living here I'd be round with a posse, I can tell you.'

'That would be against my wishes.'

'You can wish for better than this.'

FOUR

While Clyne and Ridley had been unscrolling the hurt in Hampstead the uniforms had been running around St Katharine's Dock, interviewing prospective witnesses. Not even a dog had seen a dicky bird. Manny made an appearance on *Crimewatch* appealing for information. Two days later they were still awaiting a sensible call.

No motive, no witnesses and as yet no forensic.

'How did Harper get switched off without anyone *seeing* it?' Manny raged in the incident room. The team were all there for the daily meeting.

He turned on Clyne. What had he got to show for his salary?

'Well, the reports vary considerably,' Clyne responded. 'Harper's colleagues say he was dedicated to his teenage patients. Alastair thinks he was R.D. Laing's reincarnation. His wife has yet to shed a tear. Ditto his two children. Though I think they know more than they're revealing. The daughter's a piece of work.'

Manny spun his lights off the DI and on to everyone in the meeting. 'This is all bollocks!' he shouted. 'We can't just close this one. Harper wasn't a slag, he was a doyen of the psychiatric world. There's got to be evidence. I want something in here with blood on it within the next twenty-four hours. Now get out of here, all of you.'

You get lost on an investigation, you make a return to the aetiology of the case. The crime scene.

From the station Clyne and Ridley made a run down the Highway in the late afternoon, the engine protesting. Whenever he was feeling frayed like this Clyne drove in the first two gears only. That way he couldn't climb much above 30 m.p.h., even though his head was spinning off the clock.

At St Katharine's he didn't bother parking squarely and he didn't lock up. He left the car door swinging on its hinges and took a walk around with Ridley.

'Good cover for murder in these masts,' Ridley suggested. 'It's like a forest.'

Clyne added, 'The wind's negligible now, but was force four on the day. That'd have made a hell of a racket.'

They greeted the uniforms on the pontoon and crossed the cordon on to the yacht. Down below they sat for a long while in the galley, smoking, looking at the blood stains on the sole where Harper had been garrotted. He'd been fucked up inside this cabin, trussed with rope, taken out and sent up the mast, a vista of the Thames spreading before him:

'"The tranquil waterway leading to the uttermost ends of the earth . . . into the heart of an immense darkness",' Clyne quoted. 'No forensic, no witnesses. This has the hallmarks of a contract killing.'

'But a contract's as routine as anything. They go in, do their work, get out fast.'

'Okay . . . Harper left his home late afternoon to go work on his yacht. He died around 0400 the following morning. He was killed, mutilated and then his killers struggled to get his body up the mast. Why do that, risk being caught?'

'The killer was emotionally involved.'

'Good, Sam. Very good.'

Ridley thought he deserved a drink for that and Clyne agreed. He took him across to the sailing club as his guest.

Inside they perched on a green buttoned-leather bay-window seat, a large telescope on a bracket between them. The club was almost empty of members at this hour. Without them the mahogany interiors promoted a dismal atmosphere. A grand-father clock chimed out the hour. The barometer glass above the bar fell in their time there.

Claude Vignisson was the only other member in, making a phone call inside a bevelled-glass booth behind the bar. The receiver was tucked under his chin and he was sipping a rum and black.

Clyne and Ridley spotted him at the same moment and shared a wry smile. Ridley scanned the giant Napoleonic sea battle in a gilt frame, the bookcases stacked with Lloyd's yacht registers, the ten-foot-high carved oak fireplace, lofty nicotine-coloured domed ceilings, Pugin wallpaper. Then he nudged Clyne. 'How'd Claude get past the membership committee, Bob?'

'Sailing club's a very ecumenical place.'

Claude had also clocked them. He knew Clyne from when he tried to send him down once. He raised his voice on the phone, putting on a performance for their benefit. 'Well, what happened was, Micky Street chinned Ron McGuire's tart. Instead of leaving it there, doing the more sensible thing and forgot the whole matter, Micky sent the tart some flowers. Ron hears of it and thinks there's some funny stuff going on between the two of 'em. Quite by chance he and Micky met in a shebeen over in Roding Bridge and had an altercation. Ron, who come off worst in the fight, went straight down to Phil's drinker and borrows the governor's tools. Then he goes back and does Micky. Put him in intensive. Now Phil's in Pentonville on a pontoon. For incitement. Shame really, I got on with him marvellous.'

Claude came out of the booth and tripped on the step into

the lounge. His face lit up with adrenalin, his eyes fierce with blame, for the steward, anybody, for his slip in dignity.

He recovered and walked over to where Clyne and Ridley were sitting in the bay window.

'Well, look who it isn't,' Claude said.

Clyne glanced away through the window down into the harbour. A billion pounds' worth of hardware bobbed in the water with nothing but a few lengths of rope preventing a steely opportunist walking them downriver.

He pointed to the mast cluster. 'My father used to say sailing's for the rich and vain. You rich and vain, Claude?'

'Me? I'm a model of virtue.'

'When was the last time you went sailing?'

'Years ago. My old bones ache in the cold.'

'But you still come to the club?'

'I can still dream, can't I?'

Clyne leant an elbow on the windowsill. 'Ever been to a psychiatrist in your life, Claude? Voluntarily, that is.'

'I don't need to see no psychiatrist.' His face was inscrutable.

'That's a matter of opinion, but we'll let it go.'

'You referring to poor old George?'

'Someone cut his balls off and stuffed them down his throat. Know anyone with that trademark?'

'You want me to mark your card, Clyne?'

'Could be worth a carpet on your next offence.'

'Now what's the use of credit I can't use?'

'You haven't heard anything then?'

'If I did know anything I wouldn't be telling the shoes, would I?'

'You've sung some psalms for us in the past.'

He twitched at that remark and looked back over his shoulder.

Ridley went to the bar on another run.

'When's the shrink's funeral, Clyne?'

70

'After the file's closed, expect. Might have to stay in the fridge a couple months.'

'Pity. Let me give you some advice. Bury him now. You want to know who killed George? Go to the funeral, see who it is who don't send flowers. Make a list. Start there with your enquiries.'

'Harper was a psychiatrist, Claude, not one of the Krays.'

'Then the killer probably come from somewhere ducky. Like Brighton. I never met a shrink who wasn't a shirt-lifter.'

'George Harper, was he queer?'

'I never fraternized with the man. How would I know. I only met him a couple of times, but I thought he was very nice.'

Their conversation came to an end when Ridley returned from the bar. Claude wandered off upstairs to the snooker room.

They ran into Claude again, in the car park, sitting behind the wheel of a ten-year-old Mercedes 500SE. He was hammering on the starter but couldn't get the beast going. The battery sounded corpse-dead.

Ridley got into their unmarked car as Clyne strolled over to the Merc. The window peeled down slowly on an ebbing twelve-volt current. 'Battery's dead, Clyne. She's been in a slaughter all week.'

'Got any leads?' Clyne asked.

'I got a rope.'

'You want a tow?'

'Yeah. I might be able to jump her.'

'I'll back up in front of you.'

Clyne reversed to within a foot of the Merc's chrome bumper. Claude was outside his car waiting with a length of nylon rope, one end already tied to his car. He lay on the ground and connected the other end to Clyne's tow loop.

Clyne pulled away from the kerb. After a few metres he got some momentum going. He felt the traction as Claude dropped the clutch. The Merc's tyres squealed as the wheels locked. The Merc coughed and backfired, and Clyne heard the engine gunning.

He pulled on the handbrake and stepped outside.

He went down under his car to untie the rope. The door of the Merc opened and Clyne saw his reflection in the high polish of Claude's shoes.

'Clyne, you couldn't drain the radiator while you're down there?'

'Funny fucker.'

Both knots loosened easily, despite the strain they'd been under.

Back in the unmarked, Clyne said to Ridley, 'Claude tied a bowline in that rope.'

'A what?'

'It's nothing, I guess. You want to drive back and get another drink?'

Sunlight was pouring through the window of the bathroom as Clyne considered the silhouette in the doorway: David with a football under his arm was staring quizzically at his father on the floor, half out of his trousers, half out the door.

He could not recall when last night ended and this morning began. David bounced the football on his head and he figured some of it out. Like Sam putting him into a taxi. The football felt like a brick.

Clyne scooped up the ball and they threw it around. He was enjoying the simplicity of it before David decided to try to kick for goal. The ball crashed into the window and cracked the pane of glass from one end to the other. They both looked at the broken window. Neither one said a thing.

It was Saturday morning and Clyne was off the roster until later, when the kids would be at their mother's. He went to wake Lucy, but no show there. Trying to get her out of bed was heavy-duty business, like coaxing Dracula out of his tomb in the midday sun. He gave David that detail before going to start the household coffee brewing downstairs and cooking bacon and eggs for three.

Twenty minutes later Lucy dumped into a chair and leant her head back. She looked terrible, thin and drawn. She wouldn't eat anything either, just sipped a glass of pineapple juice, watching in disgust David necking down his egg yolks.

After breakfast Lucy returned to bed. David and his dad caught up with lost time. They went to the first show at the local Odeon. *Batman Returns*, with Michelle Pfeiffer. With a dustbin of sweet popcorn and a gallon of Coke on his lap David kept asking for explanations. Why does Catwoman purr in a tight situation with the men? But Clyne was less than eloquent when it came to explaining a woman's cynicism.

They wandered out of the cinema into the mid-morning haze and into the arcade across the road, where Clyne spent a small fortune on the virtual racing car. It was blood money, guilt bonds. David kept racing, his father kept paying. The noise of sluicing coins, automatic rifle fire, galactic warfare, the penny drop, lucky dip, pinball machine was hard on his ears; music of the spheres for David. After he'd totalled his 918 Porsche for the twelfth time they left.

On the way home they called into McDonald's for a Big Mac and a chocolate milkshake. Before he'd even finished his fries David was asking what they were doing next.

'We've been to the pictures, the arcade, McDonald's. What else is there?'

'We can go to a nightclub like Lucy.'

'Lucy goes to nightclubs?'

'Of course she does.'

'I didn't know that.'

'She goes to one where they play jungle music.'

'You have to be at your mother's in a couple of hours.'

'Lucy gets to do much more than me.'

'Because she's older. You'll not always be seven.'

'I'm eight!'

'That's right, of course.' (Where *had* all the years gone?)

'Lucy doesn't bother about me. She treats me like I'm not there.'

'It's her age in life.'

'Mick pisses me off sometimes.'

'Watch your language. Who taught you to say that?'

'Lucy says it all the time.'

'I'm going to have to have a word with her.'

'Are you a good policeman, Dad? I think you must be because you can afford to pay Mick to look after me.'

'That's one way of looking at it.'

'I worry sometimes when you're at work a murderer will come in through the window. It's open because it's so hot and then he'll kill me and you won't be there to save me.'

That was Clyne's fear too. His waking nightmare. Oh fuck, yes.

He put his arm around David's shoulders and hauled him close, toking on the Johnson's shampoo in his hair.

At 1400 he ran the engine for five minutes before calling Lucy and David. Lucy ran out of the house and into the warm car. David ambled after her. He didn't feel the cold any more than his father did, but Lucy could freeze in a sauna.

Clyne examined her beside him. 'You look anaemic.'

'That's because I'm pregnant.'

'What!'

'Only kidding.'

'And since when have you been going to nightclubs?'

'For about a year.'

'You're fourteen years of age.'

'So?'

'*So?* I'm sending Mick to chaperone you next time.'

'Very amusing.'

'Do you drink, take drugs?'

'Drink, sometimes.'

'Jesus, Lucy. You're a cop's daughter, you shouldn't be doing these things.' He touched his chest with an open palm and felt his heart palpitating.

They drove to the Angel on the way to Mother's. From a metered street they walked to Café Flo. David held his father's hand. Lucy went ahead on point in case some boy she knew might by chance appear.

They passed a lingerie shop and Clyne's eyes were drawn to the window display of lace underwear wrapped around mannequins. Suspenders and bras in vermilion, gold and yellow; adventurous colours. It was what he saw deep inside the shop that stopped him in his tracks. A yawning gap in the changing room curtains; black leather jacket draped over a wooden chair; pair of cuban-heeled boots placed underneath; a woman rolling blue lace knickers over white thighs; a flash of a pubic beard; fingers crawling inside the waist band. She looked into a mirror, turning to examine her profile, then hooked a matching lace bra off a peg. She shook the straps over her arms. The bra cups rested over her breasts as she reached around to clip on.

He possessed enough decency to have passed on his way long ago, but he knew what he was looking at. He knew who he was looking at. George Harper's daughter, Alice.

With police work there is the expectation of causality. With sexual attraction there are no such rules and he stood before the window disabled by what he'd seen.

Lucy had stopped to wait outside Barclays Bank. He shouted for her to take David and reserve a table. He didn't want him around right now, wanted the same appearance of independence as Lucy. Clyne wanted to be orphaned.

'Go with your sister,' he pleaded.

But David wouldn't budge.

'Go with Lucy, there's someone I've got to see.'

'Who?'

A devil in blue lingerie. 'A suspect in a murder case,' he said to frighten him, then immediately regretted it. He just knew it was going to backfire.

'A murderer?'

'Just go and catch up with Lucy.'

'I'm not going without you.'

He was still negotiating a separation from David as Alice walked out of the shop. Her complexion was sheet-white against black leather, her crimson lipstick shrill. The leather jacket was antique, her jeans ripped at the knee. But what lay under was very new.

She turned in the opposite direction. Seeing his chance fade he called out her name. His voice sounded pathetic, charity-seeking. She turned and looked, without recognizing him.

'It's Robert Clyne, Inspector Clyne . . .'

I scramble to remember and say 'Hello' to give me more time.

'I thought I recognized you.'

'Really?' I smile. 'When exactly?'

'Just this . . . second.'

'Who's that little boy?'

'My son, David.'

The boy scowls at me and pulls on his daddy's sleeve. 'My dad said you murdered someone.'

'Did he?' Now I remember.

I look at Clyne and enjoy watching his face collapse, like a piece of solid geometry.

'We're just going to have a coffee. Want to come? My daughter's gone ahead.'

'You have other children?'

'Just the two.'

I walk over with a smile for him and for his son, who beatifies Clyne whether he knows it or not. A son makes him more than just a murder cop.

We trail down towards the Angel, like a little family. David, who is not so sure of his ground, snaps off and walks ahead.

His daughter is crammed behind a small table in the café.

Clyne introduces me to her as we climb into our chairs. Lucy shakes my hand and I feel thin fingers inside my palm. She is a slender, pretty teenager with three silver earrings in her right lobe.

Clyne and I spark up the fags while Lucy helps her brother select the most potent milkshake from the menu. I puff away, watching their sibling covenant. Like me and Max when we were young.

'You're a long way out from Wanstead,' Clyne says.

'This is where I used to live, go to school.'

'Your brother was saying he hasn't got a job. You seem to, though. That right?'

'I'm a freelance journalist.'

'What kind of journalism?'

'Celebrities. Actors, pop stars, that kind of stuff.'

'Good living?'

I eyeball him. 'You've seen how I live.'

'I had a run-in with an actress and a poet once,' Clyne says. 'Copped the two of them around three in the morning. They'd a punch-up at some party. The poet said, I'm more important than you. And the actress said, But it's me they ask to open supermarkets.'

'Is that why he hit her?'

'Yes, it was.'

'Fucking hell!'

David looks up from the menu at me. Something I said?

He asks his dad, 'You going to sex her, then?'

I cross my legs under the table and hold my cigarette over the shoulder. 'Get out of that one, Inspector.'

'David, don't be personal,' Clyne mumbles.

I prolong his embarrassment. 'I noticed you didn't deny it.' This makes Lucy laugh, who begins to bond with me.

'Have you ever interviewed the Manic Street Preachers?'

She has been listening to me. 'Before or after?'

'Before.'

'I went to Norwich to interview them the night Richey cut 4Real in his arm.'

'Do you think he's dead?'

'No. No, I don't.'

This seems great news as far as she's concerned. A journalist has confirmed it: Richey Edwards lives!

Clyne looks lost in translation.

'A self-mutilating kid from Wales vanishes into thin air and half the population get dewy-eyed,' I say. 'If the Prime Minister disappeared . . . who'd notice?'

'You think he's still alive, Lucy?' Clyne asks.

Lucy nods, her eyes welling up.

'Richey's just trying to survive a dead idea,' I suggest to her.

'My mum and dad are divorced.' David comes back in for airtime. 'We're going to our mum's today.'

He's only just met me and already I'm a rival to his mother.

Lucy touches my fingers and makes me feel embarrassed by my dirty knuckles. But it's the nail varnish she's interested in. 'Rouge Noir?'

'Yes.'

'I can't get that anywhere,' she says.

'There's a waiting list since Uma Thurman wore it in *Pulp Fiction*.'

Clyne looks lost again. He is nowhere in our code.

'Put your hands up here.' I spread Lucy's hands on the table and produce my bottle of Chanel.

Clyne watches me paint his daughter's bare nails. A simple tribal act of union that fills him with admiration.

'How old are you, Lucy?'

'Sixteen,' she says and slides her father a cruel smile.

'She's fourteen,' Clyne corrects her. 'Put two years on your life you put two on mine.'

Blowing on Lucy's nails I ask Clyne, 'Since you're on your own tonight, want to go for a drink?'

He looks across at David. But David doesn't understand what a woman asks for when she asks for a date. Nor does Clyne apparently.

It's his daughter who has to spell it out for him. 'Go on, Dad.'

He says he'd love to but is heavily booked up. 'I've got somewhere I have to be at six, then the police station at seven.'

'How long will you be?'

'If my boss has his way I'll still be there in the morning.' Then the engine starts shuddering behind his skull and seeps smoke into his eyes. 'But I think I'll be free after an hour.'

'I'll meet you there if it's easier.'

'Sure. It's on Commercial Road.'

'I can hang around Islington until then.'

'Will you visit your stepmother?'

I screw the brush back into the bottle of nail varnish. 'I think not.' Lucy flutters her fingers in front of her face, admiring the work. 'Here.' I give Lucy the bottle. 'You can keep this.'

Lucy grins, won over.

David drops his chin in his hands, irritated by all women.

The venue was my call, a tapas bar near Euston that made good margaritas.

We sit at a corner table near the door and order a pitcher. And a plate of olives, calamari, deep-fried mushrooms. Clyne smokes and drinks but doesn't touch the food. I notice every time he takes a hit of margarita he moves his glass round to get at the salt on the rim.

'Your kids at their mother's now?'

'Yeah, south of the river. Whenever I go over the water I feel like I'm going abroad. The fact she can live over there explains

80

why we can't get on. Apache country. She's shacked up with an investment banker name of Justin.'

'But your kids live with you, don't they?'

'Ever since she's been living with Justin I've not seen her in a pair of jeans. She came to the door just now in a mohair dress, string of pearls, lycra stockings. And four-inch come-fuck-me heels.'

'How do you manage, with your job?'

'I get help. I have a bloke called Mick who looks after them when I'm at work.'

'You trust a *man* to look after your children?'

'This man I do.'

'Nice children. How did you get custody?'

'Simple. She didn't want it.'

'Most women fight tooth and nail for their kids.'

'Jenny isn't maternal.'

'Sounds to me you're still chewed up about her.'

'I guess.'

'See a therapist?'

He just laughs, inhaling smoke voraciously.

'It might help.'

'I got this DS, she's been nagging at me about the same thing. Just because she's been up to her eyeballs in shrinks for years. She says, talk to me, I know the nomenclature. Fuck that, I says.'

'It might help you with this investigation. Even if you are still fucked up at the end of it.'

He thinks that through and suddenly brightens up. 'I can see my way forward on those terms.'

Now it is my turn to laugh. 'You'd do anything to solve a case, right?'

'Sure. I'd tell Kelly I like to wear women's knickers if it helped the investigation.'

'Why did you divorce?'

'She said I didn't share with her, like my day. I said, My day is best left inside my head.'

'Is that why the divorce rate's high among police?'

'How'd you know?'

'I'm a journalist. I'm an investigator too.'

He pauses to light a cigarette, the last Camel in his pack, and he's already fretting about where he can buy more, looking around my head for vending machines. I understand that feeling. Without a cigarette I can't talk, don't exist.

I flick my cigarette with a fingernail and ash falls into the olive bowl. 'I might like to interview you one day, Inspector.'

'Call me Bob. Why would you want to do that? I'm not a star.'

'I could make you one.'

'I don't think so.'

'I could invent you, like Agent Cooper.'

He looks overstretched, vexed. Then a connection dawns in his eyes and makes its way gradually down to his lips. 'My daughter writes letters to friends in the style of Laura Palmer's diaries.'

'And Laura Palmer's not even in *Twin Peaks*. She's the murder victim.'

'Actually, it bugs me she's more influenced by Laura Palmer than Agent Cooper.'

'By her mother more than her father.'

'Very perceptive. What you're saying is, cops aren't real. If you can make us up.'

'You're real, just not original. Like crimes are real but not original.'

'Yeah, I get that. Did you know your father believed the same thing? That we're not originals.'

'We may be originals at some point. Before the age of five, say. But then we start constructing a character from archetypes. Did you construct yourself from watching detective shows as a kid?'

'Jigsaws. I liked jigsaws as a kid, trying to find the last piece. I've always liked patterns.'

'Like serial killing?'

'Yeah. It's nice to work on a case with continuity.'

'Don't serial killers usually leave something behind, a personal signature?'

'Like slitting a throat from left to right, you mean?'

'R.D. Laing called the criminal a mystical explorer in a mechanized world.'

'Back to your father again. One of his friends said he was R.D. Laing's heir apparent.'

'Did he?'

'Yeah. Both believed parents screw up children's lives.'

'"They fuck you up, your mum and dad . . ." Famously misquoted once as, They *tuck* you up, your mum and dad.'

Clyne laughs into his margarita.

'Was my father murdered by a serial killer?'

'No, at least we don't think so. Maybe a contract killing. Though I've got my doubts about that too.'

'Someone paid to have him killed?'

'It's one assumption we're working on.'

'How much does a contract killer cost?'

'Three hundred fifty for a frightener, thou for a cut. Murder starts at five rising to twenty grand for a policeman. Hundred for a Triad. Your father would have set someone back forty, as a ball-park figure.'

'More important than a policeman, less important than a gangster.'

'That's it.'

'Not many people have forty grand to spare.'

'It's a lot of fur.'

'Say I had it, how'd I find a contract killer? How's that work?'

'You'd go through an agent. Man gets recommended by the agent, investigated independently to see if he's all right, you

wouldn't even know his second name. The agent would introduce you to the man and that's the agent finished. He'd fade
away. You carry on the business with the man. You tell him
what you want done, to whom and when. You could be there
when it goes off, if you wished, to make sure it was done, shake
hands and then the man would go, fly. You'd not see him again.
But that would be dangerous for someone like you.'

'Why would it be dangerous for me?'

'If they could get another five grand from the police for
grassing you up, they would. Only thing that stops them is
knowing beforehand you'd diss 'em. You have that sort of
clout, Alice?'

'Are we going to be friends?'

'Why not?'

'When will that begin?'

'As soon as you like.'

'Now?'

'Okay.'

'Then stop interrogating me!'

'Sorry, it's a bad habit. How old are you? Last question.'

'That depends.'

'Depends on what?'

'The light. If you saw me in the noonday sun five years ago I'd
look older than I do tonight. Time's not progressive when seen
in terms of light.'

'Really? Well, I see a lot of dead bodies in my line of work,
gonna need more than light to resurrect them.'

'Do you want to fuck me?'

'It crossed my mind.'

'If we do and you discover I killed my father, what happens
then?'

'I turn you in.'

'Sounds fair to me.'

Our conversation suddenly dies. In the tapas bar customers

are swelling in number, pushing themselves ever closer, looking at us, smiling, some laughing. I wonder, do they know? Do they know what I have in mind to do to this cop?

'Let's go,' he says, rising. I rise with him. His voice has that power. Like one in a dream you can't refuse. 'Your place or mine?'

'I doubt you'd want me back at your house.'

He doesn't answer, just reaches for his wallet. As he's forking out thirty quid to cover a £25 bill, I wander to the next table that has recently been vacated and drink the remains of the wine from four glasses.

On the drive to Wanstead I ask if his kids like fairy stories. His face lights up as he recalls something his daughter did, aged three. He said to her, 'Lucy, stop picking your nose, you're making it bleed.' And she replied, 'I'm not Lucy. I'm Snow White.' So he said, 'Go look in the mirror then, Snow White, if you don't believe me.' She went to the wardrobe and looked at herself in the mirror – believing such sights were negotiable – and saw her nostrils were rimmed with blood. She stamped off, muttering, 'You skunk!' over her shoulder at the mirror.

And when his son was two and a half he was sitting in the garden one afternoon eating fishfingers on his red plastic table. He was looking up at the trees, thinking laterally. Suddenly he announced: 'The seven dwarfs don't wear nappies.'

It gives Clyne such obvious pleasure to recall these stories, even after all these years, that I feel reassured about him. It's an act of love to remember such fleeting moments in your children's lives. This is a man who knows how to love.

On the Flats the dogs are running in packs. Crusties copulate in the bushes. My bus is another scene again. A gang of six have gathered there to watch TV. They sit on the mat, cooking up.

Clyne looks at me. 'We gonna get any privacy?'

I shrug and so he gets down on the carpet, an alien among the Wild Bunch. I squat on the arm of the sofa and play with Rainbow's hair. Max is nowhere in sight.

On TV a man seems to be imitating Liam Gallagher. The gang all protest: 'Liam Gallagher's not dead!'

The host comes on during the applause and hugs the Gallagher counterfeit. Other lookalike contestants are shown waiting backstage: Elvis Presley, John McCormack, Sarah Vaughan.

'What's this?' Clyne asks everyone in general.

They look at him as if he's the one off his tree. Someone hands him the joint, as if that's his problem. He waves it away. 'I'm a cop, I can't.'

The crusties laugh loudly. They like that one.

'It's an imitation singing contest, right, but they're meant to do dead people. But Gallagher's not dead.'

'It's English culture,' I say from behind, then add: 'Imitation.'

'I thought it was warm beer and village cricket,' Clyne offers, craning his head round.

'Imitation. None of us are originals . . .' I smile at him. 'Where's my brother, Rainbow?'

'Max?' says Rainbow.

'How many brothers have I got?'

'He's sleeping.'

I take Clyne's hand and lead him past the galley and through Max's room where he lies in the bed facing the wheel arch. We fade through the curtain into my bedroom. I switch on a coach light and the room opens up. Clyne goes off inspecting the paperback novels piled precipitously on my dresser, their spines bent. He rifles through the stack of CDs on the floor. Hardcore rappers with their anti-police lyrics: GZA, Smooths Da Hustler, Shyeim, Gravediggaz. Also the Brand New Heavies, Massive Attack. And the Manic Street Preachers.

I light a candle scented with Yves St Laurent and hit the light. Nodding to the front of the coach, I apologize for the family.

'One of them's Rainbow's baby's father, though she's not sure which one.'

'Not even a hunch?'

'No one's coming forward, put it that way. In the event the Child Support Agency makes him pay maintenance.'

On the floor by the bed is a half-full wine bottle and an empty glass, Evian water and an ashtray overflowing with butts smeared with my lipstick.

I take my clothes off and stand in front of him in the blue underwear I bought earlier today.

'How much of your salary goes on lingerie?' he asks.

'About a quarter.' I hesitate before adding, 'Some things you can't skimp on.'

'What did you say you earn . . . five grand?'

'So maybe I don't want to work any harder. I earn enough to get us by.'

'You and Max?' Then he asks: 'Where do you take a bath?'

'I don't. Still want to shag me?'

'I'm having some doubts.'

'Really!'

I stomp out of the bedroom, the bulkhead curtain swishing behind me, into the galley. From the Belling I take a kettle of warm water, a blue plastic bowl from the sink and a tea towel back into my room. I remove my underwear, and force him, in his preacher-black suit, to watch me washing my arms, stomach, feet, between my legs . . .

He stops me with a strong grip, pulling my arms down to my sides, and touches my cold, clammy skin. I unbutton his shirt, peeling it down his arms. In the candlelight we explore each other's bodies with the tips of our fingers.

I take him in my mouth and feel not so merry as I perhaps should. He holds my hair from my face so he can have an unimpaired view. I perform my work, varying the pitch and depth, sucking so hard I pull him inside my head. Then I gag, making a sound like muffled laughter. I close my eyes and concentrate on giving a smooth, oiled passage, taking care not to connect with my teeth. I open my eyes again and bring my leg into my stomach. He stares at the contour made by my upper thigh where it joins at the abdomen. This extract of a woman's body has been so commercialized that his response is Pavlovian. I swallow an enormous lashing of sperm.

His mouth finds mine and wolfs the emotion I exhale.

'Now what?' he says, deflating.

I take his hand and lock it between my legs, moving his fingers in small circles, shifting his hand, making millimetre adjustments, spreading his thumb and little finger, anchoring them on my pubic bone. I lighten the pressure, increase the velocity.

I think about what should be in my head and there is nothing. An empty head is a vulnerable target. In an instant it can fill with the worse of fears. 'Talk to me,' I demand. 'Tell me stories.'

'I don't know what to say.'

'Say anything that comes into your head. Tell me sailing stories.'

This is what he tells me . . . sort of.

The skies darken and a thousand moths cling to the deck. There comes a wall of pelting rain. The yacht heels over. The sea makes a sizzling noise like bacon frying. The wind's in a state of senseless fury. Stays, sheets are taut with the strain. There is phosphorescence on the lips of breaking waves. The yacht surfs, the bow buried in the waves. I put out a thirty-foot hawser to produce drag, slow the boat. The small amount of sail I have goes limp in the troughs, blasted by gusts on the crests. The water level in the cabin has risen to above the chart table. I engage the self-steering, detach myself from my lifeline. As I start to go below there's a tremendous rush of water, a splintering of wood. The boat lurches, breaches and I fall overboard. I watch my yacht sail away from me like a ghost ship. It's oddly calm, this feeling. I wouldn't mind dying like this. But the human instinct is a survival instinct. I pull off my oilskins and swim into the wake of the boat and get hold of the trailing hawser. I pull myself up to the stern along the hawser and climb back on board as sheet lightning exposes this whole cold madness. Seas break at fifty feet, like avalanches in the Swiss Alps, leaving behind acres of white water. And I see myself as if in a painting that people are admiring in a gallery. But they don't see me, alone in a corner of the canvas.

My legs stiffen and my feet shake, the muscles in my stomach stiffen. The wave rolls right over me and lifts me off the bed. I hold him there for the ten seconds it lasts.

Then I sink into the bed and burst into tears. The gap between our naked bodies opens up.

Moments later I'm swigging from the open bottle of red wine. I move back over and kiss him, trickling the wine down his throat.

FIVE

A warrant dropped on Clyne's desk for the Seizure of Confidential and Special Procedure Material under Section 9 Schedule 1 of PACE. Stokes' smiling face was there to meet his as he looked up. Her trip to the Old Bailey had taken less than two hours.

An hour further on they were flashing the warrant card at the senior consultant at the Marwood. Oppenheimer studied it gingerly. 'I'd like to see the information,' she demanded.

'You know the legal procedure?'

'Yes, I do.'

'Fine. You may see the information any time you like, at the Old Bailey. Meanwhile you have to hand over Dr Harper's patients' notes.'

Oppenheimer left Clyne and Stokes in the waiting room. She returned with a large pile of manila files which she dumped into Clyne's open arms, declaring, 'If just a single one of our patients gets hurt in all this you'll be at the brunt end of a prosecution yourself, Inspector.'

She turned and marched out. The manila files slid out of his arms on to the floor of the waiting room. Stokes went on her hands and knees to retrieve them.

As they were escaping that long white frightening corridor in the main hospital, Clyne asked, 'This is the place where you come to have low self-esteem reversed, right?'

'A hundred Anadin'd be more effective.'

'You try and solve one of their own's murder and get treated like a pimp . . . Kelly, I've been thinking. About your offer to be my therapist. It could help me, all the parlance, with this investigation.'

'That wasn't exactly the point, was it?'

'I'll do it on those terms.'

'In the car?'

'In the car, Kelly.'

'The most private consultation room in London.'

'It better be fucking private.'

Driving to the station along Kingsland Road on to Commercial Street. Rain clouds were massing in the sky. It was cold outside but Clyne rolled the window down anyway. He wasn't feeling anything but heat. At a red light he glanced down at the manila files piled high on Stokes' knees – all that teenage angst – and then looked up at a shop window. An Elvis Presley curtain showed stills from all his old films Clyne had seen as a teenager: *Kissing Cousins*, *Fun in Acapulco*, *Girls Girls Girls*, *Love Me Tender*.

The light changed and Clyne chugged on. Every shop displayed the same sign: Import–Export.

'Importing-exporting what?' Stokes asked.

'That's what Cary Grant asks Van Damme, the villain in *North by Northwest*.'

'And what was it?'

'State secrets.'

'More likely to be saris around here,' Stokes said. 'Even an old pub's at it, look.'

'Thing is, I don't really care, do you?'

'I don't care, no. I've never had to come out this way once on business.'

91

'The Indians are all right,' Clyne said.

'Yes, the Indians and the Pakistanis.'

They let it drop. Then they looked at each other.

STOKES: Let's talk about your ex-wife. Why did she leave you?

CLYNE: She left because she's absolutely raving top of the roof, what else can you say about a woman who used to sleep along the north–south magnetic axis for health reasons? Actually she left me because I'd stopped talking to her.

STOKES: Where did you meet?

CLYNE: A county court. She was a young solicitor, I was a DC. She was defending some guy we were prosecuting. She lost and I walked over, to offer condolences. Then she completely wrong-footed me by asking me out. I was going to say no, but when I opened my mouth the word that formed on my lips was yes. A man can't turn a woman down even if his life depends on it. So anyway, next night we go to this bistro place in Frith Street. You know the kind, menus all in French, waiters're all American. She orders a main course, and this waiter corrects her pronunciation. She says, You're American, right? and the waiter goes, Yes, ma'am. So she says, Well, for your information, this French word has been part of the English vocabulary for so long now, like three hundred years, that it's pronounced the English way. It's a mid-Channel word. In America you may pronounce it with a French stress but then that's the difference between us. It's like old and new money. I guess you're what we call over here new money. Boy, was I impressed. Three hours later we were in bed and that was her idea as well. I didn't seem to have any control over what was happening. For months we fucked like rabbits.

Everything she said was wonderful. Her voice was a river.

STOKES: Why did you stop talking to her?

CLYNE: Because she started asking too many damn questions.

STOKES: That's what lawyers do. Ask questions.

CLYNE: Except these wouldn't have won no prosecution.

STOKES: What made you happy in the relationship?

CLYNE: What made me happy? Playing football in the park with Jenny and the kids. She and David against me and Lucy. Moments with heart.

STOKES: What made you unhappy?

CLYNE: We're unhappy when we're being critical, aren't we?

STOKES: Why've you started talking about yourself in the third person?

CLYNE: Have I?

STOKES: Because the criticism comes from somewhere else.

CLYNE: Police are big on criticism, making judgements. We can find something bad to say about almost anyone. Why does being critical make us unhappy? You tell me.

STOKES: It fails to get you what you want.

CLYNE: But it's hard not to be critical sometimes. Like that time when Jenny had a case defending a bloke accused of raping five women. It was a racing certainty he was guilty and even she knew it. But she and her barrister got the bloke off on a technicality surrounding a point of evidence. I went to meet her that day in some bottom office. She and the barrister were slapping each other on the back, breaking open the champagne. I said, Police aren't angels but at least we only celebrate when we move justice forward, not backwards.

STOKES: You spoilt the party for her.

CLYNE: Yeah. Afterwards we walked out to where I'd parked

off the Holloway Road. We get in the car and I start to head off in a direction which I know will get me on to Tollington Road and back on to Holloway, when she says, You can't turn right down there. She's correct, of course, because she's thinking about Seven Sisters Road and Seven Sisters is one-way to Finsbury Park. But then I was going such a way as to cross Seven Sisters at Hornsey Road. So I just kept going, thinking it's not worth mentioning. Which is a mistake as it happens because Jenny is now shouting that I am going to end up going the wrong direction. So I tell her that she's wrong, which strictly speaking she isn't, but then nor am I. And that's my second mistake. She screams, You're the one who's wrong. So I say, It doesn't matter. And she says, You always say it doesn't matter whenever you're wrong and I'm right. It does fucking matter! It matters a lot. You are wrong and that's something you will never admit to . . . And so it goes on until all I can hear is so much noise. So then I say, Shut up, shut up! And she says, Don't you dare tell me to shut up! I hit the brakes and the car skids to a halt. Get out, get out of the fucking car! She is only too pleased to get out, but not before she tells me to grow up. It is all too painfully obvious now, with hindsight, what was going on back then. The marriage was on the rocks. We could both smell the smoke in the air. When she told me not to tell her to shut up, she was saying, in effect, You're not listening to me, you don't respect me, you don't even understand me when what I'm saying is right. This is not love.

STOKES: Tell me about your children. Are you able to be intimate with them?

CLYNE: I'm a man, Kelly. Men aren't intimate.

STOKES: Masculinity's a denial of the feminine. Feminine is the primal force, masculinity a conditioned response.

CLYNE: If I've to become feminine in order to be intimate, how would I do the job?

STOKES: How do you think I do the job?

CLYNE: You know what I mean. You don't rush a blag and say to the guys, Hi, I really feel a lot of sympathy for your social disadvantages, please put *down* those shotguns. You chin the assholes hard as you can.

STOKES: Let's get back to your kids. My sense is that your children are important to you because they help you over the hump.

CLYNE: My children are important to me because a) they're important little people on their own merits and b) they're all I've got. My ex-wife granted custody to me. That's unusual. She said that without the children I'd be irredeemable. *Fucking hell.* I said to her, if the kids redeem me, will you return? And she said, what she said was, You could be St Nicholas and I wouldn't come back.

STOKES: You must be their hero, though?

CLYNE: I don't look so heroic in an apron.

STOKES: What do you think are heroic qualities?

CLYNE: Don't know that. But heroes, they're loved by multitudes. That's what I want . . . a thousand people standing outside my door, waving flags. I have this recurring fantasy. I'm a military adviser for all the peaceful tribes threatened with genocide. In Kurdistan, East Timor. And because I never lose a war, when I turn up in the middle of a fight the bad guys get understandably nervous. No one exactly knows my true identity. Media speculation has reached fever

95

pitch. I'm a household name. Pictures of me appear in the tabloids, on horseback, camelback, my face hidden. Beautiful divas sing ballads about me. Songs go straight to number one in the charts.

STOKES: But war heroes get shot at. They're often fascists. Beat their wives and children.

CLYNE: Not my kind of war hero.

STOKES: Not your kind of *fantasy* war hero. Your fantasies are psychotic.

CLYNE: Didn't Freud say that culture is a product of psychosis?

STOKES: Psychosis has also produced war.

CLYNE: And war poetry. And boy scouts. Where else would I have learnt to erect a tent if the scouts hadn't been invented?

STOKES: If Baden-Powell was in therapy you'd have been allowed to wear long trousers.

CLYNE: Oh, very droll, Kelly.

STOKES: Therapy does not destroy culture.

CLYNE: Well, actually, it does fuck with your imagination. You know what I'm fantasizing about now? Since this therapy started? I'm fantasizing about saving my local butcher from bankruptcy.

Clyne and Stokes spent half a day reading the case notes. Oppenheimer was right: nothing more consequential than severe acne, a bad haircut. Harper's omniscience peppered them up, adding worldly significance.

Manny came into the incident room and scanned the patients' notes. 'Any percentage in these, Bob?'

'Here's one,' Stokes said, touching a manila file in a tender way. 'This kid could suffer for England.'

The client's name was Michael Rivers, who'd been admitted to the unit under a supervision order. The Youth Justice Team had presented a package of six months' therapy at the Marwood as a condition for a suspended sentence for common assault. Rivers had agreed to those terms and saw Harper as an outpatient once a week.

It was only a partial disclosure. The notes were written longhand, signed and dated.

From Michael's first-person accounts I have been able to compose a picture of his mother, who is worth mentioning in some detail. Michael was her only child and they lived in a council estate in Canning Town. Without his father around she emerged as the devouring central figure in Michael's life. Her narcissistic vulnerabilities in relation to male sexuality and aggression have created in Michael an intolerable burden. 'Depressed' and 'paranoid' (his words) throughout his childhood, she would lock herself and Michael in the flat, not answering the door or telephone for days on end. She would crawl on all fours, claiming it made her feel safer. The idea being that intruders would associate her with an infant and would be less likely to harm a child who could not yet walk. On the few occasions she ventured outside she convinced herself that graffiti on the estate was addressed to her. The graffiti she claimed was 'filth written by filth'.

Because men were 'dangerous, evil forces' she had a pathological need to suppress Michael's masculinity. Paradoxically it was also her idea that he take up boxing, because she hoped it would channel his 'aggression'.

Michael was made to sleep in the same bed as his mother because she was afraid of being assaulted by intruders. She started coercing him into a sexual relationship from the age of seven or eight.

Somatic expressions of anxiety: when Michael goes to bed now, he first touches the knots on his wooden bed and

97

the soles of his feet, as his mother had done. He develops rashes, high temperatures and acne.

Today we discussed how whenever he tries to experience himself as separate from his mother, Michael undergoes a crisis of self-confidence. He feels 'hollow, helpless and stupid'. He is convinced that all people who talk to him are bent on destroying him. He believes they wear listening devices. At the beginning of our session I had to take off my shirt to show him that I was not 'wired up'.

Michael admitted today for the first time to cutting his arms. It seems obvious to me that the psychogenesis of this pathology is the relationship with his mother. He cuts himself because he was erotically stimulated by her. The blood produced represents the internalized mother as transitional object. Mutilating helps him separate from the original object. Michael tells me it is pleasurable. I tell him I'm not surprised that it's pleasurable. By turning pain on himself and experiencing it as pleasure, he defeats the object of the original abuse. I suggested that mutilation is for him a means of self-control, of independence. By abusing the body his mother once abused he is expressing ownership. However, any such relief is short-lived. While cutting discharges the taboo of incest, self-mutilation is another taboo with its own shame. Cutting enhances differentiation but immediately plunges him back into the Oedipal conflict.

I further suggested that self-mutilation is an act of empathy with his mother, by harming the masculine body that she vilified. Intercourse was 'punishment' for her. Her husband 'stabbed' with his penis. Michael 'attacks' his body as his father had once 'attacked' his mother.

His self-mutilation is replacement masturbation, an auto-erotic activity providing him with orgasmic-type relief –

enuresis, encopresis – as well as punishment for this impulse to stimulate himself.

With the exception of Bill Haines, a boxing 'character' Michael holds in high regard, I am the only person in his life with whom he has been able to develop some sort of trust. That is because we have a transitional relationship. I am only partially real to him, a 'therapist' more than a 'man'. Yet he has developed a growing belief in the authenticity of my concern for his wellbeing.

However, Michael's efforts to maintain me as a trusting, caring person – which contain aspects of his lost relationship to his absentee father – are frequently interfered with by his destructive and persecutory fantasies relating to the internalized mother. In therapy he often makes Oedipal overtones in his relationship with me. Although he consciously wants a heterosexual relationship, his masturbatory fantasies are homoerotic, ego-distonic. Before he comes to the sessions he grooms himself in the toilets, applies make-up on his acne. This is for my benefit and indicates a pronounced feminine identification.

To foster this transference through interpretation may be inappropriate, although I admit to a desire to father him, take him home into an environment where he could build a belief in himself and a trust in others. This is a way of saying how fond I am of Michael, how sorry I feel for his situation. He is tall and strong and his face has potential for real beauty, if it weren't so scarred by acne.

Our initial contract has been for weekly sessions for six months. In a review session Michael said that the therapy was causing him concern because he was beginning to have fantasies about 'harming' me sexually. These sexual fantasies were interwoven with violent thoughts, activated by our impending separation. He called my words 'sharp', 'cutting', 'painful'. He attempts to force me into taking control of his body, by having physical contact with me. Whenever I try to establish a positive therapeutic alliance with him he attempts to enact with me sado-masochistic transference fantasies.

I do not yet understand the countertransference.

'Strewth!' Manny said the moment he finished reading. 'How can anyone get as fucked up as that?'

'Rivers doesn't sound all there, does he?'

'What's countertransference mean, Bob?'

'Like shagging your patient,' Stokes advised.

'That's countertransference?'

'One kind,' she said. 'A therapist is trained to deal with it. He's meant to keep his own problems out of the frame.'

Manny got out the smokes, passed them around. 'This kid Rivers, sounds like he's handy with a blade. We're going to have to pull him.'

Some uniforms were sent out to pick up Rivers but came back from his address empty-handed. Trying to think where else he could be found, the name Bill Haines tripped out on Ridley's tongue – the boxing 'character' mentioned in dispatches. Ridley knew a few things in the boxing department, like who Haines was and where he lived. Sailing was Clyne's bag, pugilism Ridley's, having been an ABA junior middleweight in his youth.

They drove out east together. On the way Ridley briefed Clyne about the man. Haines was born in the 1940s on the Monteith estate off the Old Ford Road. When he came into the money as a fight manager a few years ago he moved into one of those colonnaded gentrified houses on Cadogan Terrace, a few hundred yards from the estate. The houses have an unimpaired view of Victoria Park to the front and the A102 (M) flyover at the back – for a quick getaway through the Blackwall Tunnel. He didn't do crime any longer, but old instincts, etcetera. At least one of Haines' former associates was buried in the concrete foundations of that flyover.

Haines was now rich enough to buy one of the palaces on The Bishop's Avenue. But he remained a guy with impeccable working-class credentials: big on money, short on the uses of money. He'd gone on record saying, I was born in Hackney, I will die in Hackney. Although he wasn't planning on a funeral in the Monteith estate.

Clyne stared into the security camera above Haines' reinforced front door and held up his ID. A female voice, that hadn't roamed far from the Bow Bells, crackled over the intercom. She told them they'd find her husband down Swift's gym on the Isle of Dogs.

They got back into the car and took off down the A102 (M), dodged under the East India Road, taking Cotton Street and Preston's Road on to the Isle of Dogs.

The island was in a state of frigid motion. There were police controls everywhere after the IRA had made a flying visit a few months back. Mounted cameras followed their trajectory. On each side of the road heavy plant machinery ploughed up what was left of some new architecture. A pub stranded in the middle of the bomb site glowed in the twilight of the afternoon.

The gym they were looking for was above Swift's pub in Cubitt Town. The bar was doing unnatural business as they walked in, serving up fruit juice, tea and biscuits to the fighters who had worn off their aggression in the ring and now made for serene company, helped by the interiors which the landlord's wife had made comforting: dripping deep-red velvet curtains parted over the door and the windows, displays of dried hops above the small stage, fresh lilies in vases, gold-leaf wallpaper, scrubbed pine bar and tables.

Upstairs in the gym it was business as usual. The two-to-five

training session was in progress and the place felt claustro-
phobic to Clyne. In the small ring a trainer was taking a ban-
tamweight through his sequences on the hook and jab pads.
Two other boxers were working on the bags, another on the
speed ropes.

They couldn't see Bill Haines anywhere. But Ridley knew
one of the trainers by name. 'Spade . . . you seen Haines anywhere?'

Spade looked them up and down, remarking scathingly, 'Managers don't come near training sessions. I ain't met one yet who
knows nothing about boxing.'

'His wife said he'd be here.'

Spade leant his chest on the ropes, his gut well outside the
ring. His face was flat as a dinner plate. 'Bill's here all right.
Biting his fingernails off in the office.'

A little girl in a tutu sauntered through. Clyne blinked once,
just in case she was a mirage, but the girl was still there when
he opened his eyes. Spade asked her to go tell Bill that 'two
shoes is waiting to see him'.

As she ran off on her mission Ridley said, 'Bet she packs a
punch.'

'Don't mess with her,' Spade replied. 'Bill's daughter.'

While waiting for Haines to appear they watched a lumbering
middleweight, Paul 'Sweet P' Winslow, strap his hands. He put
on 14 oz gloves, head guard and jockstrap and climbed into the
big ring. Spade had three fighters standing by to spar with him.
One in the same weight division, one below for speed and one
above for power. The heaviest went in for two rounds and from
the moment Spade told them, Go, enjoy yourselves, they gave
each other what for. He talked them through it the whole time.
Clyne couldn't hear what he said over the rock-and-roll music
rippling from loudspeakers. There was not much headroom
either, between the fighters and the hot-water pipes snaking
around the ceiling.

Clyne sensed Ridley's excitement. 'You miss the game, Sam?'
'Sure I do.'

'But not the pain, right?'

'I hate to say it but I liked it better when the pain came.'

'Did you ever think about going professional?'

'Thought about it. But you know, boxing's a life-threatening form of employment.'

'So is coal mining.'

'Health and safety's improved coal mining,' Ridley said.

'Yeah. They closed down all the pits.'

'Some people want to ban it. But no boxer I know would support a ban.'

'What about shorter rounds, shorter contests?'

'Definitely not.' He was indignant. 'That would be a feminization of the sport.'

'A feminization, huh?' Kelly Stokes came to Clyne's mind, her bullshit. 'Is boxing intimate, Sam? It looks intimate to me.'

'Boxing's very intimate,' he said. 'You lay your chin on your opponent's shoulder, bite his ear lobes. You can even smell what he had for dinner the previous night.'

'That's good, I like that.' Clyne stored it away for ammunition.

Haines made his appearance in an expensive cream linen suit, white shirt, silk tie, with his daughter on his shoulders. Without a word he looked at Clyne's ID and sat down on the viewing gallery, while his little girl tried on a Ringside headguard, Reyes boxing gloves.

His face bore the marks of other men. There were maps of scars around his mouth and eyes. Veins in his cheeks were broken and his grey hair was yellowing from too many dinner-show cigars. On his knees he rested his bulldozer hands, the knuckles permanently swollen.

He watched the fighters nervously, his small eyes canopied beneath swollen lids.

103

'That your boy?' Ridley pointed to Sweet P.

'Yeah.'

Haines did not want to be there in the gym. His nerves twitched in his thick neck. Nothing to do with the police, more because his contender was warming up his moves. The trainer didn't want him around either, and froze him out.

'What you want to see me for?'

'We're running an investigation into the murder of a psychiatrist called George Harper,' Clyne explained.

Haines took his eyes off his fighter to look at Clyne. His face was just a little too blank to believe. His lips were chalk. The boxers stopped sparring at that point and came to the corner to spit in 'Spade's bucket' – so labelled, presumably, in case anyone mistook it for his hat. Spade spread white petroleum jelly over their lips, noses and eyebrows.

'One of his patients was a boy called Michael Rivers. We understand you know him?'

'I know him, so what?'

'We're looking for him. We need him to help us in our enquiries.'

'Whenever I hear the Bill make that remark it always sends me running for cover. Is Michael a suspect?'

'Not yet.'

'Not *yet*? Then I'm saying fuck all.'

Haines walked away across to the far side of the gym. Clyne looked at Ridley for answers. This was his territory. 'He won't budge now,' Ridley opined. 'I know that much. He's a stubborn fucker. Secret to his success.'

'Then what do we do?'

The middleweight had started boxing with the lighter of his sparring partners. He was good too, this second one, a portsider who brought his punch with him. Sweet P had to chase him a bit and gave his opponent too many opportunities to get inside.

104

'When's your boy fighting?' Ridley shouted, his question finding Haines on the other side of the gym.

'Thursday. York Hall,' Haines replied, starting to drift back. 'We got Sky covering.'

'Why do you managers always sign with Sky?' Clyne asked.

'Because they offer the best deal,' he said.

'They offer the best deal, but most of the population can't see the fights. My kids can't see the fights.'

'We sign with Sky because terrestrials only want the big contests. I want all my boys to get a piece of the money. Tell your kids to hook up with satellite.'

'My kids watch too much TV as it is.'

'That's too bad.'

'Did you know that whenever the media focus on a boxing fight it affects the murder rate?' Ridley added.

'No shit?' Haines leant his back against the ropes.

'Theory is, fights reward one person for inflicting violence on another. Which is the opposite idea of our system of justice.'

'You one of those girls who don't approve of boxing?'

'Yeah,' Ridley said. 'One of those girls. And I'll tell you something else . . .' he added, rising in stature, 'I could pan that boy of yours any day of the week.'

'Oh, that's very cute, that is.' Haines snapped off from the ropes.

'Give me a shot at him now,' Ridley said.

'You want to spar with Sweet P?'

'I'll knock him out inside two rounds.'

Haines laughed heavily, his shoulders rising and falling inside his suit. Clyne couldn't find anything to laugh about. He didn't like the way this was developing. He tried to catch Ridley's eye but it was fixed on Haines.

'Hear that, Spade? This bloke wants to go a few rounds with Paul.'

Now Spade joined in with the laughing. 'You got a gun or something?'

'I don't need a gun,' Ridley said.

'Maybe he's got a knockout fart, Spade.'

'What you all frightened of? Sweet P . . . you want to give me a couple of rounds?'

Sweet P spat out his mouthguard. 'The chance to diss the Old Bill? Come on in.'

Spade knotted his fingers around the top rope. Haines rested his hand on his daughter's head. They both needed all the support they could get to avoid falling down.

Spade said, 'You serious about this?'

'Sure he is,' said Haines. 'Fit him up with some gear.'

'He's sitting on it.'

Sweet P's sparring partner gave way. Ridley took his tie and shirt off, trousers, shoes.

Clyne approached. 'Are you fucking crazy? He's bigger than you.'

'I'm faster than him.'

'You're joking, right?'

Ridley ignored him and squeezed into a pair of black shorts. *Small but perfectly formed.* Size seven boots they didn't seem to have, so he waded into a pair of Adidas nines. He strapped his own hands and rolled on the gloves.

There was no turning back now.

Spade insisted he warm up for five, so Ridley did a little work on the bags, some shadow boxing. Haines and Spade went suddenly quiet. Now they could see the footwork Ridley put in, they'd lost their sense of humour.

He finished off the warm-up on the bike. His lungs were barely holding out. All those Marlboro reds.

Spade held the ropes open and Ridley in a headguard climbed into the ring. It took him only a moment to find his feet and start rocking. Sweet P came at him, dancing to the music. Ridley took

106

a one-two combination in the head, but there wasn't any heavy hammer on them, and he just rolled off the punches.

He bent too low and lost sight of his opponent. Sweet P didn't miss the chance and landed a sickener.

Ridley stuck on to his chest like a limpet. He rolled punches off his guard, back in again, legs apart, rocking, took one himself, rolled out of it. Chin on chest, breathing through his mouth, he jabbed a few more. Sweet P made contact with an uppercut that nearly put Ridley on the ropes.

Sweet P had got Ridley angry now. He jabbed and missed. Jabbed, made contact, then went inside for some body. He took so much punishment inside he had to hold on to Sweet P again. He flung Ridley away and followed with a left hook that was already fading as it found his head.

Ridley went back in, ducking, and made his first serious contact. Sweet P knew it too and moved out of reach. Ridley waited . . . waited for punches to come from him that he didn't know he had.

Spade shouted, One more minute to kill. Then Ridley did explode. Rapid fire.

He was giving as good as he got . . .

Spade and Sweet P were both on their knees. Haines and Clyne hung on to the ropes outside. Ridley was lying flat out on his back on the canvas with Spade prising his eyelids apart. He couldn't lift his head from the canvas. The silvered water pipes in the ceiling clicked as they expanded with hot water.

Spade was repeating, 'What's your name? What's your name?'

'Detective Sergeant Samuel Riley.'

'He's okay,' said Spade, getting up.

It was Ridley. Not Riley. But close enough.

Ridley lifted his head off the canvas and looked around for reassurance. Bill Haines cast his vote. 'You got heart, crusher.'

Ridley turned over on all fours and climbed to his feet. Sweet

P patted him on the back with his glove and Spade sponged his face with water that was pink with blood. He just managed to climb out between the ropes without falling in Clyne's lap.

Haines was still laughing as Ridley sat next to him on the viewing gallery. With his arm around Ridley, he began paying out. 'Michael would never have killed that shrink but I can't say I'm unhappy about it neither.'

'Tell us,' Ridley said.

'Kid trains here when he can bother getting out of bed. Lot of promise, but fucked up. Royal A1 headcase, he is. In and out of detention centres, the business. I tell him, he can't fight with all that what's crashing around in his nut, so he tells me he's seeing this head straightener about it. So I think, okay. Few weeks on I ask him if it's sorted and he tells me his therapist's been touching up his jacksie.'

'He could have been lying.'

'No way the kid would lie to me. Said the shrink told him it was part of a healing process, to help him take control. The kid don't talk like that!'

'A lot of parents complain they don't like what they've paid for when the kid comes out of therapy. Don't like the results,' Clyne said.

'I ain't his fucking parent, am I? Anyway, I go straight in to the senior consultant there, the management.'

'Beaky-looking bird of fifty?'

'That's the one, parrot fucking face, stands up for this quack. So I threaten to whack her once or twice around the snout to bring her to her senses. She tells me to leave or she'll call the police. I'm the one who's going to call the fucking police, I say.'

'Did you? Call the police?' Ridley asked.

'No, because I get a letter from them saying the kid suffers from delusional memory, whatever the fuck that is. I call the NHS but they can't do nothing because it's private over there.

They tell me to go to the General Medical Council. *They* told me I need a court order before they can move on it. So I go to the Crown Prosecution Service. Week or two later they come back saying there's no evidence. Now I'm thinking it's because I've got a criminal record that they don't want to know. What I need is some hot-shot personal injuries lawyer.'

They all stopped talking to watch Spade drying Sweet P with a towel. His muscled torso was sleek with sweat and blushing in places from where the leather of Ridley's gloves had embarrassed the skin. The way Spade wiped him down suggested someone polishing a bronze trophy. All he was short of was the Brasso.

After shining every crease and contour Spade led him to the scales. The boxer stripped out of his shorts and boots and stepped up naked. He held on to his genitals as he studied the scales. He'd still got a few grams to lose before the weigh-in later.

They broke out of their trance at the same time.

Haines shook his head, shaking out the bad vibes. 'That cunt Harper was a nonce and got what was coming to him.' He addressed his next remark to Ridley. 'You want to go another round with Paul? Help him shed a few more ounces.'

Ridley declined. 'I've taught him a lesson as it is.'

'Oh yeah, you put the frighteners on him.' Haines' laugher was now more or less permanent. 'Why don't you come and see him in York Hall? I'll leave a couple of tickets on the door for you. Michael's fighting too, as an undercard. That's if he bothers turning up.'

'We might just do that.'

Then Haines said something that Clyne was never to forget. 'Boxing makes you into a good man. This boy, he'll be a good man too one day if he sticks with it. It's as straight and honest as that.'

As they were walking down the stairs to the pub Clyne

said, 'You did good work up there, Sam. I think we deserve a drink.'

'But your round.' He sounded shaken. 'I've just had mine.'

At the bar Clyne ordered a pint of Guinness and a pint of orange squash for Ridley. There were a dozen men in; faces full of bad weather drinking fiercely at four in the afternoon. The verbals and the fibre were getting flung around. A scene straight out of *Get Carter*. Bollocks-in-a-vice *sotto voce*.

Ridley had cooled down in the ring but Clyne was feeling frisky. He had an urge to hit someone that the company standing next to him did nothing to soothe: a Jamaican in a pork-pie hat, and a colossus with an artificial hand fixed around his gin and tonic. He did something clever with an arm muscle and closed the claw. The metal made a crunching noise against the glass.

They clocked Clyne looking their way and could tell from his expression that they were fighting on different sides. He finished his Guinness and stubbed his cigarette under his shoe.

Sam went ahead towards the exit. Clyne felt a weight on his back as he followed, a thickness spreading across the shoulders. The pub went silent as they reached the door. Ridley grabbed the handle and they both glanced back. From the bar the two men were eyeballing them. They weren't smiling. And nor were the detectives.

The light in the street was blinding. There was half an hour left before dusk. Clyne decided on a stroll along the top of Mudchute. Ridley didn't want any more exercise, so went to the car to convalesce.

When his kids were small he used to take them up Mudchute Hill. It was there, in City Farm, where Lucy found her love of ponies. She lost it a year later when one bit her, trying to steal the Polo mints clutched to her breast. And before the kids existed, long before, Clyne's father had fired 4.5mm shells into the skies from Mudchute Hill at the Luftwaffe. After the war he joined the Customs and Excise. Back in uniform again.

From the hill Clyne meditated on the glass rafts of West India Docks, where his father's office used to be and where he once watched him pour gallons of contraband alcohol down a sink. He wanted his son to witness him doing good works. Not a drop of that free booze passed his lips.

The sun set on Millwall and Canary Wharf, the old world facing off against the new. To the permanent residents those pyramids were fast-track-exclusive giant carnivorous VDUs.

Clyne did not understand Canary Wharf either, what it means. It was like an airport departure lounge without the duty-free. Camelot maybe, or a sex industry. All those phallic totems. At the top of Harbour Exchange Tower was a sperm bank.

Canary Wharf Tower's shadow darkened St Katharine's Dock, the Royals, Millwall, Blackwall.

It is designed to piss you off, looking at it. No place to kennel the King's dogs any more.

Once, Clyne saw a woman on East Ferry Road hawking 'dream catchers' to the suits leaving for home at the end of the day. They laughed at her contraptions: colanders with valves, allowing dreams through but not out.

He wondered now, was she so eccentric? Those guys who laughed, well, they sell telephone calls. They sell debt at the banks. They don't get paid a salary, they get 'compensation'.

He returned to Swift's as night was falling at the same moment a fox was wandering down Plevna Street. The fox nosed into the bins, very casually, giving the impression he'd have a word if he could. Grass anyone up for an oven-ready chicken.

Clyne invited me to go to the boxing at York Hall with him.

I asked, Police business or pleasure?

He said, There was a suspect he had to pick up.

A suspect. I didn't feel jealous exactly, but some element of competitiveness, certainly.

One suspect to go out there with him and two to bring back home. It takes a suspect to catch one.

Hot date, I said.

In the car approaching Hackney he passed a Manila file across the seat; said I should read it. It contained case notes composed by my father on a patient called Michael Rivers. When I saw the old man's handwriting I flushed hot and cold. I pinned my ears back. There was the black ink of his Mont Blanc, his worm-like ss, the looping ds, ls like a carpenter's right angle.

I'd never seen any of my father's case reports before. And as I digested these, thought, Where's Michael Rivers under the cascades of analysis? If I believed what I read I'd lock him up and throw away the key. That's one dangerous fucked-up kid. On the other hand his character had so much movement. He might even make a good citizen, on Mars.

I felt an urge to bring him home too. You never know, he might find his milieu in Wanstead Flats; the crusties the best nexus for his condition. He could swine himself all over the fields for all we cared. None of it would be recorded, no file would be lodged with the authorities.

I should have been his therapist, I am not my father's daughter for nothing. But I'd not worry about his 'enuresis', 'encopresis'. That language of therapy is the fog that covers the wellsprings. And camouflages the countertransference.

We get to York Hall early with an eye to buying a drink before the off. The bar is closed until seven, so we wander around instead. The hall looks as though it might have been a municipal swimming baths at one time, with windows in the ceiling and black and white marbled walls, where Barry McGuigan's picture on *Daily Express* fliers now hangs.

Clyne says he'd gone by there a couple of years ago and it was full of people sitting exams. There's a different kinetic again now with the place set up for fighting. A large banner advertising Sky Sports is strung up high. In the gallery behind a glass window sits McGuigan himself, slicking back his hair, having his make-up prepared. Next to the gallery the Sky cameras are veiled in darkness, with a little background light alternating green and red. Waiting for the aggro, the gore, the blood on the ropes to flash into subscribers' homes.

The bar opens and we get that drink. We miss the first fight which ends on a knockout in the second minute, then leave when we hear the MC announce the next undercard: Michael Rivers' ABA three-rounder.

Rivers' opponent, C.J. Donleavy, is first to reach the ring. His London-Irish partisans from Kilburn chant and stamp their feet with such force it makes my eyes water. That's something the cameras can't capture. The aggression of the fans.

Then Michael Rivers canters in from the dressing room in a baseball cap stuffed on the wrong way and sparkling red shorts.

Inside the ring he removes his cap and throws it to a girl sitting at ringside. He starts hopping around on the canvas, rolling his head on his shoulders. He's not a kid you'd want to mess with. Five-ten, olive-skinned, built. A few long strands of hair are tied in a ponytail, the rest of his head scalped. TV lights shining on him give the illusion of a halo.

The MC and the seconds leave the ring and the boxing commences. The hall maintains an eerie silence each time Rivers lands a points-scoring punch; the only sound the acoustics of leather expelling air. But when Donleavy replies his supporters come to their feet. Their shouting makes the air tremble more violently out of the ring than in.

I don't know anything about boxing, who might be winning, who losing. But it does occur to me that boxing is the total inverse of what most people consider the right condition for normal life, a life absent of pain. For Michael Rivers, on the other hand, boxing makes sense, while the rest of his life probably doesn't. Life is like boxing, as one observer has said, but boxing is only like boxing.

How organized he seems now, how in control. *This* is his milieu, I realize. If Clyne's everyday emotional journey is a shuttle from victim to victimizer, in Michael's case he can save himself the fare: he's got it all in one. The hunter and the hunted cancel each other out.

The second realization I have is Clyne's going to cop this boy when he gets out of the fight. Maybe he hasn't begun thinking about him yet, reserving judgement until he's talked to him. But by then it will be too late. Rivers' only forum for eloquence is here. In the police station he will talk himself into trouble, take the fight to the police and stitch himself up.

This kid needs me in his corner.

I determine to affect Clyne's pre-judgment. But how can any agent affect the will of another character?

'Doesn't look like he's got any following, does it?'

114

'What about this bloke?' Clyne nods to an old man standing immediately behind us, shouting advice. (Left hook, over the top . . . Make him walk around . . . Right hand, left hook and double it up. That's better. Hands up. Hands up . . . Bob and weave, that's better.) 'Who you supporting?' Clyne asks him. 'Any relation to Rivers?'

'Who?'

Clyne rolls his eyes at me.

The referee stops the fight in the first minute of the third and final round. In Rivers' favour.

The crowd turn blue, very pissed off. But I'm with the referee, we're on the same side.

'Grab a chair, Alice,' Clyne shouts over the noise. 'Protect your head.'

But the moment passes safely. Rivers is crowned, as a knave, then bows out to the sound of boos.

He can't win even when he wins.

There is only one human face I can see among the tumefying red orbs at ringside. It belongs to a middle-aged man who leads Rivers out of the hall with his arm around his shoulders.

'Who is that man with Michael?'

'Bill Haines. Manager,' Clyne says. 'Now I go and claim him. That boy's mine.'

'Bob, have a heart. Let him enjoy his victory a while.'

'Okay.'

So we end up staying for the main event. The bar empties and the hall packs out. Bloods work the security around the ropes. The atmosphere is choking, the most violent oxygen in London. At ringside old boxers share cruel jokes, equivocal smiles, bone-crunching handshakes. Fighters, managers, trainers, villains – whoever they are – have the same bristling presence, heavily gelled haircuts, cheap double-locking suits. They've emerged from their lairs in good gear, £500 of clobber strapped on their backs, to engage marginally in the boxing while bobbing and weaving around the hall, working the crowd, with a fixed smile that a single wrong word could shatter. When they connect, engage each other, they make the sound of a car crash. Tearing metal.

Of the crowd I am most curious about the women. There are mothers and girlfriends attending on sufferance, but as many glimmering morts have volunteered to see the fights. They sit in little clusters among the bar brawlers and the outlaws, their hands folded on laps and clutching embroidered purses. Manicured nails, painted faces, dyed hair seem as much a demonstration of their gender as the boxers' display is, as if they too have something to prove.

Men go to fights to see pain and violence inflicted. Boxing may be a brave sport, but the spectators are cowards. The only dignity is in appreciating the tragedy inherent in the game. But these women are not witnessing it as tragedy, they don't fit in at all. And the men avoid all association with them. A boxing tournament is no place for a man to score.

'Who are these women, Bob? They can't all be social anthropologists.'

'You're too young to remember the bare-knuckle fights?'

'Too young? Why would I want to see bare-knuckle fights at any age?'

'The boxers' wives were the revelation. Came to gee up their husbands and started fighting one another. Tore into each other, bloodthirsty as hell. The local street bookmaker would take bets on them.'

It is then I notice the girl clutching Rivers' baseball cap, looking as out of place as I feel. She hasn't moved from her ringside seat. 'If that's Michael's girl,' I say, 'why hasn't she gone to the changing rooms with him?'

'Women in the changing room?' he grimaces.

I move down to ringside and ask her if she's with Michael. It's really a rhetorical question. Her solidarity with Rivers is graphically displayed, in her shaved head and tattoos of crossed knives inked into her skull. Dressed in a white vest, her bare forearms show a complex map of self-inflicted scars.

She turns her face away. Clyne asks, 'You want a drink, love?'

Without a word she gets up and walks towards the dressing rooms. Now Clyne is eager to follow her, doesn't want her to spook his quarry. But he seems just as eager to stay and watch the main event that is about to start.

A rock fanfare. A middleweight contender, Sweet P Winslow, is trumpeted into the hall. He chats to people on the way as if he has nothing special on, no worries. He climbs into the ring and empties his nostrils on the canvas before settling into his corner with his trainer, dressed in a crimson shirt and white trousers. From the other direction comes the Commonwealth title holder, Amos Obu, sleek and indifferent as a horse.

The fighters are announced, the seconds retreat from the ring and they connect. Clyne is lost to the enfolding drama. I look away, just for a second, and when I turn my attention back to the ring Sweet P is lying on the canvas. I never even saw the punch. There is a roar of surf in my ears. For a moment I think everyone around me is fighting.

Sweet P's trainer appears at ringside. His face looks crestfallen. He looks godmother-worried. Sweet P gets up before the count and chases his opponent, who puts him down again inside thirty seconds. Sweet P gets up, but more slowly this time. The referee stares into his eyes, declares he's fit to fight on. Obu marches in and punches him out of the ring on to the judges' table.

'Bloody hell.' Clyne sighs heavily. 'My bag carrier's going to love this when I tell him. As it is, every time Sam thinks about Sweet P his nose starts to bleed.'

Obu's wife comes to the ropes and hands in their two-year-old child. The infant gets the treatment, exposed to Sky cameras by his father, who trails him down the line of microphones, flash bulbs, steady cam. The child's then lowered to the canvas while Obu fits on the championship belt. He poses for the cameramen before climbing out of the ring with his seconds and trainers.

They have forgotten the kid, mother included.

He toddles around inside the ring wondering why everyone has suddenly lost interest in him. A symbol of virility a moment ago, a good piece of PR, he's just a child again.

I've seen enough. And so has Clyne. He is shivering and looks quite pale.

Then he cancels me. He hands me a twenty-pound note for a cab. There is no discussion about this. He leaves the hall for the changing rooms alone to pick up Michael Rivers. I am out of the picture.

SIX

Michael Rivers was fed and watered and offered counsel. He ate the food but refused the brief. He could fight his own corner, he said. His eyebrows were swollen and his jaw beginning to discolour.

Clyne put him in Interview Room 2 then went down the hall to find Manny, who was shooting the shit with Ridley and Stokes in the incident room.

'This kid . . .' Manny inhaled on a Gauloise. 'Do you believe what he told Haines, about Harper?'

'Probably not,' Clyne said, 'but I'm keeping an open mind.'

'What kind of shrink would give his teenage patient a browning anyhow?'

'A creative psychopath with insight,' Stokes butted in. 'Unlikely to be Kleinian.'

Both Manny and Clyne looked at her. Then they looked at each other. Then the two men walked away to the interview room.

Rivers was rolling a smoke in there. A WPC stood motionless in the corner. As Clyne and the DCI noted their entry into the room for the benefit of the tape, Rivers looked up at Clyne, his acne flaring from all that leather treatment. In front of him on

119

the table was a vending cup that he'd ripped into a little pile of polystyrene.

The DCI conducted the first phase of the interview. Clyne stood behind him, listening in.

'Michael, you have a complaint about your therapist at the Marwood?'

Rivers seemed to consider his answer, then said, 'I couldn't fucking tell if he was for real or what they was.'

'You mean Harper, your therapist, wasn't for real?'

Rivers laughed in Manny's face.

'What's that meant to mean?'

'Old George's an uphill gardener.'

'How do you know?'

'I know. All right!'

'Did he come on to you?'

'None of your fucking business.'

'You came on to him?'

'You want a fucking smack?'

Clyne pushed himself forward off the wall and spun a chair round. He sat with arms resting on the back. 'You trust Bill Haines, though, don't you?' he asked.

'Bill's like a dad to me.'

'Yeah . . . What'd you say to him?'

'I ain't telling you. Not with that woman in here.'

Manny glanced quickly at the WPC. 'Would you prefer if she left the room?'

'Nah, you probably get off on it more than her.'

'Bill told us what you told him, Michael.'

Rivers' eyes widened, smarting with the betrayal. Nothing was sacred, no secret safe, not even with him who was like a dad. It was a shame to have to drag his trust in Haines through the mud.

Clyne continued. 'What did Bill say when you told him that Harper was a nancy boy trying to give you one?'

'Bill said, I'll have the cunt.'

'So you did tell Bill that Harper sexually abused you,' Manny added. 'Is that correct?'

Rivers lowered his head and mumbled, 'Yeah.'

'Could you speak louder, please.'

'Yes, yes! Fucking hell.'

'That's a very serious allegation. Not that I'm totally convinced.'

'Michael,' Clyne said, 'tell us how Harper persuaded you. What were his words?'

'Harper said, what he said was, it was an experiment like, me and him, and that in some countries like Denmark they had sex therapists who shagged their patients and it's on the level. What it is, it wasn't just meant to talk about things that have happened. I could do anything I liked to make up for all the wrong that has happened to me.'

Manny cut to the chase. 'Did you ever see Harper anywhere other than at the Marwood?'

'Like where?'

'Did you ever go on his yacht?'

'I didn't know he has a yacht.'

'You've never been on his yacht . . .'

'I just said no, you fucking deaf?'

'Well, Michael,' Manny knitted his hands together behind his head, 'I tell you something. If I was your age and my shrink started taking liberties I'd be inclined to diss him.'

'It's what grown-ups do, innit?'

'Like your mother, you mean?'

Rivers' eyes widened. He catapulted himself out of his chair across the table at Manny, sluicing paper cups and tobacco pouches off the formica top. Manny leaned back out of reach. Clyne took Rivers by the collar and hauled him back into his seat.

'Easy, son. Get angry with Harper, not us.'

'That shrink was doing my head in.'

'Were you ever violent to him?'

'I bit his cock once.' Rivers glanced quickly at the WPC and smiled coyly. 'He screamed like a pig.'

Manny hit the turbo. 'Dr Harper was murdered last Thursday, Michael.'

Rivers looked up, genuinely surprised. Either that or he was a good actor.

'Where were you on Thursday morning, around four a.m.?'

'In bed.'

'Can anyone confirm that?'

'Yeah, my girlfriend, Rosine. I got up round eleven and went for a run to Blackwall Tunnel.'

'How can you remember for sure?'

''Cos it's what I do every day. I sit tight for a stretch and watch the traffic going through the tunnel.'

'Fascinating,' Manny said. 'How do you feel now about Dr Harper. Are you sorry he's dead?'

'No. I ain't sorry. I ain't sorry he's dead. Fuck him.'

'You gay, Michael?'

'Fuck you.'

'Harper said you were. Said you used to put on make-up like a girl before you went to see him.'

Michael's self-control was impressive. He just stared back at Manny and said quietly, 'You know nothing . . .'

'I know that your mother used to lock you both up in your gaff for weeks on end and made you poke her. What was it like having to give the old girl one? Must have put you off women for the rest of your life.'

Rivers sheered off again, in another violent attempt for Manny's face. Manny pinned him to the table, and whispered in his ear, 'Is this what you did to Harper when he made you confess to fucking your mother?' Rivers started screaming, struggling to get out of Manny's half-nelson. 'You're a strong boy, Michael. Like an ox.'

'Let me go!'

'If I let you go will you sit down quietly?'

'Let fucking go!'

'Say, I'll sit down quietly.'

Rivers shouted, 'I'll sit down quietly . . .'

Manny released his arm. Rivers slithered back into his chair, his face burning red.

'I want to see Bill.'

Manny and Clyne left the interview room for a conference. Clyne said, 'You've just undone six years of therapy in there.'

'Six months, Bob. He only saw Harper for six months.'

'He's a short-fuse merchant, ain't he?'

'But is he a killer?'

'He's got an alibi for four a.m.'

'We'll check it out.'

Tranquillizing himself with another Gauloise, Manny offered the pack to Clyne. Clyne waved them away. 'I don't need to smoke in your company, Manny. I get enough of a lungful.'

'You think Harper abused this kid? I can't believe it myself.'

'Maybe he didn't,' Clyne said. 'But Harper made him feel vulnerable, getting him to talk about all that stuff . . .'

'So he lied to Bill Haines?'

'Maybe. But Haines doesn't know that. He's walking round with it in his head like an infestation of lice.'

'So Haines sends out someone to whack Harper,' Manny suggested.

'But why would he do that, if he was going through the official channels?'

'That investigation was getting nowhere,' Manny reminded him as they walked to the incident room. He thought it through some more. As they got there he said, 'No, you're right, Bob. Haines had nothing to do with it.' He laid his hand on Kelly Stokes' shoulder. 'We can hold Rivers forty-eight hours if we want to.'

'Let him go, Manny. For now.'

It would appear that my interview with Claude Vignisson isn't of a sufficiently revealing nature for the commissioning magazine. A new editor's come in and has turned it into a dirty mag. Tit, cunt and ass. He inherited my copy and insists I spice it up.

He wants me to get into bed with Claude. 'I want it *that* close,' he tells me. 'If you can't fuck him, then fuck his wife.'

Even as metaphor that's a sinful concept. He's the one man with whom I have no sexual frisson. Claude's propriety is above board. We've met several times since our first encounter in the Ruskin Arms and I've shared a lot of intimacies with him. I'm perfectly aware that Claude Vignisson's a dirty old dog, but I still respond to his paternalism. There is a certain atavism in the way I react to older men treating me as a fragile child. Pathetic, but true.

I suspect he's an awful father in reality, better at play-acting papa than being papa. Suits me too, play-acting his child. Certainly he's spawned kids all over the place that he has no contact with now. The only reason the CSA hasn't gone after him is because they know he'd slice their fingers off with a razor. Why make it hard for themselves, they only go after soft targets anyway.

So I've invented him as a kind old daddy, a consortium of fathers, a whole father*land* in whose fields I wish to fall. The way he opens the door of a pub for me, gets each round, lights up my fags, touches my wrist every time he needs to punctuate a point, rests his freckled hand on mine, asks how I am, saying how pretty I look (Pretty! What a lovely word that is on the mouth of an old man), leaves me feeling light-headed. It's the kind of solicitude long overdue me. He doesn't care that my clothes are permanently creased, or the knuckles of my fingers are ingrained with coal. I'm still going to make some boy a lucky guy one day. And Claude's going to give me away at the altar.

We meet at the sailing club at St Katherine's Dock and I tell him my woes.

He tells me another one of his tales.

'So after I join the navy I come back to London on my first home leave. I'm seventeen with the first serious money I've ever had. I goes down the West End for a night out. I want to see a strip show. I goes to this sort of kiosk in Soho and pays my money to a man. He suddenly ups and lifts the counter like a bar and tells me to follow him. I follow the geezer up Old Compton Street and around the loop. I remember him walking fast, never once looking back to see if I was still with him. Big shoulders and hair crawling over his shirt collar. He points me to a door on Brewer Street and tells me to go in. Down some stairs in the dark there's another open door. From there I can see a stripper on a little stage beyond. Xanadu! I'm just about to walk in when another bloke steps out in front of me and says, "Five pounds. Tax." "I just paid five pounds to that bloke outside," I says. "Membership," the bloke goes. So I turn to go. Suddenly from out of a side door in the basement a great big hairy cunt steps in my way. "Five pounds to get out," he says. So I runs at him. He was quite a bit taller than me, so I had to jump about a foot to get a good shot. I nutted him in the face,

I could feel his nose break under my forehead. Then I ran back and did the other bloke. He was big and slow. I dodged his swing and clenched his balls in my hand until he crumpled. Then I went in to see the strippers. They were fat too, old and terribly unhappy-looking women. I was thinking about leaving when this suit comes up to me and drops a twenty on my table. "What's this for?" I says. "For showing me what a worthless piece of shit my security are if they can't stop a punk of a kid like you getting past them. They're on their way. You want their job? Take that twenty as an advance." And that's how I started in the business, after I left the navy. Blue corner game. Orange box hookers.'

You may be able to tell from this what my problem is. Claude has no inner life. He is all exterior. He tries to respond to me in the same confessional language that I speak to him, but falters. He has a limited emotional vocabulary. All I can glean from him are adventures.

'That's a funny story, Claude. But what I really need are some insights into your thinking.'

So then he thinks. And then tells me Vignisson isn't his real name. He adopted the surname of the last man he killed, an Icelandic book-keeper. Before Vignisson it was Barrow, after the boxer he knifed in a pub brawl. His original surname's English, and English Claude is. How else could he have got off on manslaughter pleas in both cases?

He insists he never murdered the original Vignisson. It was self-defence. Self-defence, self-defence, he repeats over and over.

As a natural progression we get on to the case of my real, biological father.

Claude first offers his condolences.

'Thank you,' I say, bowing my head.

'How you feeling? Gutted?'

'No, nothing. Not a thing.'

'That's the best way, gal. Have the Old Bill told you who they think topped him?'

126

'No, they don't seem to know.'

'Well, that's too bad.'

'I'm a suspect, Claude, although I've not been told as much. But the DI, Bob Clyne, he's keeping me in the frame.' I tell him about Michael Rivers, how he's the main suspect now. 'And he's just a kid.'

'What they collar him for?'

'My father was his therapist.'

'Well, well. Life's full of surprises, ain't it? But I guess the kid won't be seeing your old man again, unless he's holding sessions down the mortuary.'

'First of all he gets abused by his mother, survives that, then gets abused by my father, allegedly. That's the motive they think ties him to it.'

'So now they're going to fuck him a third time.'

'You know the police.'

'Do I know the police! They always go for the sad ones. Easier to pin a conviction. You like this boy?'

'On paper. He's a solid kid. But he's had a rough life.'

'He's had a rough life.'

'He's got no support, money. No prospects unless he can make it professionally as a boxer. He's fallen through all the safety nets.'

'That's not right. Even if the kid did top your old man. Where's he peck and perch, this kid?'

'Clyne said he lives on the Cypress Court estate.'

'The fucking Wild West. I wouldn't go in there without a gun.'

'You don't use guns, do you, Claude?'

'No, that's right. I don't need no gun.'

SEVEN

Manny put together a team drawn from the social services, NSPCC and a number of DCs from Area 3 AMIP. They were given the job of tracing Harper's adolescent patients. The kids started drifting through the doors within hours. Some with their parents, some alone. Some broodingly aggressive, some so incapacitated by shyness they were entirely silent. Not one of them directly accused Harper of malpractice. Manny didn't think he could push it further and handed the case load over to the social services and the NSPCC. That was now a separate, pending inquiry.

Then forensics came up with something and lifted the gloom. One of the fingerprints they'd made from inside Harper's yacht had four points of familiarity with Michael Rivers' fingerprint. Short of the sixteen features required by the CPS for a conviction, but enough to get the investigation back on wavelength.

Stokes and Clyne went to pick up Rivers from his address in Cypress Court, E9, in convoy with a squad car.

Clyne drove as Stokes, swivelling around in her passenger seat, made him feel uncomfortable saying things like, 'How's it going with the shrink's daughter?'

There was a tone of mockery in her voice but then Clyne

128

noticed she was not smiling. Rather, she was trying hard to show a sympathetic countenance with her back against the door.

'Fine. It's going fine,' he replied.

'Making progress?'

'There was no love lost between her and her father, but that's all I know. In any case that's hardly motivation to murder, is it?'

'I mean, are *you* making progress.' That sympathetic countenance cracked like plastic.

'What are you insinuating, Kelly?'

'I'm free, and you're out chasing suspect skirt.'

'Manny's free too. That mean anything to you?'

'Manny's not my type. Too northern.'

'Well, I'll try and fix you up with someone else.'

'Fuck you, Bob, you're not my pimp.'

She turned square on and glared through the windscreen at the housing estate looming ahead like a bad idea.

The streets around Cypress Court estate are named after composers. Mozart Drive, Schubert Gardens, Chopin Avenue. They parked on Elgar Close and walked around looking for Rivers' apartment block, called Sojourner's Truth. The two uniforms followed the blue signpost to 'Harmony'. Kelly and Clyne took the trail to 'Optimism'. Which they assumed to mean if they got to the other side without being mugged they'd lucked out.

Demolishers from south London had removed large chunks of the estate, whole fifty-storey blocks. Of the buildings remaining, half the snake-eyed windows punched into grey concrete had been boarded up with chipboard. From lower-floor windows the chipboard had been stolen. Or flagged with graffiti. LEROY'S MUM AINT A VIRGIN! was one of the notables. Clyne lost count of the satellite dishes, and illegal pit-bulls with an overripe male torso on the end of the leash standing in every high-rise entrance.

They located Sojourner's Truth on Chopin Avenue, a low-rise

building propped above garages painted in pastel colours. Stokes went in with the uniforms while Clyne went back to rescue the car, his VW Passat with a Blaupunkt stereo. He drove back and parked in front of a wall of sliding metal windows and grey net, facing a treeless grass bunker. In a children's playground a car tyre swung on its chain in the breeze. No kids to be seen, only a few muscular carrion crows standing in the sandpit/dog toilet who showed their backs to him, indignant at the intrusion.

He lit up and put his head back in that street named after a Polish musical genius. What was in a name? If the idea was to beatify a slum then he had doubts about that. He couldn't hear anyone singing arias in that narcopolis.

There was a little snow in the air and Clyne willed a blizzard on the place. Let it come down, a whole year of flakes to rise up the sides of these forlorn edifices. One uniform blanket, one big freeze on hopelessness.

Stokes returned before he'd finished his cigarette. She was empty-handed. Rivers had fled. But she had met the girlfriend. 'She's got a vicious scar on her nose.'

'She was covered in them when I saw her. Cuts herself, like the boyfriend.'

'This one's the work of a different artist. Still has the stitches in.'

'Did she tell you how she got it?'

'Said Rivers threw a glass ashtray at her before he fucked off.'

'Parting souvenir. Where's he gone, did she say?'

'"Wot it is, he got no gaff, no relatives. Anyfink else you wanna fucking know?" . . . Christ, I was bleeding in there.'

Clyne started the car. 'How old is she?'

'Said she was nineteen. I'd put her on the sheet as fifteen.'

'What about her parents, they know where she is?'

Stokes shook her head. 'I don't think they count, somehow.'

*   *   *

130

STOKES: Do you get depressed ever?

CLYNE: Yes.

STOKES: Depression is only suppressed anger.

CLYNE: You have an answer for everything, don't you?

STOKES: Anger is compensation for needs denied. None of us have all our needs satisfied, so sometimes we must feel anger. But that's okay, providing you allow it to come out. It's when you suppress anger that it becomes depression. Or violence. The two extremes.

CLYNE: Before I sailed around the world I was on the verge of killing someone. A cop in the murder squad, he gets so close to it. You can smell it. You couldn't get any closer. So yeah, I set keel for open sea, but if there'd been a war going on at the time I'd have enlisted instead. Do some real killing of my own. War's the get-out clause in the fifth commandment.

STOKES: What you want is the experience of going to war, while keeping the head of someone who hasn't been. Experience without the consequences . . . a fantasy.

CLYNE: I fantasize about killing dozens of men all in one night. It's how I send myself to sleep, like counting sheep. I shoot them in the head. Or I kidnap a few at a time to be killed later. I've got quite a large collection incarcerated in a barn down in Somerset. Each night I go and feed them, giving them a stay of execution.

STOKES: In a fantasy like that you are both the executioner *and* the prisoner.

CLYNE: Where I am, the places I go at night . . . murder is committed in those hours. I'd come home to Jenny, in with the morning sun. Walk into the bedroom with the smell of blood on my breath and exhale it into her mouth. I was half torn away.

STOKES: How was the sex?

CLYNE: How was the sex? One night I came home and she

131

tells me this thing *as* we are fucking . . . about some builders working in our house. She was home alone. It was summertime and they were stripped to the waist, up on the scaffolding, smashing heavy hammers into the brickwork. Their bare torsos were very eloquent, she said. Later, but before I came home, she was getting out of the bath and one of them returns. She opens the door and he says, 'You know what I've come back for, don't you?' And Jenny thinks . . . Aah, should I take off my bathrobe, or do you want to rip it off? And the builder says, 'The torch. I've forgotten my torch.' She shares this with me as we are locked in an embrace! So I start attacking her politics, her weakness for designer clothes, her rape clients, anything but that fantasy she had about the builders. Then I turned my back to her . . . Oh fuck, I can't go on with this, Kelly. I'm going to get pissed off all over again. Let's get off the subject.

STOKES: Someone says something to you that makes you feel vulnerable and you immediately take flight into anger.

CLYNE: I don't like feeling vulnerable.

STOKES: How would you know? You never give the emotion a chance.

CLYNE: Jenny doesn't like men who're unsure of themselves.

STOKES: That might have been *your* fantasy. The trouble with fantasies that go unchecked is they become internalized as facts. Women are often compassionate when a man admits to failings of confidence, when they show themselves to be vulnerable.

CLYNE: We must all worry about sensual women left at home with the builders, is what I say.

He felt so down driving alone from the station en route for the sailing club that he had to stop the car. He got out and walked along Tower Bridge. From there he looked over at St Katharine's Dock. His marriage had failed as a direct result of his work. About this he was certain. So whenever he couldn't close a case he always felt he'd lost her for nothing.

The river below was in flood. A tug pulling two refuse barges sheered into the main stream, stemming the tide. The pilot backed his load against a wharf at Bermondsey, to pick up another two barges. Lightermen ran around the gunwales, lassoing cleats. The stretching of nylon ropes echoed in the steel hulls.

The freight passed under the bridge and Clyne could smell refuse leaking out of the containers. His own anger leaked though his seams. A green darkness fell across the river. The clouds broke above him and rained blood.

He watched the tug pilot lean out of the wheelhouse and negotiate the buttresses on the bridge. A false assessment of just a few degrees with that kind of length on tow and thirty seconds later his tail would swing off course. He laid two fingers delicately on the wheel and made constant minute adjustments to his course.

It was a perfect piece of navigation.

The pilot made it through, and so did Clyne.

The sailing club had a few in. Leaning against the bar was Alastair O'Kane, speaking into a cell phone. Clyne hated cell phone users, even though he was one himself. In a train he could always tell when someone out of eyesight was speaking on a cell phone, rather than to a fellow passenger. The way they raise the volume, converse too formally. Like talking to yourself. It's haunted, clone-talk, unnatural.

Clyne strolled over to O'Kane while he was still on his Ericsson and said, 'Let me have a word with what's-his-name, will ya?'

And O'Kane went, 'Excuse me? Excuse me?'

'You're bringing your office into the bar, Alastair. I can even smell the coffee brewing.'

He called an abrupt halt to the conversation and switched off the cell phone.

'Hello, Bob.' O'Kane turned to the man beside him and introduced him. 'This is Rusty.'

Clyne and Rusty shook hands. Alastair, caught between, added, 'Rusty was a friend of George's too.'

'Really?' Clyne said. 'Rusty what?'

'Rowlands,' said Rusty.

He was a new one on Clyne. He hadn't seen his face before. Rowlands was wearing a blazer with four-button cuffs embossed with ship's anchors, a blue-striped shirt, pearl cuff links and a polka-dot bow tie. His ginger hair was thick, low on the brow, edging into the corners of his eyes and disciplined into a sharp parting. His face was heavily freckled, like a pox. Clyne had never liked ginger-haired men. Never got on with them, never trusted them. Who else but a carrot top would smoke a menthol cigarette? Now that's something Clyne hadn't seen in a long while.

Rowlands was trying to order a margarita from the barman, who didn't know how to make one. 'Two tequila to one lime juice, spoonful of Triple Sec . . .' Rowlands instructed.

'Where'd you all meet . . . here?' Clyne asked.

'No. We go back further,' O'Kane said.

'How much further?'

'Actually, through a schoolteacher from Eltham. I was going out wi' her. She was going out wi' George at the same time . . . before he was married, to his second wife. And wi' Rusty as well.'

'This woman sounds interesting,' Clyne said. 'Don't suppose you still have her phone number?'

'None of us knew of the others' existence in her life,' Rowlands smiled.

'So how'd you find out?'

'Well, that's quite a story.' O'Kane grinned at the memory.

'I like stories,' Clyne said.

'Okay, well . . . I'd been going out wi' her for about six months when I start having trouble with ma waterworks. Nothing much, a little thrush maybe. So I tell her go get checked out. Clarc goes to a VD clinic. Overreacting, really. But that's what she did. Next thing I hear is she's got gonorrhoea. She's very distressed. Then she tells me about George and Rusty.

'She organized a trip for us all to go to tha clinic. Clare picks me up first in her old Morris Minor, then we go get George. George and I shake hands and start making light of the situation.' O'Kane broke off to look at Rowlands. 'For obvious reasons she couldn't pick you up from your house . . .' He turned back to Clyne. 'Rusty was married, see, so he waited for us at a pub in Chancery Lane. Rusty sits up front and makes polite conversation wi' us in the back. Clearly he's the most anxious about all this. That right, Rusty?'

'That's right,' said Rowlands. 'If I was positive I was going to have to tell the wife.'

'With all of us on board,' O'Kane continued, 'Clare drives in complete silence, way out a' London, somewhere beyond Chislehurst. On some country lane she gets a flat tyre. She doesn't have a jack in the car. We have a debate and decide the best thing's for us to get out while she drives back on the flat to the garage we passed a mile up the road. As we're standing on the side of the road, waiting, we begin to see the humour in this. Like, how come three strapping men let a woman go back to fix th' car? We start to relax wi' one another. Then George asks if they still use the "umbrella" at clap clinics.'

'The umbrella?' Clyne asked.

'A thin metal rod shaped like a folded umbrella and razor sharp. Victorian medicine. What they do, George says, is insert this into the urethra. Then they whip it out fast, scraping the scabs off from inside the urethra. Rusty and I buckle at the knees as George starts exaggerating the doctor's action, placing his boot into my groin and pulling the umbrella out wi' both hands, while making a rasping noise in his throat. Rusty and I have fallen on the ground now, laughing. Laughter in the dark. Fuckin' murther!

'At that point a car pulls over. We're in field city, ploughed over for winter. This driver rolls down his window and asks directions for Newton. He's American and pronounces it New Town. We're laying on the grass verge. George tells him to drive about a mile down the road and take a left at the lights, to get rid a' him. He drives off, stops, reverses back. The window rolls down again. You guys okay? he asks. You want a lift somewhere? Then he smiles. What the fuck are you doing rolling around in the dirt in your suits? We're civil engineers, George says. There's going to be a new bypass running along here soon.'

The barman coughed. O'Kane stopped talking.

'We don't have any fresh lime juice, sir,' he explained to Rowlands.

'Lemon juice then. Use lemon juice.'

'I don't think I can do this anyway. I don't have Triple Sec behind the bar either.'

'What about Cointreau?' Clyne suggested. 'Use Cointreau instead of Triple Sec.'

'Can you?' Rowlands asked. 'Use Cointreau?'

'Sure. It's fine. You got any salt?'

'We've got salt,' the barman said.

'Then mix enough for two. I'll join Rusty in one.'

'You want to hear the end of this?' O'Kane asked. 'It's a beauty.'

'Carry on,' Clyne urged.

'Okay. Finally Clare comes back wi' the car, tyre repaired. We drive to the clinic, all of us laughing about that American, trying to keep our minds occupied. In the clinic Rusty leaps to the counter to be registered first. Sorry, Rusty, but it's true. You were up like a ferret. He gets to go first to give blood and urine samples. I go in next, George after me. Then we wait. Rusty has his head in a newspaper the whole time in case someone recognizes him. The doctor comes through eventually and calls in Rusty. A few minutes later Rusty reappears wi' a huge grin on his face.

'He's just been given a clean bill of health. George and I go sick. I'm in next. Same result. Negative. Now we're all looking at poor old George. He's crushed. He's going to be on the Coca-Cola while the penicillin goes to work. But when George does come out he's jumping up and down. He's in the clear too. This is incredible. Then the doctor summons Clare to his surgery. A minute later she comes out laughing. The doctor explained her blood samples must have been mixed up wi' someone else's. We end up in a pub boozing it up, laughing about that poor woman wandering around with gonorrhoea and thinking she's okay.

'That was the last we ever saw of Clare. I think she was too humiliated. But me, George and Rusty, we stayed in touch and became friends. George had a boat. It was him who got us all interested in sailing.'

'Poor George . . .' Rowlands said.

'Aye . . .' O'Kane added.

Then Clyne's cell phone started ringing in his pocket. The other two men laughed as Clyne pulled it out and took the call.

'Rusty, can you smell tha' coffee brewing?' O'Kane jested.

It was the computer nerd at the lab who'd called Clyne on the cell phone. He needed him to come in urgently. Clyne never even got to taste his margarita.

The lab was as dark as Pandora's box. The blinds had been pulled down on the world outside. VDU screens lit Clyne's way to the computer programmer in a swivel chair, his face six inches away from a screen. Electro-static was making his hair hover like dry ice. His hands, Penelope-like, unravelled the wool from the hem of his dressing gown. On the toe of his right foot balanced a plaid carpet slipper.

The man was so obsessed by information technology he slept with it.

The moment he saw Clyne enter he threw his arms in the air. A solicitor had come in two hours ago and tried to take away Harper's computer equipment. Mrs Harper had obtained a court order claiming proprietorial interest in the property under Section 19. Manny called in their solicitor, who invoked powers under Section 8. The computer programmer didn't know how long they'd be able to keep hold of it. He was as anxious as a child whose toys might be confiscated.

'Is it that important?'

'Could be.'

He was keyboarding like Franz Liszt – on the Internet, the World Wide Web. Clyne fired up a Camel, lost in all that on-line shit.

'Please tell his widow I'd like to keep hold of this stuff a while longer.'

'I'll try.'

'See what you can do in the charm school department.'

'I'll give you a call.'

'So you'll give me a call?'

'Yeah, I'll call you.'

Clyne arrived at Mrs Harper's house as she was coming home with the shopping. She looked flustered, fitting the wrong keys in the locks, spilling fruit out of her Marks & Spencer carrier bags. He was offered no formal invite inside but the bag she left on the doorstep was as good as any. He picked it up and followed her down the hall, past a row of Hogarth prints, into the kitchen where the table shone and the sink sparkled. On the table was a large vase of orchids and a ceramic bowl of fruit.

They maintained the silence as she uploaded the food from

the floor into the fridge and freezer. There were lots of frozen meals, he noticed. Chinese, Indian, Italian. A big ladder in the back of her tights articulated loudly.

She moved to the table and emptied a bag of kiwi fruit into the overflowing bowl. The pears, bananas already in there were turning brown and mouldy. Apples rolled off the table on to the floor.

Clyne picked up the windfalls. 'Do you work, Mrs Harper?'

She stopped unpacking, a tangerine in each hand. 'I used to,' she replied. 'Not any more.'

'What did you do?'

'I was a counsellor.' She looked tired, her eyes bloodshot and dazed.

'A county councillor, or the other kind?'

'The other kind.'

'Is that how you met your husband?'

'We met at the Tavistock. I was taking a course in family counselling.'

'He was a medical doctor too, wasn't he?'

'George was a lot of things.'

'Why did you give it up?'

'Why did I give it up?' Mrs Harper lowered herself into a dining chair, crossing her arms around the back of the chair. She was as flat-chested as a boy. 'Oh, I don't know. George was not so keen for me to work in a similar field.' She looked him squarely in the eye. 'What do you want to see me about?'

'Mrs Harper, why are you trying to get his computer equipment returned?'

Her hands untied from behind the chair and she sat forward. Clyne watched her folding her arms across her stomach.

'I don't need to answer that.'

'That's a shame.'

'What do you know about psychotherapy, Inspector?'

'A little.'

139

'A little knowledge is a dangerous thing.'

'W.R. Bion says something interesting about knowledge. He says there is plus knowledge and minus knowledge. Plus K is used towards enhancing life, minus K to gain power and control. I feel a lot of minus K coming from you, Mrs H.'

'Where did you learn about Bion?'

'My shrink's a Bion freak.'

'You're in therapy?'

'In a manner of speaking.'

'Who with?'

'No one you know,' he said. 'So can we keep the computer stuff?'

'What can you possibly find out from my husband's computer equipment?'

'The people he talked to on-line might lead to his killer. I don't know. The lab think it's important.'

'I was advised to get it returned by a friend of ours.'

'Who?'

'A magistrate, actually. He sits in the juvenile courts.'

'How'd your husband know this magistrate?'

'I thought it a good idea somehow, if a magistrate suggested it.'

'What's he called?'

'Rowlands.'

'Rusty Rowlands?'

'Yes.'

'I just met him as it happens. And he advised you to interfere with police procedure?'

Mrs Harper picked up his static. 'My husband had a very fine reputation as a therapist. I intend to keep that reputation intact.'

'I'm beginning to think it's your own reputation you're protecting.'

She grew from her chair, like smoke rising. 'I want you to leave now, Inspector.'

My father had been filmed by Sky news returning from the 1994 *Observer* transatlantic single-handed race. He'd kept a video copy of the interview, which Clyne brought round to my bus so we could watch it together. Although I rather suspect he wanted to watch me watching the video. They were the most recent pictures of my father I'd seen and I smoked voraciously for the duration.

He was interviewed while motor-cruising up the Thames through Greenwich Reach, heavy industries pumping out steam in the background. My father stood in the cockpit behind the wheel, bronzed, in a white Lacoste golfing shirt. His greying hair was stiff with salt blast.

I feel a little stiff myself as he is saying to camera:

'I hit a half-submerged oil tanker on the Azores route under bare poles. I had to go into the water in a hurricane with a snorkel to inspect for damage.'

He taps the coaming affectionately, and for several seconds. 'She protected me from a hell of a buffeting. God bless the designer. The hull was okay, but the keel damaged. Storms at sea . . . they're just obstacles to be conquered, really. Either they win or you do. But submerged oil tankers, well, the hull could've been ripped right off.'

'You won this time,' a voice with a Scots accent comments, off-camera.

'But I lost the race.'

His yacht passed an abandoned jetty mid-stream in Greenwich Reach. Under a derelict crane a portakabin bolted on to the gantry had been tagged with swastika graffiti. My father joked, pointing at the swastikas, 'They weren't there when I left. Don't tell me Britain's had a right-wing dictatorship installed since I've been gone!'

I lean across to the VCR and switch it off. 'There's only so much of him I want to see.'

'Why's that?' Clyne says.

'The face that launched a thousand ships.'

'I'm not with you.'

'Did you see some storms at sea?'

'They snap up and snap off, followed by peaceful, silent moments. That's when I'd crash for an hour. Always a charmed sleep, that one hour.'

'No time for nightmares.'

'No, nothing.'

'Like the rest of your days out there, I suppose. Full of nothing.'

'Nothing is always something at sea. I'd wake to the off-course alarm trilling away in the silence, take my first sun sights. In the afternoon take a shot off the moon's edge as it first appears in the daylight, a sight of the Pole star at dusk. Peaceful, like I say, silent, but after three days, you start pining for just a breath of wind. Then get a force ten on the nose.'

'Let's go to my room, Bob,' I breathe in his ear. 'Tell me more stories in there.'

The dogs roam Wanstead Flats combusting into free-for-alls every now and then. Labrador crossed with bulldog, spaniel with lurcher, Dobermann with Alsatian. Deformities, bad tempers, dirty fighting, desperation.

We are as naked as dogs ourselves and slick with a sweat of our own. In our hour of self-possession we had neglected to feed the stove. The room is dark and cold around us. The only light comes from the tips of our glowing cigarettes.

I light a candle by the side of my bed. The watercolour nailed to the wall of children playing on a beach, Clyne starts looking at intensely.

'You like that painting?'

'It reminds me of our summer holidays,' he says. 'Me, Jenny and the kids.'

'Haven't you noticed it before?'

'No. How long's it been there?'

'Longer than you've been coming.'

'I've not noticed it before. I'd like to buy that painting off you.'

'It's not for sale.'

'Then tell me who the artist is. He can do another one for me just like it.'

'That's not possible either.'

'I don't like the way you're looking at me. Your face just did a little dance,' he says.

'He was a traveller. And I used to go out with him until he committed suicide. Which is why you can't ask him to paint your picture.'

'Were you in love with him?'

'You know what love is?'

'Yes, I think so.'

'I don't. I don't know what love is. Not even romance.'

'Romance is a fairy story.'

'Fairy stories aren't about romance. They're about the threat to childhood. A child's abused by a witch and goes into hiding. The witch is killed by a saviour of children who then marries the child. Snow White and Sleeping Beauty are child brides. You shouldn't presume they're happy ever after.'

143

Clyne adds in his inimitable empirical way: 'It's like orphanages. Dr Barnardo and all. The house parents turn out to be the witches. All round the country police are running dozens of investigations into these places, involving thousands of former residents dating back thirty years or more. Suspects are all men. But why in fairy stories is the bad guy always a woman?'

'I don't know. But I tell you something. Walt Disney portrays the good fairies as plump old ladies and the witch with red nail polish and lipstick. As a girl he made me frightened of my own sexuality. And Max, he was scared shitless of women. He'd watch the films with his hands over his balls.'

'Which fairy story do you like most?'

'Hansel and Gretel. Because they save themselves. They take the law into their own hands.'

'You love Max, don't you?'

'Max is all I've got. My only family. And the reason I'm living with the travellers. Max won't live in a house. It was a choice of losing him, or going New Age.'

'He needs you.'

'And I need him. You can die from want of someone to love.'

Clyne drops his head and carps, 'So what's a girl like you see in a cop ten years older? Am I the huntsman or the prince?'

'You're rough trade,' I laugh.

'*I'm* rough trade?'

'You fuck me like you want to kill me.'

'I don't want to kill you. What a terrible thing to say.'

'It's all right, I like it. Your job makes you conversant with killing without being a killer.'

'How's your job make you, Alice?'

'It doesn't. What I do isn't real.'

'If it pays you money, then it's real.'

I think about that. The stuff I write for the glossies, *Loaded*, *FHM*, *Maxim*, *Arena*, and *Cosmo*, *Elle*, may be ephemera but at least it's ephemera that doesn't stick to me. While the money it brings in keeps the wolf from our door. And it's something I enjoy, being the only working girl. Some of the guys hobble as we travel, fixing cars, sharpening knives, but it's small beer compared to what I earn. I don't even mind being collared for a few jib by the tribe after they've pissed their giros up against the wall. It's to me they come begging. Aunty Alice, the *good* witch with the Rouge Noir nail polish.

We go down for the second act. He circles his finger around the lips of my vagina, anchoring his thumb and little finger on to my pubic bone, like I'd taught him to do. I can smell heat rising off his skin, like the warmth of the sun.

He fucks me holding on to my ankles. I turn my head to the side, dreaming. I see my stomach swelling, as though with an ectopic pregnancy.

And all the time Clyne tells me stories. That's my idea. The stories, fables and sex fantasies during which he talks about himself in the third person. ('He's coming inside you now. You can't see his face. You *wouldn't* want to see this guy's face.')

Yet all the while I feel there is something he can't reach. He's entered through a narrow aperture into my dimensionless space, a nebulousness. Not an unhappy experience, just an incomplete one. A freefall through a sky frisky with stars. We are out of synch by a single stroke. One key, one shout away from . . . well, what?

EIGHT

Clyne woke up in Alice's bed alone and disorientated. Only on a seaborne yacht had he ever slept so soundly. He looked at his watch, realized he'd been asleep for about one hour and quickly started to dress.

He didn't want to be found on this coach where he so obviously didn't belong.

He felt vulnerable. And didn't have Kelly Stokes with him to explain what that meant.

Beyond the curtain he could hear amorous noises. To get out he had to walk through Max's room, disturbing whatever was going on in there. He pushed back the curtain and immediately wished he'd knocked on the bulkhead first. Like some trap laid for him, he saw Max fucking a woman lying on her stomach across a trellis table, her head turned away. Four piles of Alice's magazines under the table legs brought it up to Max's preferred height.

Clyne tried backing off but the momentum went the wrong way. He thought for a moment that the woman was Alice.

Max spotted him cowering. 'Hi, Inspector.' He waved gaily.

The woman ejected herself from the table and crashed into

the coaching, dreadlocks covering her face. Her pubic hair was shaved off, exposing a rather delicate tattoo of a butterfly. Yet it was her breasts she wanted to cover from Clyne. Her hands, like her face, were weathered brown, the rest of her body a luminous white.

'Hi, Max. How's you?' Clyne's limbs came back to life.

'All right, yeah. Okay really,' Max sniffed. 'Apart from this cold I can't shake.'

Clyne sliced through the rancid air of Max's room. 'See you another time, Max, when you're less busy.'

'No, wait, I'm coming.'

'Don't take too long, I'll be in the front.'

Clyne joined Rainbow in the lounge, who offered him one of her Roses chocolates. 'When's the baby due?' he asked.

'In a month, but wish it was today.'

'Last part goes slow.'

'Have you any children?'

'Yes, two.'

She stared at him wide-eyed, as though he were a veteran of the same war she was fighting. 'Were you at the birth?' The battle.

'Both times.'

'Did it turn you off sex with their mother?'

'No. On the contrary.'

'There's no way I'd let my baby's father watch. I don't think he'd want to give me tongue again.'

He remembered what Alice said, that Rainbow could only guess who the father was. 'It's going to be tough going it alone.'

'Not as tough as the other way. You married?' she asked.

'Used to be. I'm divorced.'

'Then I rest my case.'

'Do you know where Alice is?'

'She's gone to interview the Manic Street Preachers.'

Clyne had no further questions and flopped around until Max came out. He was naked apart from his boxer shorts and smoking a small Hamlet cigar, to keep up appearances.

First thing he asked, 'Would the police want me, do you think?'

'What have you done wrong?'

'As a copper, I mean.'

'Since when have you wanted to be a policeman?'

'Since you walked in.'

'Something I'm wearing appeal to you?'

'You see some sights, don't you?'

'Nothing like the one I just saw.'

A boyish grin spread across his face. 'That's my girl, Malakite. She's just got back from Newbury.'

'How old are you, Max?'

'Twenty-six.'

'Might be too old to join the police.'

'Aw, really? Twenty-six too old? I'm in my prime.'

'I joined up when I was twenty-one, after university.'

'I want to do something meaningful. I got up today, cleaned my teeth.'

'But did you do a thorough job? That's what I ask my children.' Clyne lit up a Camel.

'Have you caught our father's killer yet?'

'No, Max. All I've done so far is meet his friends.'

'Which friends?'

'Alastair O'Kane, Rusty Rowlands . . .'

'I know them.'

'You know them . . .'

'Rusty, I know Rusty best. His son's my friend.'

'Where's he live?'

'Here, in the camp. We joined up together.' Max looked out of the window of the bus. 'He was one of my father's patients, long time ago.'

148

'Perhaps you'd make a good cop after all. Can you take me to meet Rowlands *fils* . . . what's his name?'

'Kevin, alias Troy.'

'Troy?'

'He changed his name.'

'Yeah, of course. Like Alice is Wave.'

'And I'm Fawn.'

'Okay, Fawn, take me to meet Troy.'

'What, now?'

'Why not? You got something better to do?'

A dozen more vehicles had joined the travellers' camp. Veterans of the A30 Road War had come home to graze. Folks stepped out of buses to shake hands with these tree architects. Accounts of oaks abseiled and lived in Clyne overheard, of sheriff's men chain-sawing the branches under their feet. And he felt a little admiration for them, for fucking with the basic contradiction of a free market democracy: say what you like but do as you're told. The fight had lent them atmosphere, like tango dancers.

A horsebox in the corner of the field was painted orange. As they approached, a dog posse snapped at Clyne's ankles. A tin bath tumbled out of the horsebox door, just missing Max. The tub was followed by a mattress and lastly a traveller who fell on his ass in the mud. Shitfaced. What impressed Clyne was the way he managed to keep hold of his can without spilling any.

'That's him,' Max said.

Kevin Rowlands, alias Troy, got on his feet and lunged for the door as it slammed closed in his face. He smashed his fist into the coach panelling, then howled in pain.

He still hadn't noticed Max and Clyne standing in the dark.

Max made a low-gear approach. 'Troy . . . ?'

'Whaaa?' Troy examined his bleeding knuckles.

'What's going down, man?'

'Dillybag in there's kicked me out. It's my fucking box.'

'What you do to her?' Clyne asked.

'I didn't do nothing. She just flipped.'

'Sit down over here,' Max offered. 'Give her indoors time to cool off.'

'Yeah, right.'

They sat on the damp grass outside his horsebox.

'This is Bob,' said Max.

'Oh, right. Cool.'

Clyne ran his hand down his tie. It felt like a noose. Then he came out. 'I'm a detective inspector, Kevin.'

Kevin was clearly not happy to be addressed by his real name and by a policeman to boot. He hissed at Clyne, crossing two fingers in front of his face. The gesture made Clyne smile, at this tramp who'd just been thrown out with the bathwater.

'What's the Old Bill doing here?' he asked.

'What are *you* doing here?' Clyne countered.

'I'm an air breather, that's what I do.' He took the cigarette Max offered him. 'You come to run us off the Flats then?'

'No.'

'Because we've got as much right to live here as a farmer has to live on his land.'

'So where's your crops?'

Dogs' barking broke up the conversation, relieving their boredom by having a scrap in the grass.

Troy suddenly said, 'Do you believe in hell?'

'I'm in it, son.'

'This is heaven *and* hell, together. Good and evil. That's why people are petrified of us. They look at us through their windows and . . .'

'If I lived in a house here and saw your dogs fighting, saw you falling over and busting your hand up, I'd be petrified too.'

'What goes on here's no more troubled than what goes on over there. It's just we're more visible.'

'Granted,' Clyne said, recalling when the Flats was a haven

for flashers who stepped out of their houses on Capel Road and performed their rituals on the common. Men who were rarely apprehended. 'But people who pay their council tax have a few more rights than you do. That's just how it is, Troy.'

'They can't stand it that we're free and they're not.'

'Free from what?' Clyne retorted.

'They accuse us of defecating and leaving litter, as if that's all we ever do.'

'Where do you take a dump, as a matter of interest?'

'In the fucking Dorchester.'

Clyne suddenly felt very tired. It was time to raise the issue. When he mentioned Rusty's name Troy looked sharply at Max. 'How did he know he was my father?'

Max said nothing.

'What is this? What you want from me?'

'I'm on your side, Troy. I don't particularly like your father either, and I've only met him once.'

Troy let out a shrill, bitter laugh, and grew small inside his combat fatigues, fighting the war against himself, the war no one ever wins. He looked skywards, casting his mind back in time and place to when he was a sour adolescent, living in affluence with a lawman in a resplendent London house. It hurt him, clearly, and Clyne felt sorry for him. Whatever that hurt was, he had tried to disguise it with hair dye and tattoos and mud from a London floor until Clyne came along snooping, scraping the camouflage away.

Clyne lowered his voice. 'Tell me about your father?'

'My father's a very charitable man.'

'But not to you?'

Troy laughed again, with less conviction. Now the lid was open and his cover blown, he became suddenly articulate. Even his voice-tone changed, from estuary hard-ass to a more dulcet Englishness. 'He adopts other people's kids, takes them under his wing, spoils them. When he gets bored he puts them back on the street, where they come from.'

'You were in therapy with Max's father. That right?'

'Yeah.' Troy addressed Max. 'He got murdered, didn't he?' Max nodded. 'I'm sorry, man.'

'Was he helpful, Dr Harper?'

Troy stayed mum. He glanced at Max. Max was as unmoved as ever. Clyne wondered about Max then, how much he actually knew, disguised by that Hansel lost-boy act of his.

Hansel and Gretel take the law into their own hands.

'Why do you live here with the tribe?'

'We're on the Ninth Wave.'

'I asked you a straight question.'

'And I'm trying to give you a straight answer.'

Clyne bristled and then sighed. 'Okay, set me right.'

'The Ninth Wave's the boundary between life and death, land and sea. The last outpost before permanent exile. Go beyond the Ninth Wave and you die. But there are survivors. The survivors perform great deeds.'

'And you intend to be the survivors?'

'If we survive we will pioneer the next new world.' Troy shook with laughter on the verge of tears. 'A world without families, I can promise you that.'

The days rolled on but the momentum was sluggish.

In the incident room Manny's steely gaze roamed across heads, his eyes glowing. He was waiting for someone to come up with fresh ideas. But no one had been home in two nights. They were beat. Everyone needed a bath, a shave, women included. And the reek of Manny's Gauloises was gassing them into a state of narcolepsy.

Clyne was off the roster now, jacking in the aggro for the night. As he was putting on his coat Manny pounced on him. He wanted Clyne in his office.

He told him to close the door. When Clyne turned round he found he was staring at the end of Manny's rotating pencil, the lead six inches short of his nose.

In his other hand he waved the reports of Clyne's interviews with Alice Harper.

'I didn't raise these actions, as I recall.'

'I raised them in arrears.'

'Bob, you've had your dick on the perch for a long time now.'

'What's that got to do with anything?' Clyne paused. But Manny held off for longer and won the game. 'Who said I'm fucking her, anyway?'

'Sam said she's an oil painting by all accounts.'

'Maybe he's fucking her.'

'You denying it?'

Clyne stared at him. Manny lowered his pencil in grim satisfaction. 'You should know better. If we bring a prosecution against her you won't be able to offer evidence.'

'I'm getting her to open up, Manny.'

'Wrong orifice, Bob.' Manny calmed his voice. 'Right now it's Michael Rivers you should be thinking about. He's our main suspect. Our only meaningful forensic points to him. Go find the little fuck before this investigation goes out of shape.'

'How do we know what we know, Manny?'

'Ay?'

'This is like science. You can't have the results until we get to the end of the experiment.'

'What d'you want, a Bunsen burner?'

'A little more space to explore.'

In the incident room Clyne was again setting out for home when Manny loaded him up with an action. This action had nothing to do with the Harper case.

Clyne was convinced Manny was punishing him for his indiscretion with Alice. 'Come on, Manny, I'm off the roster. And I'm beat.'

Manny said, 'This one's open and shut. Should take you no more than an hour.'

Clyne made Ridley go with him. He had a bone to pick with his DS. In the car he asked, 'Did you tell Manny I'm balling Alice Harper?'

'No, of course not.'

'Then how'd he know that?'

'It's what made him the DCI, I suppose. Intuition.'

'The intuition of a celibate.'

They were driving through urban desert again, bearing east. Through the windscreen they half watched the clinker ruins go by outside like so much downbeat TV.

Ridley said, 'Have you ever been to his gaff? Manny's?'

'No.'

'I went there to pick him up once. It's spotless, like no one lives there. And nothing in the fridge but ice cubes and a cucumber.'

'A cucumber?'

'He puts slices of cucumber under his eyes at night.'

'What an old fruit!'

It was to an everyhome in a Victorian everystreet that they went to. Housing association or council stock. There was a primary school at one end, park at the other, the road between the kind of lick you make every day walking the dog, the kids to school. Plane trees lined the way up and the way down. An Austin Metro was parked neatly outside, a baby seat in the rear. The path to the door was littered with crisp packets, free newspapers – palm fronds under a policeman's feet.

But inside, inside the door and up the stairs, Clyne felt the temperature drop. He knew instinctively that this was all wrong. It was tundra six feet inside the flat.

An eighteen-month baby had been found dead in her cot. The parents were standing against the living room wall, making a stony-faced statement to a WPC. They looked nonplussed. Clyne could smell their unwashed clothes, greasy hair. He could smell their bleeding gums.

The baby's room was so cold the two officers inside had dewdrops at the end of their noses. In the cot with the baby were crushed beer cans. Fag ends had been ground into the wet carpet – like a sponge under his shoes. Clyne examined the little corpse up against the bars of the cot. He examined it for about one minute.

When he turned away a Home Office doctor was just coming through the door. Clyne said: 'I want to know what caused this two-inch contusion to the head. I want to know what kind of force was used to snap the ankles like that. And this looks like a screwdriver's been drilled into the neck. And these are bites, you can see the teeth marks.'

He walked out of the little bedroom through the lounge, avoided eye contact with the parents. He merely pointed at one of the uniforms. 'Take them down to the nick. *Now*.'

One last glance back towards the baby's room as a scene-of-crime officer was framing the cot in his camera lens. Clyne blinked in his flashlight, one-sixtieth of a second of respite, then walked out into the street through the rain.

A couple of miles on in the car and he realized he'd forgotten Sam. He pulled over at a tea van parked in a lay-by. Lining up at the service hatch lorry drivers and salesmen were sharing their day. Clyne bought a hot dog. Down each side of the frankfurter he squeezed a line of mustard and a line of ketchup. He walked back to the car and ate the hot dog before driving home.

David was standing on a chair in the kitchen as he walked in. He was trying to swat a sluggish fly with a metal spatula. Each time the fly passed he'd swing at it with all his might. Mick came downstairs then, appearing in the kitchen with the *Evening*

Standard. He was reading the centre pages. Headline on the front page was: Government To End Neutrality On Family.

Clyne said, 'That's rich.'

'What is?' Mick asked.

'How much is a politician's morality worth?'

Mick turned to the front page. 'The family's knackered. Someone has to do something.'

'It's all your fault.' Clyne jabbed a finger at Mick. 'You voted them in.' To David, Clyne said, 'You're going to fall off that chair in a minute.'

'I vote for the best party for the times,' Mick asserted. 'You vote for the party your father voted for, in case he turns in his grave.'

'If you were Catholic,' Clyne said, 'but didn't agree with the Pope's policy on abortion, would you become Anglican?'

So Mick said, 'Some Anglicans are threatening to go Catholic if the Church starts ordaining women priests.'

David swung the spatula. It hit Clyne in the eye. He screamed, but not because David had really hurt him. The piercing cry came out of some greater place.

He tried to run it out, into the bathroom, and locked himself in. Seconds later Mick was trying the door. 'Bob, David's upset. He thinks he's hurt you. Open up. What the fuck you doing in there?'

What was he doing in there? What was he doing . . . ? He was talking into the mirror and a corpse talked back. Sometimes a dead body can be more eloquent than a live one. The bathroom was full of steam, a vestige of his daughter's lingering hot bath. Toothbrushes lay like spent missiles in the sink.

He rifled around inside the cabinet, looking for something, an antidote, pick-me-up, rescue remedy, when a sharp edge cut into his hand. And in an instant the smoke and unreason blew out the top of his head. He yanked out his hand with a Wilkinson Sword razor blade stuck in the palm.

156

He ripped his shirt, forcing up the sleeve. He pressed a corner of the razor into his forearm by the watch strap and cut a line. The muscle bunched into a stone and raw flesh peeled back like a red rose. Hairs on his arm sprang through the streams of blood. The pain was scandalous, but focused. His voice was repealed, but as a woman's, a whole octave higher than his own, as though he'd crossed a frontier, abandoned one sex for the other.

Mick was still on the other side of the door: 'Are you all right?'

The razor came free with a sucking sound. He slumped on to the floor, resting his head against the toilet bowl with this wonderful afterglow. Seeing so much of his own blood felt terrific. He felt alive again. Shame had been vanquished, the original sin avenged. A new, pristine flag ran up the pole. He looked out of the window into the sky and the sky was purified.

The Manic Street Preachers are good ambassadors for their nation. What marks them out is their furious intensity, an almost Latin temperament that characterizes their race. They don't try to make an issue communicating in that arcane and domesticated language, they don't pluck harps or employ male-voice choirs for their recording sessions, or sing songs about pit ponies and the Davy lamp being man's best friends. They are political in a personal way. They are the bards of the lost tribe of youth: junkies, suicides, anorexics, self-mutilators. They trade in tortured polemics and have no peers, apart from maybe Elvis Costello, that Englishman's Welshman. A hundred years ago the Manics would have been fire and brimstone evangelists conducting revivals in the mountains, below the snow line. They may have guitars under their arms instead of Old Testaments, but the song remains the same: 'Weep! As though the day of judgement has dawned.'

Good universal chuff. Good boys too, nicely modest and unspoilt. A maturity that is helping them come to terms with the loss of their front man, Richey Edwards. His disappearance is like a death, but less than a death, which prevents the survivors from mourning.

I get back from interviewing the Manics in Shepherd's Bush to find Clyne waiting for me in the bus. He's come round to tell me that a skip driver who'd been working near the north entrance of the Blackwall Tunnel had found a pile of clothes on the river towpath. He wouldn't have given them a second look were it not for the way they'd been neatly folded and stacked. Jeans, shirt, bomber jacket weighed down with a pair of Nike trainers. Wrapped in a sock inside the shoe was a wallet. Inside the wallet was a monochrome photograph of Michael Rivers and girlfriend. They were protruding their arms for the camera, blood running from their wounds.

It looks as if Rivers jumped into the Thames, ending it all.

If so, Clyne has lost his main suspect.

And I move up a rank on the grid.

He wants to talk it over with me.

People go missing all the time, I say. Richey Edwards, Michael Rivers may have different motives for vanishing but the impulse is a common one. Not everyone believes that life is continuous, with one day following the next, one week, one month, one year without interruption, as if it's all one long train journey. The point is, people do fuck up along the way. Then it becomes an issue of: do I stay a failure, a victim until the day I check out? Or do I check out early? Or vanish, change names and identity and become someone else? Happiness is not a matter of luck, but hard work.

If we've invented ourselves anyway, if we have constructed our characters from the fictional world, then we can do it again. And again. And again. A failure in love? Turn homosexual. If you're one of the abused, you can change that status too. Fuck, abusers do it all the time.

The American police facilitate this very thing, Clyne adds, with their witness protection scheme. Turn state evidence against the Mafia and the FBI find you a new life.

Actually, I say, the United States was invented by missing persons. Petty thieves from Poland with names like Mikhail Mienzevich leave on a boat for Ellis Island. Twenty years later they turn up in Washington DC as Micky Mann, running the country.

What joy it brings, to know all is not lost after a bad start, that you can begin again. The Christian cults have always understood how seductive this offer is. The cults tell you to abort your original character, shed your family ties. Then fill yourself with information hitherto denied.

And you're still out there, still somebody.

I tell him in the Grimms' version of Hansel and Gretel, Hansel is transformed into a fawn after they escape their wicked step-mother. Gretel finds an abandoned cottage in the woods and there they raise themselves, exiles from the family. By the time the King and his huntsman find them years later and the King proposes marriage to Gretel, her integrity is indelibly forged. What will change with age is style, the texturing of language. But her conviction is a miracle of parthenogenesis.

Clyne interrupts. In the version he grew up on, Hansel and Gretel kill the witch in her gingerbread house, then go back to their father with a fortune in pearls and diamonds.

Well, there you are. Even the stories themselves are trans-formed with every new telling. They alter shape, even though their compositions stay the same.

NINE

Clyne and Ridley found Rowlands in a private chamber seated round a table with the court usher, clerk, secretary and two lay justices – one a charity worker, the other a doctor's wife. The pine furnishings and wall panelling were redolent of a chapel of rest. Trying to make upbeat something intrinsically downbeat. Rowlands had one big foot up on the edge of the table, the leather sole cocked like a Zulu shield. Laid on the table was a picnic lunch: French loaves, goat's cheese, vine tomatoes, black grapes, small bottles of Volvic water and orange juice decanted. No one had touched the food; they were listening to Rowlands speaking in a full-mouthed lisp, pronouncing the soft syllables with a whistle.

'The Law Society came to me to ask what they should be doing. You're the only one who knows what's going on out there. I said, All judges in the crown courts should spend time as stipendiary magistrates in the youth courts. Because in the youth courts you have to shift from the justice mode to pay equal attention to welfare. We see how crime begins, they don't. They sentence eighteen-year-olds the same way as forty-year-olds. That is wrong, to turn them into symbols. You have to communicate to young people, it's so important.

161

Can they take it in? Is there eye contact with the defend-
ants? If you see their eyes glaze over, you can't have an
impact. You've got to communicate an idea of the future,
which, being youths, they don't have. I feel very strongly
about this. I told the President, make your circuit judges
spend four weeks a year in a youth court. It's where you
see how a life starts to go off the rails. Do they listen?
You bet they listen. To me. They know what I've done here,
what I've achieved, they can't argue against the results. I do
not like to see boys and girls come back to this court. I
rarely sentence. I never mix a fine with a supervision order.
What I do is compensate for bad parenting. Or no parenting.
London's like *Lord of the Flies*. Pastoral care is what is needed,
not punitiveness; pastoral care backed up with the threat of
punishment, suspended sentences. This isn't a court in the
usual sense of the world, it's a school, a home, a family. Now
. . . let's eat.'

Rowlands' suspended foot dropped heavily on to the floor.
The heel of his shoe dug into the blue carpet. Without cueing
their visitors from the police, all hands were suddenly joined.
Clyne felt Rowlands' hand around his own. His grip was tight
and his palm sticky. Ridley too had been had by the two lay
justices. All these law-brokers were now one unbroken circuit,
handcuffed in prayer. Clyne bowed his head, involuntarily, as
Rowlands said grace. Then Rowlands released his hand and
broke a loaf of bread.

'So,' Rowlands said finally, 'what can I do for you?'

'You advised George Harper's widow to take back his computer. Why was that?'

'Because I don't think you understand the nature of his
work.'

'Did you know he was subscribing to pornographic news-
groups on the Internet?'

'So?'

162

'So!'

'George was a therapist. Therapists need to know *all* the arguments. You think a man surfing pornography must be a pervert. You don't understand youth work.'

'I understand youth.' Clyne looked at Rowlands but couldn't defeat the gaze. His eyes ended down with his boots.

Clyne and Ridley were sitting in the car outside the courts half an hour later.

Clyne was too mad to drive. 'We were set up in there, Sam.' He tried cooling down with a cigarette, recreating his own world with smoke for boundaries. 'We *were* set up. By the time I'd realized, it was too late. Holding fucking hands. Saying fucking grace.'

Shortly a Lotus Elan in British racing green snaked out of the court compound. Both Ridley and Clyne were surprised to see Rowlands behind the wheel. A Lotus didn't seem a sober vehicle for a stipendiary magistrate.

Clyne jumped to it and followed him up on to Talgarth Road.

'Is this a surveillance, Bob?' Ridley asked nervously.

'No, I just want to see where he goes.'

The Lotus drove north through Shepherd's Bush and White City and east along Marylebone Road. At the junction at Seymour Place he jumped a red light, turning into Lisson Grove. Clyne went through the red light after him with a squeal of rubber.

He caught up with the Lotus near Lord's cricket ground in St John's Wood. The traffic had gummed up with the school runs. At a private school nestling beside the barracks on Queen's Terrace the Lotus pulled over. Clyne parked on the opposite side of the road, turned off the engine. A boy of around eleven or twelve jumped off a wall and walked towards Rowlands' car. He was wearing a brown uniform, with bag slung over his shoulder. The passenger window rolled down. The boy briefly put his head inside the window before the door opened and he got inside.

Clyne rubbed his chin. 'What'd you think?'

'Guilty as fuck.'

'If this was a woman we were watching, would we be giving it a second thought?'

'He ain't a woman, though, is he?'

'Let's keep him under a ready.'

They waited for Rowlands to pull out from the kerb, started the engine then drove off in the same direction. 'He is a magistrate, however,' Ridley cautioned. 'I presume you still want us to have a job to go to in the morning?'

Clyne explained how he'd met Rowlands' son, Kevin . . . Troy.

'That's still not going to get us authorization for a surveillance unit.'

'So . . . we'll monitor him now.'

Half an hour later they were easing along the eastbound carriage of East India Dock Road. The car ahead was Rowlands' Lotus Elan. As they crossed the mouth of the Blackwall Tunnel Ridley asked, out of the blue, 'Why would Michael Rivers strip before he jumped? If I was topping myself I wouldn't bother undressing first.'

'Maybe he's done a Richey Edwards, Sam.' But Sam didn't understand the reference.

Below the flyover was Canning Town, twinning with Gotham City. Its industrial sprawl pushed towards the river, factories, plants, breweries all squeezed together.

Heading south on Silvertown Way they followed Rowlands as he took an exit to the docks and cruised through a world of scrapyards, car breakers, sweatshops and semi-derelict assembly plants. Flanked by blind walls growing headsets of barbed wire, Clyne grew uncertain inside himself. Windows were frosted, encased in wire mesh, painted out. You couldn't look in and they couldn't look out.

The Lotus pulled into a courtyard that extended around several buildings. On the wall of an old warehouse flanked by road and railway and facing Royal Victoria Dock was painted a name:

THE PUMP HOUSE

Parked in the road, they watched Rowlands and the boy get out of the car and walk through the courtyard. As they disappeared round the front of the warehouse Clyne pulled into the courtyard.

There was no entrance to the warehouse from the courtyard and all its windows were blacked out. Clyne left Ridley in the car and went on a recce. It was raining and a strong wind troubled a set of venetian blinds hanging in a broken window at the side of the building, making a desolate, percussive sound. He could see the dock basin from there, and a fleet of dinghies moored up along the towpath.

He returned to the car and sat tight. Twenty minutes later he was back outside again.

The basin had transformed itself in that time. In the water a dozen Toppers and Lasers crewed by children were racing around three yellow buoys. The Toppers were navigated single-handed and the Lasers by helmsman and one crew. The kids were dressed in wetsuits, having a good time leaning out, trying to get maximum speed, keeping the boats from heeling. They had been tutored well. Dinghies put in so many tacks that the water looked sewn up. Sails flapped in dirty wind and collisions occurred every few seconds.

A gust darkened the surface of the water with catspaws, capsizing one of the Toppers while gybing. From in front of the building a rubber dinghy powered with an outboard appeared. At the helm was Rowlands himself. He was wearing a woollen hat and oilskins. He motored over to the capsized Topper and held the masthead into the wind. The boy stood on the centre board and brought the boat up. He climbed back in, took control of the tiller and rejoined the race.

Clyne watched them sail for another few minutes until the race ended in chaos as the wind picked up. Rain was falling in bar codes. The dinghies made for the towpath, a weather shore, dropping their sails at the last moment.

Clyne made a note of the time: 1630 and getting dark.

'Are we waiting?' Ridley asked.

'Yes.'

Ridley laid on the dash a range of tobacco products: Malboro reds, Old Holborn, rolling papers. His wife had packed an ice cream box with tuna sandwiches and chocolate biscuits. From a flask he poured coffee into two plastic beakers.

Clyne didn't have a wife and didn't have victuals. He started eating the DS's chocolate biscuits.

Ridley shielded his lunch box with an arm. 'What the fuck did you do for grub on the yacht?'

'I dined in style, Sam, with ten gallons of wine stored in polythene casks. But no smokes.'

'No cigarettes?'

'Not even a cigar. All the stress had gone, see. Sailing's an antidote to our kind of life.'

'You don't talk about it much, do you?'

'I didn't share it with anyone. Who do I tell?'

'You liked being alone all that time?'

'It's good to be alone sometimes. In a crisis it's very good to be alone.'

'I'd have gone crazy, with all that water trying to get in.'

They maintained silence for a while. Ridley felt, after his colleague's tales of lone sailing, that Clyne needed it. Which is one reason why Clyne never talked to non-sailors about single-handed yachting. It embarrassed them.

Ridley's brow furrowed as he changed tack. 'I never could understand what a grown man sees in a kid. I mean, you know, in that way . . .'

'You got to imagine you're living in a different time, Sam, in the twenty-second century, say. Straight sex has been outlawed. You'd have to fuck your wife, except she wouldn't be your wife, behind a public toilet. Or in Thailand.'

'I'd castrate myself.'

'You positive about that?'

'Sure, I'd cut my dick off. I have every sympathy for nonces who go in for voluntary castration.'

'NHS would put you on a waiting list ten years.'

'I had a circumcision a couple of years ago on the NHS. I only had to wait six months.'

'A circumcision! No kidding?'

'I had some form of sclerosis of the foreskin. It got tighter as the years went on until I couldn't peel it back.'

'Was it painful?'

'It wasn't so bad, they do it under anaesthetic.'

'If you were an Aboriginal your mates would have hacked it off for you. In the Marquesas they perform longitudinal circumcisions. Stone knife, no anaesthetic. Then there's some places where they cut your balls off while they're down there. Just one testicle.'

'How do you know all this?'

'They're the kinds of things you hear about when you sail around.'

'When I was waiting to go into surgery this doctor sidles over to me and asks if I'd mind trying out a new muscle relaxant drug. Like, he wanted me to be a guinea pig for some pharmaceutical company. He was whispering like a pimp, shoving a medical indemnity form under my nose. I was on the point of fainting, but just had enough left to tell him to go shove it. When I came round after the anaesthetic,

167

the surgeon was standing at my bedside telling me I'd had an erection during the operation and they'd messed up the stitching.'

'Jesus. A boner under anaesthetic?'

'Yeah, surprised me too. Suddenly I saw the virtues of that muscle relaxant I refused. There was this nurse standing next to us, serving tea. Embarrassed? I was mortified.'

'What'd it look like, your dick?'

'It swelled up like a bruised peach for a week. And yeah, the stitching isn't exactly Savile Row. Wife says it's like sucking on a bottle of Budweiser with the cap still on.'

A couple of cars and a motorcycle drove into the courtyard as kids began strolling out of the Pump House. They jumped into the cars, on to the pillion seat of the motorcycle. But mostly they walked home, in the rain, in a crowd that strung along the basin road.

Rowlands' Lotus was still there after everyone had left.

Clyne drew a hand across the windscreen to clear the condensation. 'What time do we have, Sam?'

'1710.'

'I'm going to take another look.'

There were two second-floor windows with lights on facing the dock, curtains drawn on each. A fire escape gave access to a metal door on both levels. There was a wall crowned by broken glass between the building and the towpath and another adjacent wall inside that ran close to the fire escape. Between the main wall and the building the fleet of dinghies were kept.

He climbed on to the main wall as a light went off in one of the two windows. Rain hammered down and the wind buffeted him. There was nothing to hold on to as he negotiated the broken glass. A freight train passed, carrying motor cars from Dagenham. He crossed on to the adjacent wall and seconds later got a purchase on the fire escape. As he

climbed to the second-floor landing the fire escape bellied
out from the wall. Rust dislodged by his shoes fell to the
ground below. A moorhen on the water started barking, making a sound like a pop gun. He couldn't see into either of
the windows from the fire escape. A pink drainpipe passing
alongside one window was close enough for him to reach.
He held on to the drainpipe with two hands, moved one
foot across to the wall followed by the other, leaving his
sanctuary. Hanging there he looked through a two-inch gap
in the curtains at a blackboard inside; diagrams of the points
of sailing chalked on.

Rowlands appeared in the room carrying a dripping wetsuit.
Following him was a boy, wrapped in a towel. Clyne watched
Rowlands gather up a pile of clothes from a chair as the boy,
naked, rubbed himself down with the towel. As they walked out
of the room Rowlands turned the light off behind him. The light
in the next room came on. But there was no way to get closer
to that window.

The car reeked of tuna mayonnaise and tobacco as Clyne
climbed in. 'What's happening?' Ridley asked.

'Rowlands's got a naked kid in there.'

'What do we do?'

'We can go in if we think the kid's at risk.'

'Are we going in?

Clyne sat in silence. It was almost unbearable, staring through
the windscreen, hoping for something to present itself. It
felt like hours later when he asked, 'How long since I've
been back?'

'Ten minutes.'

'That all?' It was the hardest thing not to imagine what was
going on up there. Images of his son David kept floating into his
mind, sitting on a cold floor with some lupine presence standing
over him. And that was basically the problem, Clyne recognized.
For how much of this was a product of his own paranoia? Look

through the window of any house and you will witness the same quotidian scene of intimacy. Suspicion can fall like blanket snow on all men.

Ridley lit up a Malboro from the butt of his last. 'How long we gonna wait?'

'Shut up a minute and let me think . . . I'm going to take another look around the front.'

And oh, the relief just to get out of the car, to feel ground moving under his feet. He ran to the front, walked the walls and got back on the fire escape, and scaled the pink drainpipe. A light flickered on and off inside the room. He could see the boy all alone in there, sitting on the floor with his back to the wall. Partially dressed, he was holding a torch in one hand, shining the light into his own face, switching it on and off, on and off in a random use of Morse code.

Clyne's arms began to tremble holding his own weight. His shoes slipped on the wet wall. The overhead light came on in the room. He pressed his face to the crack in the curtains. Rowlands appeared, smoking a Menthol Slim. He stood over the boy and took the torch out of his hands.

A Lear jet taking off from City Airport on the Royal Albert Dock laboured to gain altitude over the roof. Huge, indifferent container lorries thundered down Silvertown Way and Victoria Dock Road, making the air shiver.

Rowlands moved outside his field of vision. Clyne tried to improve on his angle and slipped on the wall, bumping the window with his forehead. He lowered himself down below the sill. Rowlands' face appeared at the glass. His hands parted the curtains and he stared into the night across the water, his face contorted with conjecture.

The moment he turned away Clyne raised himself up, his arms shaking from shoulder to fingertip, to look through the window at Rowlands' receding back. Rowlands absented himself from the room, leaving the boy sitting on the floor. Seconds later he returned, throwing the kid his coat. He hit the light switch with a cursory glance towards the window.

Clyne climbed on to the fire escape, made the walls and ran through the rain to the car.

Rowlands and the boy appeared in the courtyard, the rain driving hard into them. The boy was in school uniform, coat over his arm, a baseball cap covering his eyes. Rowlands held his black trilby with a hand against the wind. Clyne and Ridley kept absolutely still while he went to the nearside of the Lotus and opened the door.

They waited until he had driven out of the courtyard.

'What now?' Ridley asked.

'We go home. It's all over here.'

Manny decided they needed some specialist advice. He contacted SO1(4) at the Yard but couldn't get anyone attached. They were understaffed and overseas on active duty. But he managed to find one of their detective sergeants on leave, who consented to break into his holiday for an hour.

The DS who came to the AMIP was an Oxbridge graduate. A fashion mainliner in a Paul Smith suit and canary Valentino tie, with eyebrows that met over the bridge of his nose. He had no sense of humour either. Clyne took him into an interview room and briefed him on the Harper case.

After impressing him with his grasp of the issues, the DS said, 'You don't want a transfer, do you?'

'To SO1(4)? No thanks.'

'We have the worst time recruiting.'

'I'm not surprised.'

'Blokes on the unit develop problems relating to their wives, impotence, lack of libido. They daren't touch their kids. But it's an opportunity for a promotion if you're looking for one.'

'I'm a single parent. I can't afford to alienate my kids.'

'Okay, your basic problem here is making a case stick. It's a non-complainant crime, the offence is usually committed behind closed doors. Man plans his attack over a long period of time. He courts a child through an institution where he may be employed – a school, say – or he knows the kid's parents. Surveillance doesn't work. You see a man take an underage kid into a house who you suspect might be at risk, you have to go in and prevent it. You can't wait until the crime's gone off. Same thing with evidence gathering – it mustn't put a child at risk. Good news is you don't need a warrant. Bad news is you charge through the door and they're just sitting together watching TV. No offence committed. Prevention and disruption, that's all you can do. His pornography, that's the only evidence you'll get, that's his Achilles' heel. Until '87 it was illegal to take indecent photos of children. Now, under Section 1 (60) it's illegal to possess the stuff as well. Another thing about child pornography – there's no money in it whatsoever. The porn's only circulated among a small group. And they're very careful about security, they're paranoid about police activity. They usually have a lot to lose if they get caught, their stake in society, their jobs. They're professional, often with power and influence. It's very difficult to investigate them because their social group all jump in to defend them. They stick together, but there's no such thing as a ring sharing out their catch. That's a myth. Satanic abuse bullshit. Home videos and photo albums . . . he uses the stuff to a) relive the experience, b) blackmail the child, c) share with other like minds. We still have no definition of obscene, but you don't need to be a priest to recognize it when you see it. He takes this stuff and shows it to kids to demonstrate a) it's fun, b) other children do it too. He says to the kid, Come in, have a glass of wine. You want to watch a film? What kind of film? Porno, ever seen a porno film? He shows the kid a sex scene and says, Hey, you want to jack off? Go ahead. Be a man. Have another drink. Gradually he gets the kid aroused and tipsy and then joins in with the fun. Other things you should know:

in the seventies there was an organization called PIE that came out of the bushes for a while. They were lobbyists, pressuring the government to abolish the age of consent. A group of intellectuals promoting their cause – that's still your classic profile. White, male, intellectual, over twenty-five, single, lives alone or with Mum, works with children.'

'What's the connection with incest?'

'Separate fields mostly. Why?'

'This shrink's daughter . . . I just wonder . . .'

'Don't go to the bank on that. Man attacks either his own kids or someone else's. Check your suspects against the list on NCIS. Our index is more extensive if you want to use it. Other things you should know . . . If you get a warrant make sure it's general enough to be able to search in the widest possible arc. And look out for the literature. These guys get a huge kick from writing about it, and fantasize about people reading it. Letters, diaries, scrapbooks, e-mail . . . all these'll be coded: chickens, young stags, lolitas. If you are interviewing, take a softly-softly approach. Don't make them feel like freaks. Remember, they love to talk about it. They have no guilt whatsoever about their victims, so don't try that angle, it won't wash. Any feelings of guilt they've already turned on to the child to protect themselves. That's about it. Happy hunting. Now I'm going home to finish painting my bedroom.'

When Claude Vignisson is driving he sits low in the seat of his old Mercedes and, using the emblem on the bonnet as a gunsight, aims the car like a tank. He goes precisely where he wants to go. He turns his head to face me when he talks and since he conducts long monologues there are long moments when he's not looking at the road at all. He drives too fast and uses the gears lazily, taking corners in top.

It occurs to me that he drives a car as if in open sea. But Claude is a far better skipper than he is a driver. We have just had an adventure on the Thames, cruising to Greenwich and back, and are now driving away from St Katharine's Dock having returned his friend's motor cruiser to its mooring.

While negotiating the bites, holes, eddies and whirlpools on an ebbing tide, Claude chanted from inside the wheelhouse all the names of the old wharves and warehouses that used to run in an unbroken line along the river banks. Orchard, Delta, Follyhouse, Humphery, Enderby, Lovell's, Oliver's – a valediction that brought a ghost river back to life for me. He indicated the precise location in Millwall where Brunel built his steamship, the *Great Eastern*, informed me how Odessa Wharf was converted with laundered Brinks Mat gold bullion and where,

174

at Brandram's Wharf, his old pal 'Broadmoor' Smith found Elizabeth Taylor's stolen jewels. At Wapping, the Freetrade Wharf and Cascades conversions provoked derisive hoots of laughter from him, not least because the new riparians were bent on getting commercial river traffic stopped. 'It spoils their view from their portholes. Fucking hell. If they lived on a farm they'd gag the blimming sheep.' We passed indigenous vessels on their regular beat: *Driftwood I*, vacuuming the Thames; salvage camel *Hookness* servicing mooring buoys with her sisters, *Crossness* and *Broadness*, who raised the *Marchioness*; the PLA launch, *Ravensbourne II*, keeping us under surveillance through binoculars. The *Ravensbourne II* spoilt Claude's good mood. 'The skipper's a right old detective,' he said. 'Not a broken navigational light escapes his steely gaze.'

In his Mercedes we enter the Royal Victoria Docks. He's got a bit of business down here he wants to take care of before taking me further north to Islington, to my rendezvous at my stepmother's house. Royal Victoria Dock plunges me back into the past as I stare out at the tidal basin. It was here that my father taught me to sail, in a Wayfarer dinghy, when I was eight years old.

Claude leaves me in the car to walk over to a cabin in a chandler's yard. Waiting for him I visualize my father at the helm of the Wayfarer, showing me how to detect a gust of wind. The water's surface begins to ripple, he said, like homemade blackberry jam ripples on a spoon when you blow to see if the sugar has boiled down.

The water in the dock is as black as berries.

When Claude comes out of the cabin he is accompanied by a man in a dirty white T-shirt stretched over a huge pot belly. He hands Claude a brown paper parcel from under his arm before they walk over to the car. Through the open window Claude introduces me as his daughter, and I do not contradict him. For at this moment I feel the need to be someone's daughter, in a landscape that is swollen with memories.

175

Later he tells me why he said what he said. 'Old Frank's a dirty bastard. If I didn't tell him you was my daughter he'd assume I was having my leg over with you. Women are either for shagging or they are your daughters. I remember one time Frank giving his kids a sex education lesson. He was telling his son to go out and sow his wild oats. Then he clipped his daughter around the ear. She was sixteen and he said, And you, young lady, you keep away from boys. So I says to him, Excuse me, Frank, but if we tell all our daughters to stay lily-white virgins until they marry, how the fuck is your son *going* to sow his wild oats? Frank said I wasn't thinking straight, ever since that screw coshed me over the head with his baton in Canterbury nick.

'Well,' he concludes, 'it's been an eventful day, ain't it? And I got a prize.'

'What's in that bag, Claude? Heroin?'

'Don't be cheeky. Just some chocolates for the wife.'

'You've come all this way for a box of Milk Tray?'

'There's no distance I won't travel for the missus.'

'Does she understand the work you do, Claude? Because I don't.'

'She don't neither, but she understands me.'

I had to drink one and a half bottles of red wine just to stay cool before meeting my stepmother again after all this time. Then outside her front door I feed my habit for nicotine, smoking five Marlboros in a row, just to get up to a height where I can peer at her without fright. Mrs Harper the Second doesn't allow smoking in her home, as I recall.

She stands in her sparkling kitchen in a white tracksuit, cleaning the silver service.

'Are you having a dinner party?' I ask.

She doesn't reply. I am leaning against the fridge freezer, feigning nonchalance, in reality hiding the effects of my big wine drink-out. In my hand is a tightly rolled sheet of computer print-out.

'Have you ever met a kid called Michael Rivers?'

'I don't think so.'

'Dad was treating him.'

'Unless he came to the hosue for therapy I doubt I've seen him.'

'He never told you about him?'

'No.'

The silver service is laid out on the table, a parallel space between each fork, knife and spoon. She cleans the pieces separately with a soft cloth. The bowl in the centre of the table contains a gravity-defying mountain of mangoes, bananas, apples, pears.

'Well, he's gone to ground now.'

'Why?'

'Because the police have him down as a suspect for Dad's murder.'

'He killed George?' She looks straight at me with a knife in one hand. I can see my strangled reflection in the blade.

'I wouldn't want to speculate on that. But he accused Dad of sexual abuse.'

'I see . . .'

'You didn't know this?'

'No, and nor did George.'

'I'd be surprised if he didn't know. Rivers has a mentor, some chap who's been asking questions around the Marwood. Even the GMC, so I've been told.'

She lays the cloth on the table and begins rolling it around the cutlery, piece by piece.

'How cruel. How very cruel people are.'

'Yes,' I say. 'I know all about cruelty. But whether these accusations are true or not, it may come out in court one day. You should prepare yourself. The press will come after you like a pack of hounds.'

'What do you mean, come after me?'

'How could you not have known? Did you realize you were living with a sex monster? These are the kinds of things they'll shout through your letter box.'

She is set in motion by my remarks, pacing around the kitchen. Giving that tracksuit a work-out.

'What evidence do they have that George was anything other than a hard-working therapist? What evidence do *I* have? Eleven years of marriage. That still counts for something. Do you not think I know who he was?'

'Million-dollar question, isn't it?'

'Look, Alice, I don't know why you've come round here now. After all this time. Your father was very upset. That is the kind of cruelty I'm referring to.'

I move away from the fridge. I put my hand on the edge of the table, anchoring myself. 'Were you and he sexually active?'

A stiff laugh ripples on her lips. 'I suppose you do nothing else in that travellers' camp.'

'Of course. We're all shag-meisters. Fuck like rabbits.'

She stares me in the eye, trying so very hard to believe it. At forty-three my stepmother looks ten years older on account of the way she back-combs and lacquers her hair. Her posture, even her big bone structure, reveals the genes of a well-fed aristocracy. I try to think of her fitting in with Dad, the radical phenomenologist. The R.D. Laing of the 1990s who never called a spade a spade. And then I think, maybe it was George who fitted in with her. This marriage would be a safe place to hide lurid secrets.

I feel a blast of cold air coming from somewhere, like a call to action. I unroll the computer print-out Clyne had given me and read it to her.

'"There are only two sexes, but multiple genders. Sexuality is an expression of gender, so it follows there are multiple sexualities. Yet we restrict ourselves to a single sexual identity (while our dreams are multi-sexual). Sexual identity is a construct, and of its time. Boundaries between sexualities are arbitrary because boundaries, historically speaking, are always being moved."'

I look up and see her eyes dimming, sick with thought. The bridge of her nose creases with tension.

'Dad wrote that,' I say. 'On the Internet.'

'You've been drinking. I can smell it on you.'

'I have been drinking. But if I was sober those words of his would still be the same.'

'He said to me once that desire *is* suffering.'

'That sounds like him.'

She moves away from the edge of the table. The blood has drained from her face.

'You say you knew who he was,' I pursue. 'How can you be so sure?'

She begins rubbing her face hard, trying to screw back her composure. Then she bursts into tears.

I flutter, but don't move. I keep a grip on the table for fear of floating away.

She snatches at stray hairs irritating her eyes. With her vision cleared she stares contemptuously at me. 'This is a bloody nightmare!'

'For who . . . you? Nothing touches you. You see nothing.'

'How dare you. Inspector Clyne . . .'

'I know Clyne. He has me on his list of suspects.'

This brings her up straight. 'Did you . . . you kill your father?'

'Oh, please. I wouldn't give him the pleasure. Clyne and I are having a liaison at the moment. Very erotic, knowing he could bust me while he's fucking me.'

She sweeps her arm across the table. Cutlery flies through the room. Twisting knives and spinning forks. The ceramic bowl topples and fruit pours off the edge of the table. The bowl crashes on to the floor, rolls on its rim into the wall, where it cracks into two exact halves.

*   *   *

I run out of the house straight into Clyne and his DS, Kelly Stokes, on the pavement. She looks me over with her police eyes, eyes you know are judging every move you make.

'I've just been talking about you,' I pant at Clyne.

'Alice, are you okay?'

'I wouldn't try to see my stepmother at the moment. Take a rain check.'

They take my advice and I ride with them in their unmarked car into the fading sun. Kelly Stokes up front, with Clyne behind the wheel. She arouses jealousy in me, something I rarely suffer from. Perhaps it's the way she resembles Kim Basinger. A star. If Clyne hasn't made a pass at her by now he should have. Christ, I'd even go for a night in the sack with her. But what really hurts me is to think how they talk together, their intimacies. That I was the one who suggested it doesn't help. Maybe they even talk about me.

Certain places have atmospheres where a lot of talking is done. Pubs, board rooms, House of Commons. It's like the smell of cigarettes that lingers in a room after the smokers have departed. This car has that kind of kinetic.

I can't ride any more miles with these two sitting up front like a married couple, and ask to be dropped off at the Angel.

TEN

CLYNE: Any circumnavigation's limited because you end up where you started. I sailed the globe and came home, eight miles away from where I was born. And to divorce proceedings. The accusations she made in court, if I believed them, I wouldn't have the courage to show my face again. Not even in the mirror. Jenny presented to the magistrates a shopping list of my abuse. She read from a notebook she'd begun writing on our honeymoon. Our *honeymoon*, for Chrissake! We were supposed to be in love back then and she was filling in this notebook 'to protect herself' in the event that our marriage didn't work out. I sat in court with my mouth open the whole time. Even the magistrates looked overwhelmed, in admiration for such a pure litigious instinct.

One of the entries in her opus described how I hit her while we were in bed. It was dated to the day and hour. I can dimly remember that. It was six years ago and I was asleep at the time, in the middle of a nightmare. Apparently I lashed out in the dark and hit her.

Another incident she recorded was the time I'd pushed her, quote, square in the face, unquote, while drunk. I have a clearer picture of that incident because it occurred a month after my father died. I was in mourning, in the kitchen, pacing around the table, drink in hand, when she came down from the bedroom. She said if I didn't stop pacing she'd call the emergency services. I said, Fire, Police or Ambulance? Police, she replied. I told her I was the police and that I'd be okay so long as I was in motion, so long as I could pace. She stepped into my path and held out her arm like a traffic warden. That's when I pushed her away. With a single finger. In the neck. I admitted to the magistrates to resorting to inexcusable behaviour twice in our marriage. As an officer of the law I always tell the truth under oath.

STOKES: At least you have your children. In a divorce men usually lose them as well. But your children's love and your love for them is intact.

CLYNE: Is it? I think politicians have hijacked that kind of love, through their agencies, the courts, schools, media. As a man I live in fear that someone's going to snatch the kids away. Not the ex-wife or some nonce in a Lotus or a therapist in a psychiatric hospital, but the social services, the Child Support Agency. The family's the new front line. Every citizen's been called up, recruited by the state as spies, waiting to grass me up. Does his kid wriggle on his lap? Is Daddy absent in the painting she does of the family house? Every day I wonder, How does it look to others when I'm emerging from the woods hand in hand with my son? I daren't trust my own instincts. I've driven the fear for my children inward. I feel a stranger in my own flesh.

*   *   *

182

Driving David and Lucy home from school Clyne's mobile rang. He heard Manny's voice fading out before the cell battery went flat. He parked outside an Indian restaurant/mini-cab company and walked back along the street to where there was a telephone box, and called in.

'Last night I dreamt about Rowlands,' the DCI explained. 'He was covered in blood.'

'Hardly admissible, Manny.'

'I had a feeling about him that prevented me getting a good night's sleep.'

'What's this about? I've only got ten pence.'

'Go see Michael Rivers' girlfriend. Pump her a little.'

As he walked back to the car he could hear the radio from fifty metres. He dived across the seat and hit the button. The car remained full of shock waves for seconds after.

'What the hell was that?'

'Manic Street Preachers,' Lucy said.

In the back seat David had an exercise book across his lap. It was open at a story he'd started writing in school. He wanted his father to read it, but he had to postpone the pleasure. Cypress Court and River's girl, Rosine were on the route home.

He parked on Chopin Avenue. Before locking them inside the car he left David a pen so he could finish his homework and instructed Lucy not to play the radio too loud.

In Sojourner's Truth Rosine's neighbour came out as Clyne banged on the door. She was so startled he assumed he'd woken her. He appraised the dark shadows under her eyes and thought she looked as if she could use a couple more days in bed. 'I'm looking for Rosine.'

She pulled her face back into flint shadow. 'She's down the day centre, probably.'

'Where's the day centre?'

'Elkington Street. What you want to see Rosine for?'

183

'I want to ask her some questions.'

'Is she in trouble?'

'No, she's not.'

'Then fuck off,' she said and slammed the door.

Elkington Street was just around the corner. Clyne walked it there.

The drop-in centre was an old Methodist church hall. No surprise then, to see people reading Gideon Bibles. It helped get a free lunch. Old boys were sleeping fitfully, their heads lying across fading yellow formica. Those who had the strength tried to pick fights with Clyne as he walked the gauntlet to a hatch where a couple of helpers folded second-hand clothes and blankets and handed out Marks & Spencer-donated sandwiches past their sell-by date. A Rubensesque woman leant out and offered him one.

'No thanks, darling. Where can I find the boss?'

'Reverend Brook?' She pointed to a door further down the passage. 'He's in the kitchen.'

He found the Reverend in mufti, attempting to teach a couple of Down's syndrome youths elemental cooking. Better smells came from a mortuary.

The Reverend was saving a chip pan from bursting into flames. Clyne asked him if he knew Rosine.

'Is she in trouble?'

'You're the second person who's asked me that today.'

'We just care about her, that's all.' Politely Clyne listened to his cant. He was a vicar, after all. 'Rosine's just one of the kids who come to the city looking for adventure. Five pounds in their pockets and think it will last a lifetime.'

'But is she here?'

'They're lucky if they get further than the mainline station before some pimp's moved in. In no time they're working round the back in the sidings, high on drugs. It's Satan's world we live in today.'

'Could you just tell me if she's here or not. My own kids are waiting in my car.'

He balked at Clyne's abruptness. 'I last saw her in the lounge.'

The smell in the lounge was a concoction Clyne always associated with prisons. Recycled tobacco, urine, bad breath. He found Rosine perched on the edge of an armchair, attacking the cellophane wrapper on an M&S prawn sandwich. She was surrounded by old men, a TV flickering in their weathered faces.

She looked up as Clyne stood over her. 'What the fuck do you want?'

'I'd like it if we could talk some more about Michael.'

She sighed like the lid of a Tupperware box. 'Make it worth my while.'

He looked at this kid and suppressed a laugh. She was sitting in a room of single-cell life-forms, eating a stale sandwich and trying to bargain with him. 'Name your price.'

'A bottle of vodka.'

'A bottle of vodka it is.'

'Gissa fifteen quid then.'

'Let's go back to your squat. Be more private.'

'We can talk here. Dead men don't have ears.'

'You'd be surprised. Let's go.'

'You going to rape me?' She almost made it sound negotiable.

'I've got a daughter your age.'

'That ain't no recommendation.'

'Come on, Rosine, let's get out of here.'

They left the day centre together. Outside an off-licence on Bow Common he gave her three fivers. She insisted on going in alone. 'You're too young to buy alcohol, Rosine.'

'He gives it me. Stay here.'

White clouds were tumbling through the air, their shadows racing across the Common, turning the grass black and white. Through the window of the off-licence Clyne watched

her execute a practised scam. She asked for something that
required the man behind the counter to go into the back room.
Whereupon she stretched over the counter, thieved a bottle of
vodka and concealed it in her leather jacket. The man returned
with a bottle of crème de menthe. She inspected the bottle then
waved it away before walking out.

'Did I give you enough money, Rosine?'

'A jib short, but that's okay.'

Boys were racing Hondas on their back wheels around
Cypress Court. Pit-bulls were roaming loose. Clyne's two kids
were steaming up the windows of the car. He wanted this to
be quick.

In the squat Rosine took off her leather motorcycle jacket
and threw it on the floor. She walked straight over to the hi-fi
and put on a tape. There was only one band in the world: the
Manic Street Preachers, forming an alliance with his own kids.

For the second time that day he turned the volume down.

She refused to talk until she'd worked on the vodka a little.
She took it neat without ice and guzzled fast, tooling up with a
cigarette, from Clyne's pack.

The squat was lumpy and uncomfortable; there were no
chairs or sofas or even a table. The walls were stained and
with huge holes hacked out – the work of carving knives and
bare hands and heaped-up rage. They sat on the floor with the
TV serenading silently in the background. Satellite, no less.

She began to loosen up with the vodka and he got to hear
her story, how she grew up in care, running away from the
residential home about a year ago. Her greatest fear was they'd
find her here and take her back. But for the moment she
was okay, she lived her own life, in Sojourner's Truth, with
her fourteen-year-old lover, Michael, who took care of her. He
looked out for her while she begged at the ticket booths in
the Underground. If some guy demanded a sexual favour for
his charity, Michael stepped on the mark's toes. On certain

days when it was raining and cold they could earn £30, sometimes more.

So long as she had enough to buy food, her daily bottle of
vodka, then she felt all right.

Yeah, actually quite good about things.

Clyne looked at the scars on her arms, those tangible memo-
rials to her pain.

'You and Michael liked to cut yourselves?'

'We shared everything.'

'The same razor?'

'Everything.'

'Feels good, doesn't it?'

'How'd you know?'

He rolled up his sleeve and showed her his own recent scar.

'What are you, a late developer?'

'How's that vodka?'

'Hitting the spot.'

'Good, because it's time for you to pay back. I'm still looking
for information. Do you think Michael drowned himself?'

'Has his body showed up?'

'No.'

'If Michael wanted to kill himself he'd have slashed an artery.
Jumping into the water, that don't make sense.' She looked
heavily at him. 'Why should I help you find Michael? You'll
put him away.'

'Not necessarily.'

'You think he murdered the shrink.'

'Does the name Rowlands mean anything to you? Rusty
Rowlands?'

'No.'

That closed down that show.

'Are you sure you don't know of him?'

'Maybe it's Alastair you're thinking of.'

A chink of light. 'Alastair O'Kane, you mean?'

'He come round here all the time stirring the shit. Michael is fucked up enough without that Scots twat poking his bugle in, what with his mother, it was her who done his head in. She should have been sectioned.'

Clyne nodded at the TV. 'Did Alastair pay for you to hook up with Sky?'

'As a matter of fact. So Michael could watch the boxing.'

'How did he stir the shit, exactly?'

'He got Michael going, spooking him with weird stuff. What he said to Michael was, Your life will give your death design. Or was it, Your death will give your life design . . . ?'

'I've heard that too. I can't remember either. A lot of people think Alastair's a regular guy.'

'Yeah? Well, tell me if this is regular . . .'

She disappeared into a bedroom. Moments later she presented him with an A4 envelope. 'Michael'll kill me if he finds out I'm showing you this.'

He took the envelope from her hand and drew out a home-printed, under-exposed black-and-white four-by-six-inch photograph in which Michael Rivers is slitting his forearm with a razor blade. Blood runs down his arm and collects in his cupped hand. He is completely naked. His face staring at the camera is expressionless, resigned. It is a very beautiful face.

Clyne slid the picture back into the envelope.

'It's shocking, innit?' she said, boasting.

'Nothing shocks me, Rosine. In fact I've seen one like this already. The one we found in Michael's wallet. You were in it too.'

'Alastair took those pictures. Tells you something, don't it?'

He checked her face for buried lies but it was running under bare poles. 'I'm going to have to take it away with me.'

'You show that to Bill Haines, Michael'll kill you.'

'I show this to Bill Haines, I'll lend him the gun.'

*　　*　　*

188

He got back to the car just in time. The neighbourhood junkies were leaning on Lucy's door speaking to her through the open window, expectorating down their chins at the sight of her school uniform, her unstockinged thighs. She was flirting with the hoods, the crack merchants.

He drove out at speed, leaving them inhaling the fumes of burnt rubber. The envelope containing the photo lay on Lucy's lap.

The moment they touched home base he needed to go straight out again. Lucy threw her head back in disgust and charged upstairs to her bedroom. David dumped into the sofa with tears springing from his eyes, clutching his little blue exercise book with 'English' handwritten in gold magic marker on the cover.

Clyne sat down beside him and read his piece.

It was a thinly disguised autobiography of their family, narrated by his stuffed dog, Gip. Clyne instantly recognized himself and their mother holding hands, their moment of tenderness witnessed by Gip, who barked, 'Hold the front page! They're in love again.' It was a very good yarn until the moment the stuffed dog got left on a hook behind a cupboard door while all the other characters went on holiday to Devon.

'What about Gip?' Clyne asked. 'You can't leave him behind.'

'I didn't want to take him.'

'But he's the narrator, he's got to go too.'

'You don't like my story?'

'I do, it's really good. What are you going to call it?'

'It's called "The Freedom of the Ants".'

Music started to ripple downstairs from Lucy's bedroom stereo. He went up to negotiate the peace. She was crying as he entered, listening to the Manics belt out 'She's Suffering'.

On her lap was an *Evening Standard*.

'I'm sorry,' Clyne said, down on his knees beside her. 'But I'll be home soon.'

189

She howled back, 'The band are going to play on without Richey! It's a travesty.'

Clyne looked at the page of the newspaper she had been reading, an article about the band's future plans. The byline was Alice Harper's.

Well, well.

Then he got it. Lucy was grieving for Richey Edwards, not because her father was going out again.

He sat on the bed next to her and assumed a respectful funereality. The sleeve notes to *The Holy Bible* were within reach. He started reading.

'The centre of humanity is cruelty/You will be buried in the same box as a killer/He's a boy, you want a girl, so tear his cock off, tie his hair in bunches, fuck him, call him Rita if you want/Such beautiful dignity in self-abuse/Life bleeds, death is your brithright/If man makes death then death makes man.'

'Did Richey Edwards write these?' he asked, horrified.

But all Lucy could do was blubber.

Richey Edwards disappears and the band say they will play on without him. David's stuffed dog narrator gets left behind in a cupboard and the rest of his characters go on holiday to Devon.

Michael Rivers disappears. So the men who committed the murder can walk free.

I had become quite obsessed with the women in Clyne's life. Kelly Stokes was causing me all kinds of violent headaches.

Why can't you talk to me? I asked him finally.

Because Kelly's the police, Kelly's family, he insisted.

Then why did you never marry into the police, since you're so close?

Would you want to marry your brother?

She looks like Kim Basinger.

Who's she?

I also wondered about his ex-wife, what she looked like. Clyne told me if I wanted to clap eyes on Jenny, to be at Maggie's café back of Smithfield meat market at six o'clock. He was meeting her there, a rendezvous she had initially resisted.

I went along to be a voyeur for an hour. He and I made the same time, even though we came separately, and sat on separate tables. I got a red wine from the waiter while he ordered a steak, cooked rare.

She turns up late, despite her offices being nearby, at the same moment as his steak – running with blood – materializes. She descends into the seat opposite, holding the hem of her short skirt. He is caught red-handed looking at her legs, which she crosses immediately.

A corporate minx in a linen pinstriped Hobbs suit, she makes Clyne looks ragged. Lean of build and fast-mouthed, she sounds tough and has tough eyes. Her shoulder-length hair has been bleached by Sassoon's or somewhere like that. Most of all she looks clean. So clean she makes me blush.

She orders a kir and asks how he is. Which sounds like code for why he's asked to see her.

'I'm on a bastard case. The Harper murder.'

'What's the problem?'

'Investigation's running away from me. How's your work?'

'Fast.' She takes a sip of kir and stares pensively at the glass.

He raises the fork to his mouth. 'Chrish! Jesus chrish,' he mumbles. 'This sirloin's so tender cow must have been listening to music all day.'

I start smiling to myself.

She remains stony-faced. 'So how can I help you, Robert?'

'Do you know a stipendiary magistrate in West London juvenile court called Rowlands?'

'Can't say I've heard of him.'

'Can you dig around for me?'

'My charge-out rate's two hundred pounds an hour.'

'Don't you do *pro bono* work once in a while?'

'Is he a suspect?'

'No, but there's something about him that's not kosher.'

'Where's your evidence in this case?'

'That's what I'm trying to say. I'm saying I don't have any. A kid called Michael Rivers is our main suspect, but he's disappeared. Or killed himself.'

'I'd need a client to approach me with a complaint about Rowlands before I could do anything . . . This kir tastes like shit.' She calls the waiter over to the table and holds the glass up to him. 'Is there cassis in this?'

'It's syrup.'

192

'I ordered a kir. Kir is white wine with cassis. If I wanted syrup I'd have asked for it. Please change it.'

'We don't have any cassis, I'm sorry.'

'Then you shouldn't be selling it as if it were. Take it back, please. I'll have a glass of white wine instead.'

'Add another beer to that,' Bob said.

I watch the waiter walk off, nursing his balls.

'You're drinking fast, Robert?'

'It takes the edge off things.'

'Have you tried this?' She reaches into her bag and produces a strip of green and white capsules. She hands him the foil, which he holds up to the light.

'Prozac?'

'Fluoxetine, twenty mil.'

'How did you get it?'

'I just went and told my GP I'm depressed. She wanted to know the symptoms. So I told her I couldn't sleep, that I often fantasized about harming myself, that I go to bed in the middle of the day, that I weep all the time. She had her prescription pad out in less than two minutes.'

'I didn't know you were depressed, Jenny?'

'Good God, you don't think I'm taking them, do you? I got them for Justin.'

'Your partner? Is he depressed?'

'No, no, no. He was having problems with premature ejaculation.'

Fucking hell!

'Justin says sex on Prozac is marginally more interesting than changing a tyre. But my God, he can go on all day now. With Prozac your feelings . . . you can't quite reach them, like they're on a shelf too high.'

'But he's not depressed, you say?'

'Well, he was having a kind of seasonal disorder.' She witnesses Bob's frown. 'You drink alcohol, smoke cigarettes?

193

Prozac is just a another stimulant.'

'My stimulants have been around a lot longer.'

'Anyway, it makes him feel optimistic. What's the harm?'

'When I feel optimistic I go out and buy some house plants.'

'I remember you feeling optimistic. About us. You ran out and bought proteas, a couple of ficuses.'

'Yeah, I did.'

'Three months later they'd all died.'

She flashes him a winner's grin. He looks down, at the Prozac again, perhaps thinking it isn't such a bad idea. But then he notices something else.

'The pharmaceutical company . . . Eli Lily. You worked on a class action against Lily, didn't you?'

'Opren. Correct. You do pay attention sometimes.'

'Thousands of old people crippled with arthritis got injured from Opren, death included. Now you're making a Faustian pact with the same company?'

'You think they'd dare fuck with me again?' she smiles.

'What's it do to Justin's brain, that's what I'd worry about.'

'Boosts the level of serotonin. It's a smart little cookie.'

'Even if his dick does feel like it's shot up with novocaine.'

Jenny raises her voice. Defending the client. 'What you call your sex drive, Robert, is actually an obsessive-compulsive disorder.'

'My sex drive is not an obsessive-compulsive disorder.'

Hear, hear.

'Justin says he can sit in a meeting now with a roomful of sexy women and concentrate entirely on the job for once.'

I've lost about a pint of blood listening to her sex theories. No doubt Bob has too, imagining her screwing someone else.

'Can you give me some advice on Rowlands, or not?' he demands.

'Like I said, Robert, my charge-out rate's two hundred pounds an hour. What kind of advice do you expect for free?'

ELEVEN

Clyne found a fax from Jenny waiting for him at the station. She'd done some *pro bono* work for him after all.

Rusty Rowlands was sitting when Michael Rivers appeared before his court on an assault charge. Rowlands brought in the Youth Justice Team to come up with a package of psychiatric counselling. Rivers was referred to the Marwood clinic, Harper's outfit.

'They got a neat set-up, Manny ... Kid comes up before Rowlands. Rowlands sends kid down to Harper. Maybe Harper shags him or maybe Rowlands, but in either case Harper stitches him up with a case report that makes him over as disturbed, delusional, whatever. So if the kid tries to grass, Harper just produces the case notes. As Bill Haines discovered for himself.'

'Those reports we read on Rivers are fake?'

'Embroidered, more like. Some of it's probably true. Like the crazy mother bit.'

'So the real Michael Rivers we know not?'

'It's possible, Manny. I'd say that.'

Every space in the incident room was overflowing with

intelligence-gathering materials. Tables were stones beneath paperfalls. All the walls were covered by maps marked with coloured pins; computer printouts hanging in their plastic wallets; white boards with victim's details.

The team were rehearsing familiar tunes over and over, going through all the theorems hoping to see something new in the old.

'Rivers is dead,' Manny began. 'QED.'

'Rivers is a self-mutilator,' Clyne returned. 'If he wanted to kill himself he would have bled himself to death. It's the logical development. Jumping off a bridge doesn't add up.'

'So then what have we got?' Manny conducted the team. 'Connections, anybody?'

'O'Kane's the new link,' Stokes asserted.

'O'Kane's very persuasive, we know that,' Clyne said.

Ridley added, 'His presenter at BSkyB, the actor, what's-his-name . . . If Alastair tells him to jump, he jumps.'

'You two are being heavy on the metaphors,' Manny complained.

'What Sam means is, Alastair might have talked Rivers into disappearing.'

'Why?' Manny contended. 'That's wild.'

'Because Rivers is implicated in murder, and O'Kane's into some lurid stuff with him,' Clyne said.

'So we're back to square one.' Manny raised his arms in exasperation. 'And that's why this incident room's still live. We have absolutely fuck all, apart from the rabid testimony of a crustie who lives in a horsebox, Hansel and fucking Gretel and a fourteen-year-old girl who sinks a bottle of vodka a day. While the men they're pointing a finger at – one's a magistrate and the other a TV producer.'

'Who likes the buckle end of a belt,' Clyne added.

'Allegedly!' Manny shouted. 'Come *on*, people, this is all shite.'

'I want to bring him in, Manny,' Clyne said.

'Why?'

'Believe the common people, not the politicians.'

'He'll get more from us than we'll get from him. Bring him in when you find Rivers . . . if you find Rivers, which I somehow doubt.'

'O'Kane might know where Rivers is.'

'You keep saying this, Bob. Why do you think Rivers is still alive?'

He didn't bother telling Manny his Freedom of the Ants/Richey Edwards theory. He hadn't got kids, he'd only mock it. Instead he said, 'You think he's dead? Okay, so where's the body?'

Manny demurred. 'If you think it will help, then bring in O'Kane.'

'Might be interesting to see his gaff anyway,' Clyne added. 'Can we try to get a warrant to search?'

'Without any evidence against him? No chance. Do a proxy.'

This was how the police played the game once in a while. To gain entry into someone's home without a warrant they had to be invited in. The invitation can come from anyone with a legitimate right to be inside the house, like a nanny or a builder, and not just the person they're trying to nail. Once inside they're within legal rights to seize any relevant evidence.

The proxy.

Clyne knew that if O'Kane came to the door and refused him entry, he'd have to take it on the chin. So he telephoned his TV studio first, to make sure he was at work.

He was.

A Filipino maid opened up the door to his house in Hampstead. 'Mr O'Kane, he not here.'

Clyne showed her his ID, made it good and strong. She peered into his hand, going to great pains to read it. She didn't expect Mr O'Kane home for a long while, she said.

Clyne said he'd come in and wait, while having fun guessing

how much he paid her. Two pound an hour or a nod to the Immigration Office.

She moved away from the door and he was confronted in the hall with a couple of original Picasso sketches, a Hockney, an Auerbach, several Sutherlands, a Balthus hidden behind a potted rubber plant. Treasure Island.

He passed through to the kitchen, over a floor of heather-blue slate flags. A fireplace was bordered with copper and leather fenders. There was a handpainted rocking chair, an eight-seater dining table with iron candelabra suspended above. The walls were painted mustard yellow set off by blue cupboards and Sicilian crockery on a Georgian oak dresser. Beyond tied brown velvet curtains the kitchen extended into a living quarter, with one yellow and one green sofa and a stained-glass window that spilt ochre light everywhere. Stacked up on the coffee table were various books: Alan Clark's diaries, Thatcher's autobiography.

The stairs took him past a few more Sutherlands, a Freud. In the master bedroom the centrepiece was a Chinese opium den, inlaid with mother-of-pearl. A futon thrown inside was covered with an Amish quilt. Two bergère-style chairs were draped with clothes. Hugo Boss. Paul Smith. The pictures on the walls had nautical themes. A sailing junk; a nineteenth-century ocean-going schooner. On the desk by the window sat two sailing trophies. Behind these cups was a framed photograph of a yacht in a cobalt-blue sea, the sails furled around the boom, anchor paid out. An island, somewhere like the Philippines, lies smoking on the horizon. O'Kane and Harper are both on deck, sunning themselves. Caught mid-flight, two little black boys dive into the sea.

There was nothing here that merited seizure, nothing but the trappings of wealth and power.

Although the opium den Clyne would love to have seen installed in Alice's bus.

*   *   *

'When you sailed with Dr Harper, where did you go?'

'Around the Solent. Channel Islands. Scotland.'

'And the Philippines?'

'That's correct.'

'Why omit that?'

'I assumed you meant on his yacht. We chartered one in the Philippines.'

'The one in the picture hanging in your bedroom?'

'I heard from my cleaner that you'd had a good nose around.'

'Who took that photograph, by the way?'

'I did. On a self-timer.'

'You like photography as a hobby?'

'Not really. Photography gets in the way a' experiencing the thing itself. It's more TV.'

'But that's your job?'

'Exactly. I get enough of cameras at work.'

'Do you have children, Mr O'Kane?'

'No.'

'But you like children. They make marvellous companions, don't they?'

'What point are you making . . . Bob?'

'You made friends with Michael Rivers and his girlfriend Rosine.'

'They are not exactly children,' he said without pause.

'But not adults either. How did you meet Michael?'

'Through George.'

'That's unethical.'

'George thought Michael could benefit from stable adult role models.'

'Really?' Clyne almost laughed. 'His girlfriend Rosine told me you took pictures of them cutting themselves with a razor. Is that the kind of thing George had in mind?'

'I came in here voluntarily, without legal representation. If you take that tone I'm going to just walk out. It's up to you.'

'Did you photograph Michael?'

'No.'

'Did you watch him cut himself?'

'There's two sides to every story. Yes, I watched Michael cut himself, to show him I wasn't shocked. That his attention-seeking wouldn't work on me. Whatever you've been told by Rosine . . . well, she's very literal.'

'I like literal people. They don't know how to lie so good. Photos tell no lies either.' Clyne produced the photograph of Michael. 'If you didn't take this, who did?'

'O'Kane glanced at the photograph. 'Michael took photos of himself. With my camera, yes, on the self-timer.'

'Who developed the negatives? Don't tell me it was Boots the fucking Chemist.'

'I have no idea.'

'George Harper liked children too, didn't he?'

'He dedicated his life's work to them.'

'But his own children despise him.'

'I know nothing about that.'

'But surely he must have told you he had children?'

'Of course.'

'They were pleased when he died. Their mood was quite celebratory.'

'That's terrible. I can't believe that.'

'He sexually abused Michael Rivers. And possibly other of his patients.'

'That's slanderous!'

'Well, I don't think George's going to make an issue of it now, is he?'

'How dare you talk to me like this!'

'You were due to go sailing with him the day he died. Is that correct?'

'Yes.'

'You left BSkyB at 0030 Thursday, three and a half hours

200

before George Harper was murdered. You and his wife were the only ones who knew he was on his boat. Later that same day you returned to the studio to put out the evening programme. We interviewed you there at 2200. You were intending to head straight to St Katharine's from Sky. What time were you dropping the mooring?'

'High tide: 2300.'

'Night sailing?'

'Yes.'

'Is there anyone who can confirm where you were between 0300 and 0400 Thursday morning?'

'I don't have a partner. So no. Anyway, this is ridiculous. George was one of ma dearest friends.'

O'Kane stood from his chair in the interview room. Clyne followed and moved right up close, inside his reach, daring him to lose control. He could feel Sam Ridley tensing up in the corner of the room. O'Kane took a few deep yoga-breaths of calming air. 'Is that all, Inspector?'

'One last question. Do you know where Michael is?'

'No, I don't.'

'I think he's still alive, don't you?'

'I have no idea. Let's hope so.'

Manny, Ridley and Clyne were gathered in Manny's office sharing a tray of custard slices that Stokes had brought in earlier from a bakery on Stepney Green. Manny managed to keep a smoke going while eating. His breath smelled like a garage. Something inflammable in those custard slices.

'Is O'Kane lying?' he asked. 'What'd you all think?' Clyne and Ridley shrugged. 'If someone as smart as O'Kane was going to murder somebody, you'd think he'd remember to organize an alibi.'

'Could be a double bluff.' Ridley attempted a sensible answer. 'Or it was not premeditated.'

'No, it was premeditated,' Manny said. 'When Harper's murderer cut his balls out he was trying to tell us something. Otherwise why not just shoot the fucker, right?'

Manny sat down, concentrating on the fag burning between his fingers. He spoke with an edge of desperation in his voice. 'D'you think Harper was a nonce, Bob? This a Rule 43, or are we backing the wrong horse?'

'I think whatever Harper did he justified on moral grounds. Whether it was actually moral, in the sense we understand it, I can't say.'

At that point Kelly Stokes stepped into the incident room holding a copy of a men's magazine.

'There's a three-way traffic here,' Manny continued. 'O'Kane, Harper, Rowlands. All professional men, all sailors. All clean as icebergs.'

'And just as deceptive. One-third white knights, two-thirds spiteful little nonces.'

'We have rumours circulating about them, and those rumours aren't nice. But that's all we do have.'

'Blackmail?' suggested Stokes, entering the fray.

Manny said, 'But who's blackmailing who? I can see no motive for O'Kane or Rowlands killing Harper. And that's the bottom line.' He concluded the discussion by walking out of the room.

They still had nothing but conjecture, and three custard slices lying in a cardboard box.

With Manny gone Stokes dropped her magazine on Clyne's lap. On the cover was an old picture of Robert De Niro as Al Capone. The title below was in blood-red lettering: CRIME ISSUE SPECIAL. 'Page one-seventeen you might find interesting, Bob,' she said.

Clyne flicked through the magazine until he was confronted by a black-and-white mug shot of Claude Vignisson on page one-seventeen. The article was written by Alice Harper.

Stokes said, 'Your girlfriend mixes in eclectic company.'

'She's not my girlfriend.'

'Sorry, your shag.'

Clyne ignored her to read the article. Full of Claude's rob-
beries, knife attacks and blags that had not yet come to light,
the interview was more informative than Vignisson's sheet at
the Yard. But what really alarmed Clyne were the locations in
which the interviews took place: St Katharine's Dock sailing club;
the Royal Victoria Dock Basin; the travellers' camp in Wanstead.
Clyne was even quoted anonymously in the article: 'As one
London detective said to me: "Old-time gangsters are like old film
stars. There's a glamour in the kind of violence they generated."'

Who the fuck was shadowing who?

For the next twenty-four hours the investigation went stone-cold
dead. It went night-night. Divers were sent out to trawl the
Thames at Blackwall while Manny made his second appeal on
Crimewatch for witnesses. He came back from the television
studio with make-up still on his face, like a hideous mask. It
was a hideous time to spend too, rigid with anxieties. Clyne
could not take the strain under that kind of empty load and
asked Manny for permission to monitor O'Kane.

Ways of gathering evidence have not quite eclipsed the evidence
itself, but the police won't secure a conviction from evidence
procured illegally. The means no longer justifies the ends.
Take surveillance. A police tail may lead to the CPS bringing
a case, but a conviction depends on the surveillance logs
being properly kept. But surveillance units don't come cheap:
minimum twenty-four-hour vigilance, two vehicles and four men,
several computer programmers, overtime for all after eight
hours. The budget doesn't stretch far enough to include every
super's needs. The Home Office hasn't the dough, particularly
without a watertight hypothesis to justify a big spend.

Manny's team didn't have a watertight hypothesis. They had
fuck all.

So what they did in the old days they still do occasionally now. Except they call it 'monitoring'. Surveillance by one. A pro-am game. That won't secure a conviction.

Sunday morning found Clyne alone outside O'Kane's house, waiting for his float to go under. At 1030 O'Kane left by the front door, unlocked his Wrangler jeep parked outside and snorted off down the road. All the churches in Hampstead were open for business, their congregations arriving in German cars. But O'Kane had a different destination in mind.

Clyne was hoping he would lead him to Rivers. O'Kane's bearing due east looked promising. In Hackney Road he parked on a meter and walked in the direction of Columbia Road. Clyne gave him a short lead before following.

It was a fine, cold day. Columbia Road is flower city on a Sunday and O'Kane fitted in, was as bright as any blossom in royal-blue Levis and green quaysider jacket. Outside a café he sat at a wrought-iron table. A girl came out and took his order, returning shortly with his cappuccino. O'Kane loaded it up with sugar and pocketed the silver spoon.

A boy with a knapsack, not Michael Rivers, drifted into this frame. He sat down next to O'Kane, who waved to the girl inside the café. The girl came out and took another order. Flowers spilled out of buckets and caught the sunlight. Clyne's eyes filled with vermilion, pink and white stamens, their scent suffocating. It was confusing, like a sickness.

The girl appeared with a Pepsi. Through the jungle of green stems Clyne saw them rising from their seats. O'Kane dumped money on the table and handed the boy the can.

Back at the jeep O'Kane lifted the kid into the passenger seat. The machine seemed to swallow him. He let the roof down on the Wrangler before driving away.

Clyne followed three vehicles behind, the boy's head hidden behind the seat. It was another long tail, through Bethnal Green and down Old Ford Road, on to the A102M Blackwall Tunnel approach to Abbott Road, East India Road and Silvertown Way.

His destination was the Pump House in the Royal Docks. Clyne could feel some sort of case coming together the moment he saw Rowlands' Lotus parked in the courtyard. O'Kane drove in next to it and clipped on the roof. Then they walked to the front of the building.

Clyne waited five minutes, five separate terrors.

He followed their path to the main entrance, suddenly changing course with as much thought as a breaking wave. He climbed over the walls, scaled the fire escape and shimmied up the pink drainpipe. The curtains were drawn on the windows. Behind the glass he could hear conversation.

He tried to move back on to the fire escape but the drainpipe came away from the wall. He just managed to get a purchase on the windowsill with both hands before the drainpipe crashed to the ground below. He couldn't go anywhere but one way.

He rapped hard on the window with his forehead.

The curtains were pulled apart. Rowlands' face appeared and his mouth dropped open. O'Kane was standing right behind him. Rowlands opened the steel-framed window. 'Are you insane?' he shouted.

Clyne asked humbly for their help. Rowlands took his wrists and O'Kane grabbed the back of his coat collar. Together they heaved him on to the window ledge. From there he was able to crawl down the inside wall and slide in on his belly, ploughing up the brown carpet with his snout.

The boy was standing beside a small pool table, cue in hand. O'Kane moved in front of the boy as if to hide him, his arms dangling, fingers playing with the spoon he'd lifted from Columbia Road.

Rowlands was wearing a red shirt under his Timberland jacket, a pack of Menthol Slims sticking out of the breast pocket. His voice had regained its calm, soporific effect.

'Would it be too much to ask what you are doing?'

'Looking for lost sheep,' Clyne said, brushing down his coat.

'This is a children's sailing club.' O'Kane breathed. 'Not a farm.'

'Then where are all the children?'

'They'll be here by and by.'

Clyne pointed to the boy, who had blue cue chalk on his face, like a clown, a painted whore. 'He an early riser?'

'He's in my care,' Rowlands intervened.

'In your care . . . and Alastair brings him over?'

A shadow passed between the two men.

'The boy's in my legal custody, Inspector,' Rowlands reasserted. 'You're making a damn fool of yourself.'

The boy's small eyes looked perplexed, but not panicked. Clyne's eyes alighted on a blackboard with diagrams of rigs, points of sailing. Scattered on a table were several pieces of rope tied into knots.

He addressed the boy. 'You want to go home, son? I'll take you. I'm a policeman.'

The kid said nothing.

Rowlands asked, 'Do you want to go with this police officer, or do you want to stay here with us?'

'Stay here,' he said.

'There you have it,' Rowlands smiled.

Clyne sat down on a plastic chair, took out his Camels and ripped a filter off one. He dropped the pack on the table next to a length of nylon rope. The rope had been knotted several times. He exhaled smoke into a ceiling of diamond-shaped polystyrene tiles.

'So what do you want me to do?' he asked. 'Close this investigation?'

'Of course not. But this is ridiculous.' Rowlands sounded almost compassionate.

'George, he was really something,' Clyne began. 'I've read his stuff so often I know it by heart. "Desire is feared because it's Oedipal. Original desire is Oedipal, so becomes fear. This fear later becomes anxiety. Anxiety is fear without an object. We forget the object of our fear because it shames us too deeply to remember."' He managed to untie the knots in the rope. He held the rope up in his hand like a trophy. 'You two should come sailing with me sometime, now that George has gone. I'm moored down at the Hamble. You ever go there, with the kids?'

'Sometimes, yes. The river's good. The river's safe for dinghy sailing. The Beaulieu too.'

'George, did he, was he involved in this club?'

'Yes. George did a bit of teaching.'

'What else did he say . . . "A heterosexual object is soldered on to the child's erotic instinct by parents, who fear their own Oedipal desire. Heterosexuality then becomes self-hatred." He was good, George.'

'Yes.'

'I mean *morally*.'

Rowlands puffed out his cheeks. Clyne recognized he was about to deliver a sermon. 'Childhood is monumentally important because it's society in the making. George chose to work with adolescents because it's during adolescence that the effects of bad parenting come to the surface. It's hard to detect in childhood, because children absorb all the blows. They reach adolescence and get angry. And what you can see you can cure. Adolescence is the last chance to correct psychotic behaviour. If you don't catch it then, it's all over. The adolescent goes into orbit, lost to reason, and comes back to earth an adult, hell bent on vengeance. Save the adolescent and you save society.

'As a magistrate I am *simpatico* with that view. I try to catch adolescents who are dallying with crime and persuade them not to go down that road. I feel quite evangelical about it. George and I worked together on this. I always sent offenders to him for counselling. Because he was the best.

'Now George's other thing was sexuality. Adolescence is also a time of sexual uncertainty. If they're homosexual they'll know it by now. In one sense they're the lucky ones. They are treated as deviants. If they're heterosexual they are seen as "natural" and nobody advises them. But there's nothing natural about heterosexuality in the disturbed adolescent when pinned to an object. There is nothing natural about rape, for instance.

'When children have been got at they have been got at through their sexuality. By the mother and by the father. Programmed to hate all women and all men. And there is no third sex for them to love.' Rowlands looked fleetingly at O'Kane. 'Our friend George took the fight to institutions that ruin children. Any institution, including the family.'

'"They fuck you up, your mum and dad",' Clyne quoted.

'Well, not all families,' Rowlands added, 'to be fair. But basically yes, the function of the family is to repress Eros.'

Spent, Rowlands meditated on the dock through the window, his mouth pinched tight. Clyne looked the boy over again. He was around eleven years old, three foot ten, a thin and jumpy character. His eyelashes were long and lush. His Levis, Adidas and leather bomber were all spanking new. Then he looked at Rowlands. A wavering light reflecting from the water made the magistrate appear composed of ill-fitting parts. His body was bulky and flatulent. Thick hair grew out of his ears and nostrils. In such light all men are ugly, as all boys are beautiful.

'Rusty, is anything we've touched on so far against the law?' Clyne asked.

'You can't legislate against thought.' His voice was clouded.

'What do you think, Alastair?'

'About what?'

'About what Rusty just said.'

O'Kane retorted, 'I agree. Crime, racism, fascism are all by-products of sexual repression.'

Clyne smiled at them. 'Yeah, I've always thought that too.

When I stare into the face of violence I'm looking at a guy who needs to get his leg over.' He tapped O'Kane on the shoulder, gently. 'But why keep this dynamite to ourselves?'

O'Kane stalled, then murmured, 'I think that's pretty obvious.'

'It's not obvious to me.' Clyne stubbed his cigarette out on the tabletop. 'Well, guys, this is an education. You make it sound so altruistic.'

'What?'

'All the bullshit in the world.' Clyne took three steps towards the boy. 'It's my judgement that this child is at risk. I'm removing him to a place of safety. Try and prevent me and I'll arrest you both under the Child Protection Act.'

He picked up the boy's bag and brought him to the door with a hand under his arm. There was a hollow stillness in the air as they walked out of the room.

In the car the boy craned his neck around to watch out of the rear window as they drove away. 'Am I in trouble?' he asked.

'No, son, I just want to take you home.'

'Then I ain't talking to you.'

'Does your mother know where you are?'

'She's at Coral's.'

'Putting a bet on?'

'Huh?'

'What's your name?'

'Nicholas.'

'Mine's Bob. Now we're on first-name terms, Nicholas ... you've got to promise me you'll stay away from those two men. Do you understand me?'

'Why's everyone telling me what to do all the fucking time?'

'And watch your language. Like who's telling you?'

'I'm not saying no more.'

Clyne drove the boy back to his home. True to his word he didn't talk, he was like a stone the whole way.

Nicholas directed Clyne to a council estate in Haggerston. He asked to be dropped off outside. There would be no one in his flat, so so long, mister, see you around. No need to walk me, you might as well save yourself a wasted journey.

Clyne invited himself along. Nicholas walked two paces ahead in muted rage. The apartment blocks were all ghostly white rising to fifteen storeys. Ringing in Clyne's ears were unruly big kids shouting. Nicholas kept his head down. Clyne had to wonder what the boy would do if he wasn't there.

They climbed four flights of steps, the wind howling through the broken windows in the stairwell. Nicholas stopped outside a red door.

'Is this it?' Clyne asked.

'Yeah, you can go now.'

'Open up and then I'll go.'

'I don't have a key.'

'Then how the hell are you getting in?'

He stared at his feet as Clyne banged on the door with a fist. There was no bell.

The woman had an unlit cigarette behind her ear, a sky-blue dressing gown draped over fleshy shoulders. Her face was lumpy and incurably resigned. It had been a long time since she'd seen sunlight.

'You Nicholas' mother?' Clyne asked.

She leered at his ID, then at Nicholas, passing sentence. 'What's the bugger done this time?'

'Nothing, he's done nothing. But I'd worry about the company he keeps if I were you.'

'What company?'

'Is your husband in?'

She responded with a nicotine-coated laugh.

When Clyne mentioned Rowlands by name her shoulders relaxed inside her bathrobe. She lit up that fag from behind her ear. She told of how the magistrate paid for her son's private

210

school fees. He helped her with the rent. And he taught Nicholas to boat in that club what was for deprived urban youth.

'Look, Mrs ... Nicholas might be getting more than sailing lessons from Mr Rowlands.' She looked at him so blankly he thought he was going to have to spell it out.

Then her face erupted and her small mouth filled with invective. 'Mr Rowlands's a king in this house. You've seen the filth on this estate. He's saved my boy from God knows what.' She kept the worst insult for last. 'The trouble with you police is like the social workers. You can't tell the good from the bad.'

She hauled Nicholas into the flat and slammed the door on Clyne's face.

There was only one cure for these kind of blues. Clyne asked Manny for twenty-four hours' leave.

Late morning, Clyne and I drive out of London for Southampton, our romance seeking fresh locations: his yacht on the open sea. I feel excited, knowing that in twenty-four hours we will have both changed in some way.

That's what sailing does. It accelerates intimacy.

After listening to the shipping forecast on Radio Four – gale warning, later, for Wight – we play tapes on the stereo: O.V. Wright, Aaron Neville.

I say: 'A cop who likes O.V. Wright can't be all that bad.'

'I like his speech impediment.'

We sing along with Aaron Neville's 'For your Precious Love'.

> 'Darling they say that our love won't grow
> I just want to tell them that they don't know
> For as long as you are in love with me
> Our love will grow wider, deeper than any sea.'

Driving through West Sussex he tells me his father disapproved of sailing, even though he loved boats – working boats. 'He thought recreational sailing was narcissism. For the rich.'

'You're not rich,' I object.

'Then I must be narcissistic.' He smiles.

I tell him that my father taught me to sail. From the age of eight I was sailing dinghies, later his yacht. My expertise eclipsed his own eventually.

'Yet one more version of Dr Harper to add to the list,' he announces.

At a small beach near Hamble we unload the car. Outboard engine, food supplies for eighteen hours and warm clothing in soft holdall bags. We transfer everything to his dinghy tied up against the wall.

'I want to phone my kids,' he says, 'before we set off.' He opens his mobile and can hear his son saying, Hello, hello. But his son can't hear his father.

I walk with him to a telephone box. He digs out a 20p and a £1 coin. 'Are you a member of the Friends and Family scheme?'

'What's that?' he asks.

'Let me show you.' I take his coins and insert the 20p, dial 0891 followed by six random numbers. The 20p is quickly devalued. To 9p, 7p, then I put in the £1.

'What are you doing? That's all the change I've got.'

I hit the follow-on-call button. The £1 coin ejects but the box still registers £1 credit.

'There,' I say. 'Now you have two pounds to spend. Call your kids.'

After he's talked to his family he screws the engine to the transom of the dinghy. In wellington boots he wades out, towing me and the supplies to a depth of two feet, then jumps in and starts the outboard. We make slow headway downstream. Even so, water splashes into the dingy and wets the holdalls.

Fifteen minutes later we reach his yacht secured to a pile mooring. I tie on to the rail with a round turn and two half-hitches then climb aboard, taking the bags and the outboard, which I clamp on to the pushpit.

We have an hour to stow the supplies and prepare the boat

before high tide. The fuel tank is three-quarters full with diesel and the batteries charged. At 1245 Clyne reads five metres of water off the echo sounder, then starts the engine. I pick up the mooring line with the boat hook and the yacht glides out on the tide. We motor-sail upriver through the channel as I untie all the fenders and stow them away in the cockpit locker.

We pass through the fairway. He cuts the engine the moment we leave the headland behind. Together we hoist the mainsail, feeding the luff through the mast, not once having to communicate since we both know the drills. Lastly I go forward to clamp on the genoa.

I also know how to navigate and every half an hour take a fix on our position with the hand-bearing compass, vanishing down below to sit at the chart table, where I transfer the bearings on to the chart. I make entries into the log, recording course steered, latitude and longitude, wind speed, tide rate and barometer reading. There is no real need to do all of this, the Solent is Clyne's patch, we are not in open sea. But my father always insisted on keeping logs up to date. It's a language you can forget, he used to say, if you don't practise it. The weather forecast feeds in continually on the fax, which I switch off.

It's a damp, cloudy day, the wind a force three from the south-west. Clyne steers a course of 210 on a starboard tack, changing to a port tack as we pass a cardinal buoy marking a wreck. He holds his new course of 295 for Keyhaven. Down below I strap myself in at the stove to make coffee in a blackened espresso pot.

He takes the mugs of coffee from me and I take the tiller from him. It's many years since I've been sailing but I find I can still read the sea like a familiar book. I keep up maximum boat speed, the telltales horizontal.

Clyne speaks for the first time in an hour. 'I saw your article on Claude Vignisson. Very good.'

'Did I quote you accurately?'

214

'I can't remember saying that gangsters are like film stars.'

'You didn't. I made it up.'

He looks shocked. 'I always suspected journalists of fabricating. Now I know it's true.'

'It's because we're all frustrated novelists.'

The wind increases to force five with gusts of thirty knots. We put one slab in the main, four rolls around the genoa. Clyne takes bearings off Peel Bank buoy and the East Cowes breakwater and makes the entry into the log I've started.

I suggest we reduce sail again as I detect the boat wallowing. He clips his harness to the jack stay and walks on to the coach roof as I slacken the main halyard. A cormorant flies close to our bows across the surface of the sea.

I smile to myself. This is all too easy.

Two hours later we lower the sails and motor into an inlet on the Isle of Wight to pick up a mooring.

As I am putting a meal together he perches at the galley table and opens a bottle of South African red wine. In the gently rolling boat we drink the wine, talk little and small, each conversation punctuated by the squelch of the VHF. Outside darkness is falling.

I am frying mincemeat, adding tomato puree, cutting an onion with a vegetable slicer when he asks if my brother Max sailed too.

'My father never taught Max to sail.'

'Why not?'

'It's just the way it was.' I reach back for my glass.

As I am slicing onion straight into the pan my head turns suddenly into a block of ice. I hear a loud yelp, like a little puppy. It is my own voice. The vegetable slicer sails across the galley and I slump against the bulkhead, holding my right hand in my left. Blood drips down my wrist.

I've gouged a large chunk of flesh from my finger with the vegetable slicer. Only now do I realize.

He is already out of his seat and by my side, telling me to hold my finger under the running tap. I can't do what he says because I am feeling faint, draining of blood, of energy.

He lowers me into a seat and finds the first-aid kit. His attempts to dress my finger are complicated by the blood oozing through the gauze faster than he can pay it out. Finally he wraps the gauze with cling-film and tapes it with band-aid.

We guzzle the wine and eat in silence. As we finish he asks, 'How's the finger?'

'It's throbbing like hell.'

'Will you be able to sail?'

'Of course.' I look at the two empty plates on the table. 'You know something? The flesh I carved off my finger went into the sauce. We must have eaten it.'

We laugh uneasily. And then he looks at me. I know he wants me. It is part of the deal really, but he doesn't know how to ask. I avert my eyes and tuck my hands inside the sleeves of my ragged Arran sweater. My nose is blue from the cold, my cheeks hot, my hair stiff with saltblast.

I climb out from behind the table to wash with one hand the plates in the sink while he goes wordlessly to the chart table and makes a pilotage plan to Keyhaven. The wind outside is picking up all the time.

'The forecast was for a force eight tonight or early tomorrow. We can stay here for the night if you prefer.'

'I like heavy-weather sailing,' I say.

'Even at night?'

'Especially at night.'

'There's a small bird sanctuary near Keyhaven. Good shelter. No yachties.'

At 1900 we begin the night passage under a full moon with five-tenths cirrus cloud cover. It is much colder now. The wind has turned around, blowing a force six from the north-west. We make best course to windward. Two reefs in the main and the storm jib hanked on.

The snap of canvas from the main and the genoa inhaling the wind furnish the dimensions of the yacht. Bells on cardinal buoys clang as we pass by. Each buoy has its own character identifiable by light patterns: group flashing, continuous quick, composite group occulting, isophases. Shipping lights name other universal truths: restricted manoeuvrability, trawling, constricted draught, mine-sweeping. The lights flicker in the night, talking.

And their talk comforts me, because they tell no lies; a system of symbols as complex as any language, but an exact, unequivocal one.

While Clyne and I say very little. People wait until nightfall to tell each other important things, but on this evening we communicate in neutral nautical terms.

'I've never liked the country at night like I do the sea.' I try to get us going. 'I get frightened by all the critters in the hedgerows.'

He doesn't answer. I look for him but can't see his face and nor can he see mine. A warship comes out of Southampton Water lit up like a city, flanking us for the moment of its passing, and pushes the intimacy between us.

'Are you always this quiet sailing?' I ask.

'Sorry.'

'It's not a complaint.'

'Sailing is when my mind takes a rest.'

'What you told your ex-wife ... Your day is best left inside your head.'

'Yeah, I feel a long way away from all that out here.'

Within half a mile of land we follow the transits of continuous flashing and occulting leading lights to Keyhaven, then turn upwind towards the inlet. A hundred metres from shore we take down all sails and start the engine. He traces the four-metre contour line on the echo sounder as I stand behind in the cockpit with the halogen lamp socketed in, looking for the marker buoy into the inlet. It's difficult to hold position in this wind and against the ebbing tide. The darkness is impenetrable. The wind freezes my hands. I begin to feel concerned that we might run aground when a white stripe on a marker buoy shines back the light. With his eyes fixed to the echo sounder he passes the buoy to port, and motors into the inlet river.

We head for an empty visitor's mooring lying in two metres above chart datum. I pick up the line with the boat hook.

When he turns off the engine the night unravels around us in birdsong. From the marshes, colonies of what I guess are curlews call to their partners on the wing returning under the cover of darkness to avoid the seagulls. It's an unsettling cry, like babies abandoned in bulrushes.

After unclipping my harness I go below to write in the log: '2250. Picked up a mooring in Keyhaven for the night.'

'What happened to the gale?' I ask.

'The wind changed direction around half past seven.'

He turns down the settee into a double berth and throws me some pillows, a quilt and sheets, before going up to strap the halyard to the mast, to stop it tapping all night.

I'm in bed as he returns, my back to the companionway. I hear him remove his boots and trousers then turn off the one remaining light above the chart table before getting in beside me. I smell the salt in his hair. When he puts his arm around me I clench up. He slides his hand inside my sweater and kisses my neck.

I am on my feet, moving as involuntarily as when I cut my finger with the vegetable slicer. There is a breath of cold air as the quilt floats back on to the bed. I can see his silhouette sitting up in bed, waiting.

I hold the mast support tightly. 'I can't do this,' I say. 'Sorry . . .'

'That's okay.' He reaches out for my arm.

'Don't touch me!' I fall backwards, rattling crockery on my way down to the cabin sole.

He gets out of bed and I feel the hair of his leg against my face. I push him away violently.

He says nothing, just waits for some sign in the darkness. When none comes he asks, 'Is this boat, does this trip remind you of your father? Sort of delayed mourning.'

I laugh in an inconsolable way. 'Not quite.'

'Then what's wrong?'

I inhale deeply. 'Why do you think he never taught Max to sail?'

He turns on the lamp above the chart table, the least revealing light on board. His face is damp and glistening. 'Tell me.'

'We'd be moored up somewhere like this,' I begin. 'Somewhere isolated. He'd make up a bed and we'd lie in it and he'd start telling me stories. About girls in some Pacific archipelago who sheathe their spindly legs in orange beads, wear sunfish across their navels, darken their palms with a deep-blue dye . . . dye that left stains on his cock.'

I suddenly lose my powers of speech, before I am able to tell him that my father's seduction venue was his yacht, always the yacht, far from prying eyes. My voice is as lost as Andersen's Little Mermaid's.

Clyne seems to have lost his too. He stands in the companion-way smoking a cigarette, watching the stars falling into the sea, with a woman in his boat he doesn't know any more.

A woman who likes him to tell her stories. But a good idea's a good idea, isn't it? Even if it does give 'bedtime story' a whole different slant.

There is no consolation for him. The pressure building inside the cabin is as wordless as life at the bottom of the sea.

We leave at first light. Neither of us has slept. I sit on the coaming, the hood of my borrowed oilskins tied around my chin. Clyne is sullen in the mouth, his eyes a roasted black.

The gale that was predicted has arrived. With the storm jib on we make eight knots on a starboard tack, against a strong Solent ebb. Majestic seas surround, with spindrift whipping off the tops of twelve-foot waves.

After an hour Clyne tells me he's going to gybe.

They are the first words he's spoken since last night.

I prepare the jib sheet around the portside winch. Clyne puts the stern through the wind and I spin the starboard sheet off the drum and winch in fast.

Trimming the sail, I look behind. Two-storey buildings chase us down the street.

I think: the sea has no pattern, it is anti-design. Only navigation is design.

Then a terrible fear overwhelms me. But of what? Out of such unidentified fears, religions are born. There is no religion in the sea.

Clyne is staring behind as I unclip my safety harness and move across to the heavily listing port side. *Our love will grow wider, deeper than any sea.*

I want to get in there among the waves, take on all the sea's concealed passion.

It is as straightforward as that.

TWELVE

For a second he thought it was a practical joke, her rising on the crest of a wave in yellow oilskins.

In another second she was fifteen feet away.

There was a falling-away in him. His head went cold, as if he'd just gone in to work. He let everything go inside the cockpit to wrench the dan buoy off the pushpit, and threw it out into the water.

He had to take his eyes off the sea. To make a note of his course. He started counting, loosened the jib sheets, leaning his weight against the tiller. And the boat turned round. He had lost sight of Alice completely. The boat stalled as the bow passed through the wind. He winched in the jib, counting back the seconds the whole time. Twenty-four, twenty-three . . .

He returned on a course of 150 and started the engine. He still could not see Alice, nor the dan buoy flag. Beating into the huge seas and counting down. His harness leash was taut.

He tried to think if Alice had been clipped on.

Her oilskins had a small wedge of buoyancy built into the shoulders.

There was no more Alice, just an amorphous mass of water.

He held in his mind a half-acre of sea, sifting it with his eyes as though through a sieve. His desire for a sighting – of a red flag, a yellow oilskin – was so strong, his concentration so intense that he made himself feel nauseous, as if reading a book in a moving car.

The boat stammered each time the tonnage of a wave collapsed on to the foredeck, bursting into atomized water and sluicing off the deck.

This was a winter sea. Cold winter sea.

A cutlery drawer pulled out on its castings in the galley. Knives and forks flew out, stalled, flew back in, and the drawer slammed shut, as if by an invisible hand.

In another five seconds he would have gone too far.

The boat speed registered as six knots. But with the tide behind, over the ground, it was probably making more like nine.

He had still not seen sight of her. He pushed against the tiller and the boat came round. He watched the compass until making a course of 110. It filled him with mourning not knowing the exact direction of the tide. Alice took that information with her, where it would be of no help.

He operated by part guesswork and following what he did know, the drills, the nautical instruments. The sea continued to mount assaults. The assaults never ended.

The boat rolled under a wave that came on sideways, the malformed sibling of another. Cups and plates crashed in the galley. The hull moaned loudly.

He had forgotten to count. He didn't know how long he'd held this course.

Three seconds . . . five?

He came about again.

Held a 030 course. The engine idled. A London taxi engine marinized. He needed more control. Less speed.

Then he found what he was looking for. A yellow blot dead ahead. The dan buoy he could not see. She had only her own buoyancy.

He relaxed and was immediately caught off guard.

Did Alice kill her father?

He plucked the boathook off the deck. As he came alongside he leant over the listing port side. One shot. He hooked her under her harness strap. Her torso lifted out of the sea like a skier's and travelled with the boat. He pulled up on the boathook but couldn't break her surface tension. Her oilskins acted as ballast. He stretched out as far as his harness strap would allow and gained a purchase on her strap. He clipped her to a hook inside the cockpit. She looked asleep, with her head pressed against the topside. Not like Alice at all now, just a body halfway between life and death.

He left her hanging outside and considered the mainsheet block and tackle as a possible crane. But the boat itself was working like one, the stern lifting each time it pitched forward. Clyne took hold of her harness in both hands. The stern came up and Alice broke the meniscus of the sea. With his arms behind her legs he flipped her inside the cockpit.

The galley is a mess of broken crockery, sleeping bags, charts on the sole. He lays me on the settee berth and tries to put his ear against my nostrils, but the movement of the boat prevents him. Gripping on to the bulkhead he waits for the boat to list before trying again.

He checks my breathing, my carotid pulse. I see his concerned face hovering above mine, a long distance away. He unzips the oilskins, using the motion of the boat to peel them off. He wraps the quilt around me and rigs up a leecloth to keep me from falling out. I feel made of ice, all emotion preserved.

He goes on deck to alter course for Portsmouth. It is a smoother ride now, on a beam reach with the wind behind. The waves keep up pursuit as if they have unfinished business with me.

He lashes the tiller and comes back below to check on me. I am lying on my back with eyes open. He strokes my hair and smiles, before turning on Channel 16. I hear him alert the harbourmaster at Portsmouth of a suspected case of hypothermia on board.

For thirty minutes Clyne alternates between cabin and cockpit, checking my vital signs, checking our course and keeping a look-out. At some point he puts a kettle of water on the stove. When the kettle boils he makes tea and holds the mug to my lips.

The barometer glass starts to climb.

A launch is waiting at the entrance to the harbour as we arrive. Clyne carries me in his arms and hands me over to the skipper. The launch takes me into the marina where an ambulance is waiting. I am to be taken to Portsmouth General Hospital for observation. Clyne is going to take his boat back to its mooring on the River Hamble and then come by car to the hospital.

I have not been very well since arriving at the hospital. In casualty I threw up all over the cubicle floor. They found an empty bed in a geriatric ward where I fainted even before I'd made it into the bed. Whatever your condition hospitals will make it worse. They make you sick, a self-fulfilling prophecy.

When Clyne arrives I am sitting up in bed, surrounded by ancients. I raise my hand from under the sheet as I see him looking for me among the sick old women. He walks over and takes my hand and kisses my forehead. I imagine this is how he deals with his own children when they are ill. I open my mouth to talk but can only cry. He does not know what to say either, and dries my tears with a corner of the starched white sheet.

What I want to say is: You came back for me.

And he replies: I will never leave you.

And they lived happily ever after.

Then the book closes.

And *then* he says: Come on, out with it . . . did you kill your old man? It's prison cells and porridge for you, my dear.

A staff nurse comes into the ward. She draws Clyne into a corner but I can hear her explain that they want to keep me in overnight. She advises him to go home.

225

THIRTEEN

The floor in his living room moved under his feet and his stomach lurched. He listened to sounds of bath water splashing upstairs, the water tank refilling in the attic. He stared long and hard at a framed picture on the mantel of Lucy and David in a pool in Deia. He turned the picture face down.

The bathroom door was unlocked. He walked in on Lucy lying in the tub. She threw her arms across her small breasts.

It was the first time he'd seen her naked in years. 'Let me look at you,' he said.

'Dad!'

'Just let me look at you.'

She had not seen him like this before. Her indignation shifted into a different register, was replaced by fear. Slowly she let her guard down. It was not an autonomous action. Rather, she was responding to his command. He'd had this power on ice all her life, and now he was using it, she had no choice but to comply.

In his despair he stared at her breasts. Her wet hair hung limply down her face, her skin pink from the heat. Little beads of water rested on her narrow shoulders. She held a duck-shaped soap in her hand and began to tremble.

Clyne forced himself to feel carnal. Tried to sexualize the distance between them.

He saw the tears before they'd formed in her eyes.

He closed the bathroom door and took the stairs with both hands on the banister, so as not to fall.

From behind he heard her crying before she had even started to cry.

Finally I get to go inside Clyne's inner sanctum. He puts me in this stark room and then leaves me. Interview Room 2 has a formica table and chairs, and white walls scarred with sour, illiterate graffiti. It's hot and stuffy. The windows are closed and so high I can't see anything but the sky through them. Waiting for his return I listen to Elvis Costello on my Walkman.

The door opens and Clyne brings in his whole family to meet me. Sam Ridley, Kelly Stokes and Manny . . . the big daddy of them all. His Newcastle accent still strong after all these years in the south, he ships into the room in an expensive charcoal-grey suit. His eyes lock on to me very intently, having heard so much about me, no doubt. His hand plays with his long jaw. He's a terrifying cop, this one, because he has nothing but the job to think about. No family, kids. He is pure police, his emotion wintered down by countless murders.

He gives no quarter either. 'Alice, you had the motive for this. People are going to understand. They'll be sympathetic.'

I stare at his face, and it's an empty book.

'We're maybe looking for two killers. Did Max help you?'

I stutter and rasp. 'Max can't even dress himself in the morning. Ask Detective Clyne.'

'You told me once that your favourite fairy story is Hansel and Gretel,' Clyne says, 'because they take the law into their own hands.'

'May I compliment you on the quality of your evidence, Bob,' I remark. 'But for your information Gretel saves Hansel in the story. It's Gretel alone who kills the witch.'

Manny will think I'm off my trolley but I tell him why I like fairy stories. I like them because they gave me my identity, my inner life, my language in the formative years of my childhood. Until the age of five. At five my father took me to see Walt Disney's *Sleeping Beauty* in the local Odeon. From the cinema we went to Alexandra Park. He told me that Alexandra Palace was the Princess's castle. It was semi-derelict, just like a castle would be after a hundred years of neglect. Approached from the south the park slopes up to the palace with trees masking the building, like the impenetrable briar hedge in the story. There is no such thing as an objective landscape. Dogs roaming were dragons, breathed fire, and even to this day I have an inflated fear of them. We went looking for Sleeping Beauty together. We made it to the palace and I started calling out, 'Aurora! Aurora! Where are you?' And my father said, 'But she's changed her name, remember? She's now Briar Rose and hiding in the woods.' So we turned around and ran hand in hand to the thick woods at the eastern edge of the park. I wandered through the woods shouting, 'Briar Rose, Briar Rose! Where are you?' I kept it up, just wouldn't give up that search. I had to find her, that poor abused child. I was going to rescue her. I was hunting Beauty and, unbeknownst to me, my father was hunting me. He suggested we should act out the story. I lay on a cushion of fallen leaves in the woods and closed my eyes. My father kissed me. Over and over. But on the wrong lips. I even called him on it, his head between my legs, and he said it was a special prince's kiss.

It ended when I was fifteen, the same age as Sleeping Beauty when she fell asleep for a hundred years. We were in the back cabin on his yacht and he had just asked to fuck me. 'But I might get pregnant,' I said. My dad smiled at my naivety. 'You haven't started your periods,' he said. And so I acquiesced. As I started undressing he suddenly remembered the bolognese sauce simmering on the gimballed stove. He made a very good sauce. 'I've got to go stir the sauce. I'll be back in two seconds.' In those momentous seconds when he was in the galley I became hysterical. When he returned we both knew it was over.

For the past ten years or more I have been trying to find my way back to that pre-five-year-old time in my childhood. Looking for the character I'd constructed out of fairy tales. I even *live* in the woods, with all the Grimm characters, the crusties. Look at those people. Every one is a made-up guy. For a living I interview stars, who are really only apparitions in people's fantasies.

'Alice, did you do it?' Manny asks. 'One word.'

I might as well have been talking to a wall. 'No.'

'Then who did?'

I slam on my Walkman and offer the earplugs to Manny. 'What's this?' he asks.

'Listen. And you will see.'

The four of us sit watching Manny listening to Elvis Costello on my Walkman. Singing about shipbuilding.

Soon we'll be shipbuilding.

He takes out the plugs. 'What is this, Alice?'

And diving for pearls.

I stand from my chair and slap him hard in the face.

Clyne, Manny, Ridley have all left the interview room, leaving me alone with Kelly Stokes.

She is quite a different kind of police.

Listen to this.

'Your father's big idea was there is no such thing as original character. Go looking for it, as you are, and you'll end up harming yourself. Now doesn't that sound like a justification to you, Alice? For his part in your abuse. If there's no such thing as original character then there can be no damage done to it. You can't damage what doesn't exist.'

'Maybe we aren't originals. But it's not an original self I've been looking for, just an undamaged one. But do you think this went through my father's mind *at the time*?'

'I don't know. I've never had a case like this. Sex offenders I've dealt with are usually pretty dim-witted. Which explains why they do it. They're not all there on top.'

'Or explains why they get caught.'

'That's right. Your father was not dim-witted.'

'And he didn't get caught,' I add.

'Well, that's a moot point,' she says. 'Now this little girl, Alice Harper, everything that happens to her is normal. Her father coerces her into having sex and that's all right.'

'He used to tell me stories . . . Like I ask Clyne to do when he makes love to me.'

'I like men talking to me too. When we make love. But your problem is how to get the abuser out of your head when Clyne's telling you things.'

'I keep it all in.'

'You've learnt that strategy from a very early age.'

'Strategy? What do you mean, strategy?'

'By keeping the secret to yourself you prevented your family from breaking up.'

'My mother died when I was eleven.'

'But you have a sibling.'

'Yes.'

'Who you protect even now.'

'I think you must be a fine therapist, Kelly.'

'I'm not so bad. For an amateur.'

'Lucky old Bob.'

'I'm glad we've had this chance to talk, Alice.'

'So am I. But tell me. What chance do I have of a happy life?'

'If you've had good parenting you will always fear the loss of love. In your case, your fears are all in the past.'

'I never killed him, you know.'

'I believe you. But it's Manny who will make the final decision.'

'He may make the final decision but he's not going to get even close to the soul of this case. He's not going to complete.'

FOURTEEN

The weather had been strange all week. One day of snow, the temperature minus seven, followed by spring-like hours, then rain, followed by snow again.

Clyne was standing on Baring Road, twenty metres from his house, staring down at Regent's Canal. He had just let Mick go, fired him. He couldn't have a man taking care of his children any longer. The man was distraught as he took the money Clyne held in his hand, the equivalent of a month's wages.

Clyne saw something floating in the water; just a Shell oil can, but fancied he recognized it. The last time he saw that can was in Royal Victoria Dock. The docks, and all who sail there, and Clyne in Baring Road were connected along a continuum of water.

The forces of nature were all screwed up all right. Even Lucy felt obliged to comment as he returned to the house. 'It's global warming,' she said. 'And Michael Jackson's not in town to save the planet!'

He was too busy saving the little children.

They were in her bedroom. From her Ikea pine CD rack Clyne took out a couple of the Manics' albums. From the sleeve notes on their first he discovered Richey Edwards was formerly Richey James. An early attempt to change identity? A dummy run for his final disappearance? Like Rowlands' son Kevin, who also changed his name, to Troy.

Later, in the kitchen, Lucy came down and found her father staring into a mug of tea. She fished out the teabag, touched the ceramic. 'This is stone cold.' She gave him a look of concern. The daughter parenting the father. 'Do you want me to make us lunch?'

'Sure. Like what?'

'Mick made up some pasta sauce. Before you sacked him. Which was a daft idea, by the way.'

'Pasta sounds fine.'

She started heating Mick's Neapolitan sauce. As she tore open the bag of dried spaghetti Clyne got to his feet, and took his coat off the back of the chair.

'Where're you going now?'

Clyne ran into his neighbour laying a concrete driveway for his car. His four-year-old daughter was helping, filling her beach bucket with sand. Clyne smiled at her bending over the sand, bum in the air, then wiped that smile off his face, turning it to a sneer. There was no clear view of childhood.

Driving in the rain his de-mister didn't work. It was steaming up inside the car. All he could see of the world was a cocktail of impressionist dots and vanishing points. Half an hour later he was deep inside the territory where Michael Rivers took his life. Or went to ground. Or something.

Was Michael Rivers a Richey Edwards fan?

Richey Edwards left his car near the Severn Bridge at a known suicide location, then walked to his current secret venue within sight of all his mourning fans dropping daffodils into the river. That's one theory anyway. A new personality developing within the same geography.

A desolate landscape produces desolate thoughts. *You will be buried in the same box as a killer.*

The road curved around a pale brick wall. Clyne cornered too

234

fast, skidded and crashed into a giant estate agent's billboard, its flame-red lettering stretching the length of his windscreen. THE HOUSE OF HAPPINESS.

He got out of the car. Without stopping to inspect the damage he walked back up the road. Smoke-coughing refuse lorries, pest control vans full of decomposed squirrels and rats pressed to the meshed windows, security vans built for blunt combat – all thundered past. The flyover above shook from heavy loads; below, the southbound Blackwall Tunnel moaned from responsibility. McDonald's shagged a traffic atoll, its neon sign winking through mists of diesel. Canary Wharf Tower reigned from any angle one cared to look. Phallic power. The pink light of dusk scarfed the head of steam on its black roof. He was a dead man walking among breweries, aggregate bases, gantries, oil depots, air-gobbling chimney stacks and incinerators: the dark satanic mills.

Dr Harper: *What will give my death design is the certainty of living.*

Richey Edwards: *If man makes death then death makes man.*

On the riverfront he heard the Thames Barrier siren warning, like the theme tune of *The Twilight Zone*. Traffic lights changed from red to green, green to red at a silent, windswept junction. Tyres burnt in an empty lot, sickening the bulbous clouds. It was desert here. And it's to the desert you go to find yourself.

The towpath was slippery and littered with broken Firebird bottles. He gripped the wall to avoid a fall. Walking in the rain had become arduous. One warehouse seamlessly joined another. They shut him out, walled him in. Cranes broke the skyline. Windows were wire-meshed. Fumes exhausted from flues. He smelled toxic substances.

There was nothing to project on to, no one to talk to but a dead shrink and a missing rock star. Then a break in the clouds appeared and some things seemed possible. Sunshine looted fissures in the asphalt, opened up names on the south bank.

Blue Circle cement, Spillers. Greenwich Marshes smoked in the sun. In the mid-distance cormorants glided across the surface of the water. Off Mudlark's Way a wooden jetty scrubbed clean by weather supported a sapphire-coloured crane. A military green portakabin rusting orange was bolted on to the gantry. Swastikas had been spray-painted on the side. Under the crane arm a bucket squatted on the jetty, snout up. At the end of the jetty was a diesel generator making a low-throated roar.

Clyne exhaled and ran back for the car.

The house was in a state of animation with the kids and their friends, their music and footballs, all eating Lucy's pasta on the run. Clyne was the only still point in this turning world, sitting on the floor with his face six inches away from the TV screen, the VCR control in his hand. He was watching again, George Harper on video returning home from the *Observer* transatlantic race, cruising through Greenwich Reach.

He glides past the crane on its jetty, the portakabin daubed with swastikas. Clyne froze the frame as Harper's mouth opens on the line: 'They weren't there when I left. Don't tell me Britain's had a right-wing dictatorship . . .'

From the north bank he kept the jetty under a ready eye. The generator rumbled in the wind. Fanning out behind him were all the locations of this case: Blackwall, Cubitt Town, Royal Docks, with St Katharine's further upriver. The rusting portakabin grew pink in the light of the setting sun.

A small light came on inside the portakabin. Clyne smiled and looked up into the sky developing with champagne stars. He could see the future in the constellations, looking closer than it had for weeks.

He walked back to where he'd parked.

The moon had risen over the Thames Barrier as he emerged southside from the Tunnel. Smoke issued from chimneys on both sides of the water. He parked near the greyhound track and walked along Lombard Wall and Riverside. On the refuse barges moored mid-stream rats scampered. Seagulls circling above the fish market made plunging raids to gorge themselves on offal. A JCB scooped up animal bones in a soap factory, its hydraulic bucket raised against the furnace flames, the boiling caldron. The melting calcium smelled like burnt coffee beans, high roast.

A steel crane bucket closed the entrance to the jetty from the gangway. The gangway led to the towpath and was blocked midway by a locked gate, and at the towpath by a copse of gnarly holly trees.

A castle behind briars.

He climbed down on to the pebble beach. The Thames was at a low ebb and left thick mud for him to negotiate. To reach a ladder feeding on to the deck he waded through icy water up to his waist. The ladder was narrow and perpendicular, clamped to the wooden pilings. He climbed on to the deck and from there the metal stairs to the portakabin.

Stretched out on a foam mattress inside was Michael Rivers. He hadn't seen or heard Clyne. His eyes were closed and over his ears were headphones attached to a Walkman resting on his belly. He rocked his head gently back and forth to the music. Clyne watched him enjoy his last seconds of emancipation. In the grey light the scars on his forearms looked raw, each one with a story to articulate, the same repetitive story. A fan heater blew warm air around the room.

He'd made it quite comfortable inside. Cosy, like Alice and Max Harper's bus. The mattress was covered by a quilt patterned with little teddy bears. His head rested on three firm pillows. There was a transformer and an AC/DC converter linked to two batteries on the floor. An electrician's forty-watt bulb in a wire cage was clipped to the edge of a table that was littered with tabloid newspapers, a stash of Cadbury's chocolate bars, two hundred Embassy reds, vodka and beer bottles, salt and vinegar crisps.

Clyne pressed his boot into his ribs. Rivers' eyes sprang open but his head stayed on the pillow, like he was expecting a visitor. When he saw it was Clyne he levitated off the bed, crashed against the wall, breathless. The headphones were still filling his head with music. Clyne yanked them out from the Walkman. The tinny scratching noise stopped.

'You look like you've settled in for a spell?'

'What you doing here?'

'That was going to be my next question.'

'It's none of your business.'

'Oh please, Michael, don't give me that. You're in a lot of trouble. Where's your pal Alastair?'

'Ask Alastair.'

'Why are you protecting that lowlife, Michael? He doesn't box fair.'

'He's okay. He got me Sky TV.'

'Is that it! Fucking hell. You're a cheap date. I bet it was his idea to leave your clothes on the towpath.'

Rivers clamped up. So Clyne made a seat on an oil drum, settled in and smoked. Rivers went back to his Walkman. He turned it up loud enough for Clyne to hear. Heavy industrial techno music, the apocalypse.

Rivers turned the cassette over in the Walkman. 'You're fucked up, Michael,' Clyne said while he had the chance. 'You're royally fucked up.'

'So? Ain't you?'

'Rosine told me how Alastair liked to photograph you.'

'I'll have her!'

'She's the only friend you've got.'

'Really. Thanks for the advice!'

'And Bill Haines too, perhaps.'

'Bill's like a dad to me.'

'But Alastair, he's a bad daddy. He wants to make love to you and good fathers don't do that. But how would you know, with your family background? Alastair's going to fuck you up like your mother fucked you up.'

'Don't talk about me mother. You know nothing about her.'

'I read Dr Harper's notes, Michael. If they're to be believed . . .'

'Alastair's gonna take me to Brighton. What it is, he's got a big house down there and said I could, like, live in it.'

'I don't think you'll get that far. Atlantis, maybe.'

He clicked on his tape again and Clyne lost contact.

Clyne called Manny on the mobile and gave him the coordinates of the jetty. Manny wanted to send back-up, but Clyne told him he'd call again if and when he needed it. He switched off the phone and concentrated himself.

Rivers had taken off his headphones.

'What time's Alastair coming over?' Rivers' face caved in. 'Come on, Michael. I could tell you were expecting company by the way you opened your eyes all loving when I come in. Someone must be bringing over your supper?'

'No one's bringing over my supper.'

'That's too bad. You fancy a pizza? I'll call for a takeaway on the mobile.'

When Rivers tried to plug in to the Walkman, Clyne snatched the tape machine and threw it out of the broken window into the water. Rivers jumped to the window, as if there could still be a chance to retrieve it. He turned and went for Clyne. Clyne stopped him dead with his hand forked around his windpipe. He fell on the bed, coughing and wheezing.

'You've got a lot more to worry about than a Walkman, Michael. You're in deep shit unless you talk to me. I can help you.'

'Why don't you piss off,' he croaked.

'Let me tell you a story while you get your breath back. When I was seven years old I was standing behind a door listening to my mother in the kitchen say to my older sister, Your brother can go live with his father. I can look after us. I have savings in the post office. I can get a job. Three years later, the status quo hasn't changed, except my sister's left home. I'm back behind the same door, only this time I hear my father say to my mother, If it wasn't for Robert we'd be okay, we'd get on.

'In the first instance my mother was saying, I was not worth fighting for. When the chips were down she didn't want me. And my father was saying, three years later, I was the destroyer of love. So I said to myself, I'm on my own here, Jack. Nobody out there's going to fight my corner.

'Since I've been on this case, Michael, I've been giving my folks a second thought. They were good people who made a couple of mistakes. Compared to your parents they were Mary and fucking Joseph. I will always have that. Parenting is powerful stuff. You only have one shot at it. Depending on how it goes will determine the rest of your life.'

'So?'

'So I'm a lucky guy.'

All good things to those who wait.

An hour later a small motor vessel appeared from upstream. Clyne watched the boat slow and glide towards the pilings of the jetty with the moon directly overhead.

There were two people on deck.

He turned his attention back to Rivers. 'Your dinner's arriving,' he said.

Rivers leapt to his feet to look out of the broken window.

'Let them come. I'd like a little chat with Alastair. And Rusty.'

Rivers walked out on to the gallery. Through the window Clyne saw a figure lean out on his starboard side and tie up to the pilings with a line. He then stood back from the window and waited.

Sounds outside the portakabin: boat displacing water, fenders

240

squealing, two separate bodies climbing up the ladder on to the jetty, Rivers saying something. Inside, Clyne couldn't hear himself breathing.

A moment later Rivers returned. Standing in the door behind him was Alice Harper.

Like the time she'd gone overboard in the Solent, for a second he thought it was another practical joke.

Then he felt his skull freeze over as Claude Vignisson appeared behind Alice, half in, half out of the portakabin, the moonlight shining in his dyed hair.

'I didn't expect to see you . . .' Clyne just managed.

Vignisson casually acknowledged Clyne's presence. 'Who'd you think it was, Robert Maxwell?'

His hunch had always been that tracing Rivers would lead to Harper's killer. But he never anticipated this kind of result. His head floated away with conjecture, like a helium balloon freed from its mooring. 'My money was on someone else, is all.'

They all stepped inside. Alice's eyes were filled with regret, Vignisson's an inscrutable black.

Clyne positioned himself for his last good shot. 'So who put the kid up to this . . . Alice?'

'Is he alone?' Claude asked Rivers.

'He just phoned someone on his mobile. He might have called them in.'

Clyne bowed in deference. 'You're not as stupid as you look, are you, Michael?'

Vignisson and Clyne watched each other closely. The old man hadn't broken, peeled, failed.

In counterpoint Alice looked frail and dishevelled in dirty black jeans, sandals and grey socks, a black cotton sweater with the elbows out, her face scraped clean of make-up and her hair full of wind.

Some of this was dawning on him, but nothing was clear, was all still silhouette.

241

Shaking her head, Alice stepped outside of the portakabin and walked out of sight. Clyne's anger started its slow rise to the surface. 'You're a bit old for her, ain't you, Claude?'

'It's not like that. She's a lovely girl.'

'Nice voice, too,' Clyne added. 'Even if the corners are still in there.'

'Now that's what I love about the Old Bill. See a beautiful woman and say, Nice voice. No wonder the country's gone to the dogs.'

'I suppose you can come up with an alibi for when her father's murder went off?'

'Let me think. That's right, now I remember. I was shagging the wife's sister around about that time.'

'Then sorry, Michael.' Clyne took a gamble. 'We have the forensic that puts you on the shrink's yacht. I'm taking you in to charge you for the murder of George Harper.'

'Like fuck you are,' Claude said.

Clyne didn't see Vignisson take a knife from his pocket but heard the blade flick open behind his back.

'Don't embarrass me, Claude . . .'

'We hid this kid here because he *didn't* kill Harper.'

'You police all of a sudden, Claude? And who's *we*?'

'Me and Alice. We *know* he didn't.'

'Then you must know who.'

'You never, ever considered a self-defence angle, did you, Clyne?'

'With a body at the top of a mast, his nuts removed? No, Claude, it never occurred to me.'

'Not my own defence, but the kids, you know, who can't defend themselves. But the principle is self-defence.'

Clyne's mouth dropped open. He stepped back and looked hard at Vignisson. He made the connection a second later. 'Jesus Christ. It happened to you, didn't it?'

'These days, people just, everybody just cares about money.

They don't give a shit. This quack Harper, who gives a shit what he done, forget what he done. Kids in those circumstances . . . you never say nothing, you don't do nothing. Those are the rules, you put up with it. No fucker ever comes forward and helps you. People turn a blind eye if they aren't helping themselves to the cookie jar.'

Breaking a case in this fashion was the closest to a religious experience Clyne ever had. It happens once in ten years. Yet despite the symmetry unfolding this felt more like a bromide, very low-church.

'You're a little orphan as well, are you, Claude?'

'Nobody come out the same way as they go in. It turns your head round on your shoulders six times, like in *The Exorcist*. Yeah. Fifty years ago it was, I was in an orphanage, in Shadwell. And I still get nightmares.'

'So now you'll pay for it all over again – with your liberty. What justice is there in that?' Clyne felt chronically depressed. 'You're crowding sixty, Claude, you're going to die in prison. Not so smart, really.' He turned to look at Michael but he was dead-eyed. 'So who paid your contract wages on this outing . . . Alice?'

'Nobody paid me nothing. I do some jobs *pro bono*, Clyne. That's for free.'

'I know what *pro bono* means, I was married to a lawyer.'

'Look, Alice doesn't even know *now* I did her old man. Scout's honour. She told me what he done, mind, and that was enough. She's like a daughter to me.'

'That's very touching, Claude.'

'She told me you was going to collar this kid for it. That ain't civil, so we put him in here till you cooled off.'

'You gonna be scalping the shrink's surname then, Claude? Claude Harper has a ring to it.'

'A nonce's name? You must be kidding.'

'I hope you had a nice long chat with him like you did all your

243

other victims. Perhaps you can tell me why he wanted to fuck his own daughter. Did he say?'

'I can't answer that, Clyne. I didn't think it too clever to let a shrink talk to me before I done him.'

'You mean he might have talked you out of it.'

'Along those lines.'

'Last question. You walking with me to my car or do I drag you there?'

'I got different plans.'

Claude crept forward with the precise, rehearsed moves of someone who has carried out many hits in his long life. His whole demeanour looked an imitation of an original that had long been lost. Clyne stared at him and a corpse stared back, his eyes black and bottomless. Men who were alive moments before meeting Claude and dead the next lived in his comportment and in those eyes. He could see Clyne's death in advance of the event, knew what it looked like before it occurred. He knew the sound death made, the language – as Clyne himself did.

'Don't embarrass me, Claude. Drop the blade.'

'I ain't going down for this. It was self-defence.'

Something shifted in his face, like a veil dropping. He placed one foot behind him, to anchor himself. And that is how Clyne knew it was coming. His hand flicked out as Claude's arm moved and caught the blade of the knife. There was a sudden rush of heat and pain. He pulled the knife out of Claude's hand and then watched as warm blood oozed between his own fingers.

Clyne sought out Rivers, who had never been anything but a foil in this whole pointless epic. He was burdened by sins, none of them his own. All he ever did wrong was to chin some bloated stockbroker a year ago who'd made a pass at Rosine while she was begging on the Tube. And he ends up in a portakabin on the Thames, with a stench of smelting animal bones up his nostrils.

There was something very disturbing about his expression-less fourteen-year-old face. He couldn't think his way out of there, project himself imaginatively into a better future. He was grounded in time, cement for shoes. And Clyne had gone so far out on the limb to catch him that he was grounded too, just as dysfunctional, like some actor who'd prepared too long for the role of a corpse. If Rivers lacked independence, so did Clyne. They belonged nowhere together, were permanently exiled beyond the Ninth Wave, shipwrecked on the same isolated rock.

Clyne could not cut himself free. He felt breathless. And deaf. And blind.

He turned the blade round and stabbed his chest through his shirt and carved a line from one breast to the other. Stars burst behind his eyes. He could see again. His shirt quickly soaked up blood, a warm pool collecting around his belt.

He heard a raised voice, like the crack of a whip. So now he could hear again too, even if he couldn't yet breathe. He threw the knife and it plugged the floor between Claude's open feet.

Clyne struggled to remain standing, his legs stuttering beneath him.

'Christ almighty,' said Claude. 'You're the one who needs to see a shrink!'

Claude bolted in pyrrhic retreat. From the galley he jumped off on to the gangway and from the gangway on to the beach. In the generous moonlight Clyne watched him plunge into mud to his waist and fall on his face. The mud made a sucking, intimate sound as he tried to pull himself free. But he just got in deeper. He was stuck fast with the tide coming in. Steam rose from his coat.

These were Clyne's thoughts before passing out: happy children are ones kept in a state of deception; happy adults are ones who maintain a state of self-deception.

Check into any accident and emergency department in an NHS hospital late at night and your experience may well be an intimate one. Casualties are enervated and sparking on account of their (minor) injuries. They've all had a shock that inclines them to share their vulnerability with perfect strangers. Maybe it's not such a good place to make lasting friendships, because this is raw, not real time, and nothing that comes after will feel the same. But for the moment it's all very live in here.

I accompanied Clyne to the A&E round midnight. The assessment nurse bandaged his chest wound, then told him he was a priority two. Meaning he'd have to wait three hours before they could stitch him back up.

For three hours we're part of a vivid community. Not a conversational one, it's more through osmosis that I feel a connection. Everyone is becalmed, shielded from the really bad blue-light, front-line casualties – the cardiac arrests and the road-traffic accidents – who go through the ambulance bay into the cubicles. It's just the walking wounded here, bleeding from the head and the hands and the chest. Blood may be on the wrong side of the skin in the A&E, but the rage that put it there has been left behind in the streets. On this night, at least, victims and victimizers shed their status and find solidarity in the same bunker.

A pretty schoolteacher with a broken ankle sits with her foot up on her boyfriend's lap. Her accident has done a job on their love and they look star-crossed at each other. All the while men are arriving with their arms protectively around their women, and vice versa, limping and sore. A marriage that suffers minor external injuries is a good marriage, for a while.

It's a long night of the family too. The good and happy news is the way children are prioritized, however superficial their injuries. They don't have to wait and are admitted into the inner chambers along with the heart attacks and car-wreck survivors. These little refugees from the war find a place of safety here, parented by nurses who run from one to the other, and by doctors with red-rimmed eyes. I feel happy, knowing that at least some children's maydays are answered.

And Clyne, *my* Clyne, has his head in his hands. His injuries may have done a job on our love too. He listens for sounds outside the hospital, but hears nothing of the city. Only the exigencies of the A&E department reach his ears. The powers of a child have returned to him, to block out all the tremors of the world.

Acknowledgements

Thanks are due to the following for their advice and support:
Barbara Jones, Jon Cook, John Tague, Sara Rance, Steve Kelly,
Hannah Griffiths, Nick Royle, Nelson Mews, Caroline Dawnay,
DCI Glen Gilbertson, DI Barry Howe, Paul Duenas.